She was to be the King's...

Rhoese was vulnerable, exquisitely beautiful, tempestuous yet with a hint of scaredness, and not quite as ice-cold as she would like to be thought.

Until now, Jude had only toyed with thoughts of marriage. The possibility of taking an Englishwoman to his bed permanently had never been more than a passing thought during his eight years in England. Until now.

This one presented more than a challenge...

Juliet Landon's keen interest in art and history, both of which she used to teach, combined with a fertile imagination, make writing historical novels a favourite occupation. She is particularly interested in researching the early medieval period and the problems encountered by women in a man's world. Her heart's home is in her native North Yorkshire, but now she lives happily in a Hampshire village close to her family. Her first books, which were on embroidery and design, were published under her own name of Jan Messent.

Recent titles by the same author:

A MOST UNSEEMLY SUMMER
THE KNIGHT'S CONQUEST
ONE NIGHT IN PARADISE
THE WIDOW'S BARGAIN

THE BOUGHT BRIDE

Juliet Landon

MILLS & BOON®

*First published in Great Britain 2005
Harlequin Mills & Boon Limited,
Eton House, 18-24 Paradise Road, Richmond, Surrey TW9 1SR*

© Juliet Landon 2005

ISBN 0 263 84368 8

*Set in Times Roman 10½ on 12½ pt.
04-0505-80762*

*Printed and bound in Spain
by Litografía Rosés S.A., Barcelona*

THE BOUGHT BRIDE

Chapter One

Michaelmas, September 29th, 1088—York

A sneaking cold wind whipped the light woollen shawl off Rhoese's head to reveal a rippling helmet of auburn hair the colour of ripe chestnuts. She snatched the scarf and tied it briskly around her shoulders, trapping the two heavy plaits that reached to her waist. A halo of spiralling tendrils fluttered around her face. 'One cart of timber from Gilbert of Newthorpe,' she called to the scribbling clerk at her side. 'Mark that down, Brother Alaric. Two cows worth twenty pence each from Robert, brother of Thorkil.'

'Yes, yes,' said the cleric. 'Not too fast, my lady, if you please.' With Robert's goad to prod them, the cows were not inclined to wait in order.

'Be quick, man. Master Ralph is here with his corn payment.'

Bundles of thatch, baskets of salted fish, live hens and fresh eggs, sesters of honey and rounds of cheese, sacks of malt and grain were carried into the fenced compound at Toft Green and accounted for by Lady

Rhoese, her bailiff and her clerk. It was Michaelmas, a time for the payment of dues in her first year as a landowner in her own right. Men had been coming since early morning to hand over their shillings and pence as rent for ploughland, croft and meadow, for two mills and two town dwellings, all noted down on rolls of parchment that buckled beneath the cleric's quill. Over his head, the canvas shelter began to flap and rattle with the first squall of rain.

'How many more, m'lady?' he said, throwing the quill down and taking another one from behind his ear.

Rhoese held back the wayward wisps of hair with one hand and strained her eyes towards the great stone archway where Micklegate passed through York's city wall. The light was already fading and soon the gate would be closed for the night, though there were still stragglers who had walked all day to bring what they owed. A cart passed through, rattling and jolting behind two oxen, loaded high with sheep fleeces, and a party of riders surged behind, impatient and obviously in high spirits.

'Who's coming, Bran?' she called to her bailiff at the gate.

'They're Normans, m'lady,' he replied, frowning.

'Close the gate after the cart. Quick,' she ordered. Instinctively, she took a step backwards under the cover of the canvas shelter. The steady stream of wagons and animals passing along the track towards her demesne had attracted some heed, and several of the riders had stopped to watch the distant scene of organised chaos, their attention caught by bellowing steers and bleating ewes. Rhoese's guess that the Norman party were huntsmen returning from a day's sport would not be far wrong, with a spot of harmless trouble-making already in their minds. Damned Norman upstarts.

It was this unease, born of past experience, that kept her wary of what was happening beyond the stockade that surrounded her large compound, so that when two of the horsemen came as far as the gates to watch more closely, she backed even further into the shadowy recesses of the shelter. Since the last king's great national survey of two years ago, the estates that she had inherited from her mother had gone largely unchallenged since, at the time, she was still living at home, the rents and dues from her estate merely augmenting those of her late father, a king's thegn and wealthy merchant of York. Now, she was on her own, a target for property-seeking Normans, and vulnerable. One of the many risks of becoming independent.

Lowering her voice, she continued dictating to the cleric whilst trying to ignore the two inquisitive riders until some mysterious unseen force made her turn and look. One of them was watching the scene in the yard, but the other watched her, and only her. He was tall in the saddle and powerfully built, that much she could tell in one glance, not a man she had seen before in York, nor one she could have forgotten easily. His dark hair ruffled like thick silk in the stiff autumn breeze, and his eyes looked across at her like level daggers beneath straight black brows.

He saw her start, and beckoned to her, a signal she

quickly decided that a servant would not ignore. Pretence was the answer. 'My lord?' she called, walking unhurriedly towards him. A sheep scuttled across, stopping her halfway.

'Where's your master?' he called. His voice was abrupt and deep, used to command and to obedience, taking it for granted that she could speak French.

She shrugged. 'Away, sir,' she replied.

'And your mistress? Where's she?'

'Away too.'

'So who's in charge here?'

Again she shrugged. 'All of us. We're trusted.'

'Your name, girl?'

She took a deep breath, ready to lie. But the bailiff was not happy about the number of fleeces in the cart, and his loud query was meant directly for her. 'Lady Rhoese,' he called. 'This load's two short.'

A howl went up from the carter. 'There ain't, m'lady. They're all there. Honest.'

The horseman dismounted and threw his reins to the man by his side, and Rhoese saw that he would be intent on an explanation. The deceit was already over, and she had not enjoyed even this short-lived attempt at subservience.

Defiantly, she faced him as he came towards her through the gate. 'My name,' she said, crisply, 'is Lady Rhoese of York, daughter of the late Lord Gamal of York, and granddaughter of a former sheriff. Is that enough for you, or would you like me to quote my entire pedigree? I can, if you wish it, but I'm rather occupied, as you see.'

Lazily, he strode forward as if her defiance meant

nothing to him, his hair lifting off his forehead like a thatch in a gale. 'I'm sure you could. So why the deception, I wonder? Is that your way?'

'Oh, with Normans, sir, I use any wiles I can devise to keep their noses out of my affairs.'

'You appear to have strong opinions about Normans, my lady. What have they done to deserve it, I wonder?'

For some unaccountable reason, she felt her heart hammering and squeezing her breath from her lungs, further irritating her after she had sworn never again to be affected by a man. This man was standing within her compound as if he owned it, his great legs planted like trees, his hands splayed over slim hips where a gold-buckled belt sat low on a linen tunic with bands of blue and gold. Expensive attire. Unwillingly, she noticed his muscular neck, shoulders and chest like a wrestler, and she found herself doing what she knew men did when they looked at her, peeling him down to his skin to see what lay there. She realised she was blushing, and the smile in his eyes told her that he knew why.

'As for that, sir,' she said, lifting her chin, 'if you don't know the answer, then it's clear you've not been in England long. It would take at least a week to tell you what damage you and your kind have done to us in the last twenty-two years. Fortunately, we still have our dignity and our language left. Those are two things you'll never remove, thank heaven.' She looked around for her bailiff and called to him in English. 'Bran! Get this overweening lout from under my feet, will you?' To the Norman, she spoke again in French. 'As you see, sir, I'm too busy for small talk. Another day, perhaps. Pray excuse me.'

As she spoke, however, even her show of hostility was not enough to blind her to each detail of his face, the faint shadow round the strongly angled jaw, the firm wide line of the mouth, the dent in the chin and the long straight line of the nose. His high cheeks had already caught the shine of the rain, and the eyes that had been no more than dark slits were now widening at her brave animosity, deep brown, dark-lashed and unnervingly bold. She flinched, suddenly and inexplicably uncertain of herself, her eyes sliding reluctantly away to avoid reaching any more liberal conclusions about his remarkably good looks. A bitter voice breathed in her ear: he would be no different from the rest, Norman or English.

'Yes,' he said, 'I can see you have much to do. Are you the owner of this demesne or is your husband joint owner?'

'You ask too many questions, sir. And your friend is waiting.'

Her attempts to dislodge him made him smile. 'Hmm.' He grinned. 'Another time then, lady. Perhaps you'll be at the ceremony tomorrow, eh? As a tenant of the king, you'll surely be there with your donation?'

His probing irritated her. 'Oh, who knows how much curiosity value we English landowners have these days? We're a dying breed. Why not show ourselves while we still have the chance? Is that what you mean? Good day, sir.'

He found no ready answer to that, but nodded

curtly and strode away through the gate with a word to the bailiff who held it for him. Without another glance, he was back in the saddle and away at a canter, while Rhoese struggled to drag her mind unwillingly back to the pandemonium in the yard and to breathe past the uncomfortable knot of fear in her throat.

There was no doubt at all that she had overdone the antagonism for no reason except that he was a Norman. Or *was* there another reason, something too recent to be excused or explained? Something to do with men in general, those unreliable, feckless, self-seeking creatures? For the last ten months she had been reassessing her need of them, and now no other feelings remained except contempt and a wish for vengeance. Cold, hard, sweet revenge. Submission and humility she reserved only for special occasions when nothing else would do, having discovered to her cost how severely they were undervalued.

The cleric had stopped writing and was clearing away his tools before the rain spoiled his script. A bundle of rolls bounced about in the wind. 'Who was that, my lady?' he said, sticking his quills back into his hair.

'I've no idea,' she said. 'He'll not be back.'

Brother Alaric, the lady's chaplain as well as her accounts clerk, was not a gambling man, but even he felt tempted to put some pence on the return of that admirer before the next sunset.

The two riders had passed the crofts of Toft Green before one of them smiled and glanced at his stony-faced companion. 'You should see your expression,' he grinned. 'It's a picture.'

'All right. So tell me. Who is she?'

'That, my fine friend, is one of York's two remaining women landowners, and I cannot tell you of a single male who doesn't long to get his hands on it. Yes—' he laughed '—her *and* the property. Snapped your head off, did she? Well, she would. She's been here in this corner of the city for the last ten months, since her father died, and she doesn't let a man within a yard-length of her. Except her chaplain, of course. And her brother.'

'Well, there could be several reasons for that. She's the loveliest thing I've ever seen, Ranulf. Those great dark eyes spitting fire. That body.' He sucked in his breath, recalling the thick auburn hair, the full mouth, the skin moist with rain that ought to have told him she was a lady, even without the usual head-covering. She was the stuff of men's dreams and fantasies. 'She tells me her father was Gamal. Who was Gamal, exactly?'

'A king's thegn. One of the last here in York. A wealthy merchant. Disappeared at sea last winter. Traded in furs and walrus ivory, mostly. His wharf is alongside the river by the bridge. Big warehouses and several ships.'

'The business is still going, then?'

'Yes, the trading was taken over by his assistant, a strapping young clever-dick called Warin. Not only the trading, either.'

'Oh? What else?'

'The widow. He moved into Lord Gamal's house

and settled in with the second wife. A shrew. Danish. Didn't take her long to accept a bit of comfort. But the daughter, Lady Rhoese, moved out and set up on her own. Took her father's death hard, apparently, and doesn't want any more to do with the stepmother.'

'Or the stepmother's lover, who presumably gets his hands on more than the widow?'

'Exactly. There may have been something between him and the daughter. We're not sure.'

'We?'

'The court. The laugh is, Jude, that she believes that by keeping quiet and out of the way she'll be quite safe.'

'From what?'

'Norman attention. Marriage, and the usual property take-over. It's the only legal way a man can get at her estate, unless she sells it to him, of course, although plenty of women lost theirs *illegally*, as you know. But the idea of a woman holding an estate in her own name is ridiculous when she's supposed to be rendering knight-service to the king for it. She'll have to lose it eventually.' The young man named Ranulf wiped the drips of rain off the end of his nose and looked down sadly at his soaking green woollen tunic. Even for the hunt, he liked to do his best to earn the nickname 'Flambard'. Flamboyant was what he had always been, and even as the king's chaplain there would be no sombre clothing for him at a court known for its extravagant dress.

'So the king knows about her, does he?'

'Most certainly he does. Since he saw that survey his late father did two years ago, he knows exactly who's got what, where it is, how much it's worth and how much revenue he can expect from it. He's got *her* estate earmarked for whoever will pay him most to get their hands on it. Better start saving up if you want to put in a bid.'

'Then he'll marry her off?'

'Just like that, whether she likes it or not. And she won't.'

'So she'll lose everything.'

'Everything.' He pointed to a tall wooden fort on a mound beyond the thatched rooftops. 'Over there, see? That's one of the castles, and over there—' his hand swung further to the left '—is the big castle. King William the Bastard had to dam the River Fosse to make the moat for it. The city people were not too happy about that.' He laughed, thinking of the flooded houses and orchards.

But Jude was more interested in Lady Rhoese of York than in the two castles, which he had already seen on his way into the city. 'Tell me more about *her*,' he said.

The smile widened. 'I can tell you that we took bets.'

'On what?'

'On how long it would take you to win her.'

Jude's eyebrow lifted at that. 'I see. And how long d'ye think we'll have before the king returns to London? Do I have days, or will it be weeks?'

Ranulf patted his horse's wet neck. 'Well, we've got the St Mary's Abbey ceremony tomorrow, and then the king will want to go hunting again.'

'When does the king *not* want to go hunting?' Jude murmured.

'And I expect that two or three days later we shall return to London. That doesn't give you much time, does it?'

'Indecent haste, in the circumstances.'

'Think you can do it?'

'I intend to try. But I'll want to know more than you've told me.'

'Then you'd better know that the king has begun proceedings—' he glanced behind him, lowering his voice '—to confiscate her late father's estate.' As keeper of the king's seal, the young Ranulf Flambard was in a better position than most to know that.

Their manner became suddenly serious. 'Now that,' said Jude, 'is not funny, is it?'

'No, it certainly isn't.'

'Does the Lord Gamal's widow know yet?'

'No, but she soon will. The sparks will begin to fly when she finds out before the ceremony tomorrow. She'll be prevented from donating to the new abbey. And, worse still, she'll be thrown out of her house because the land it stands on will be part of the new abbey buildings.'

Rhoese called to the men, their hair now blackened with rain, who hurried to unload the carts and pen the animals. 'Come inside to sup, when you're ready.' The storerooms were packed with foodstuffs and fleeces from the dales. 'And bring the carters in too, Bran,' she reminded him. 'They'll have to stay overnight.'

The great hall was quiet after the blustering wind, enclosing her and Brother Alaric like a warm blanket that smelt of wood smoke and the nourishing pottage that hung in a cauldron over the fire. Blue smoke swirled and hung in the wooden rafters before filtering out through the heavy thatch, and Rhoese's glance swept possessively round the substantial space that was the men's living, cooking, eating and sleeping quarters all in one. Her own small bower was situated apart, between two storehouses for more privacy, but here she was still mistress of the house. Here were stout timber pillars dividing the side aisles into curtained cubicles drawn back to reveal fur-covered benches that became the household's beds each night. There was the daily food store at one end, and another door to the croft outside.

A woman stirred the pot over the burning logs within a circle of stones, looking up as her mistress entered, at once filling two wooden cups with honey-eyed mead for her and the red-nosed chaplain. A young maid lifted a sleeping cat off a fur-covered chest where she expected Rhoese to sit, but saw that she was still looking in silence at her beloved territory as if to remind herself of its sanctity and of the time when she had first escaped the wounding intrusions into her grief.

Rhoese took the cup from her nurse with a whisper of thanks. 'Where's Eric?' she said, sipping.

'Wrestling with Neal,' said Hilda, disapprovingly.

'In the rain?'

Two young men came in at the far end of the hall as she spoke, half-naked, laughing, and dripping with wet, reddened with the exertion and the grip of strong hands. Eric's smile in his sister's direction would have given a stranger no indication that he had known of her presence by every keen sense except sight, and now he came forward with one hand resting lightly on his friend's shoulder to greet her with a wet cold peck on the cheek. 'I beat him.' He laughed.

'My lady,' said Neal with a courteous nod of the head, 'he did beat me only because I let him.'

'Rubbish, man!' Eric gently punched his friend in the general region of his shoulder. 'I had you down twice.' For all his blindness, Eric led the way confidently to the fire and stood before it to peel off his sodden loincloth, heedless of Els and Hilda, Rhoese's maid and nurse. Neither of them could quite ignore the sight, for one of their advantages was that they could indulge themselves without being seen. Like his sister, Eric was beautifully made, tall and graceful with deep auburn hair tied back in a pony-tail that the rain and wrestling had partly undone. At twenty years old he was nearly three years younger than Rhoese and four years younger than Neal, the Icelander who was his constant companion. With Neal to act as his eyes, Rhoese had no fears for Eric's safety, not even from the women whose eyes followed him everywhere.

Openly admiring, Els was nudged roughly into action by the nurse with a curt nod to take her mistress's damp clothes and give her dry ones to wear. Mechanically, Rhoese co-operated with a lack of conversation they all noticed, especially Eric who had expected an animated account of the day's takings.

Rubbing his hair with a linen towel, and still naked, he found his way to her side to perch on the edge of the chest lid.

'What is it, love? Are you not pleased? I thought it was going well.'

It had gone well, though at that moment she had been possessed by a strange sense of foreboding that had been growing since the brief visit of the Norman, who had not even offered her his name. It was usually the first thing inquisitive men did. She recalled the shiver of fear she had felt instead of pleasure while she had treated him to her scorn, and the cool self-assurance of the man as he walked towards her with his too-many questions. No, she would certainly not be at the ceremony tomorrow, not even to see the new king.

'Yes,' she said, 'I am well enough pleased. Every-one came who was supposed to.'

'Father would have been proud of you.'

Only one year ago, Lord Gamal still lived, and she had loved Warin, her father's most trusted assistant, a man with an excessive ambition that included the pursuit of his master's daughter. At the time of his first interest, Rhoese had neither understood nor cared about his reasons, being then only twenty-one years old and ready to be caught by a man with enough brash persistence. Warin's success with York lasses and his tales of escapades in Norway and Iceland had excited her and had more than made up for his lack of sophistication and finesse. He had been eager and impulsive, and she had been swept into his big love-making arms with hardly time to savour the chase, such as it was. Her father had approved, and neither he nor Rhoese had seen any weakness in the man that could not be put down to the ignorance of youth.

Ketti, her Danish stepmother, had also encouraged the relationship, having taken quite a fancy to the young merchant whose affability towards her as Gamal's young wife could not be faulted. She was, after all, only a few years older than Warin, and to take on the role as future mother-in-law to a twenty-four-year-old man did not come naturally to her.

It was only a few months before Warin persuaded Rhoese to become intimate with him, since they intended to be betrothed as soon as he came back from the next trip to Iceland. Rhoese had truly believed that nothing could go wrong with her plans, even going as far as to clear out her father's merchandise from her property on Toft Green ready for their eventual occupation as a married couple. She had given herself to him here, in this very hall, just before he went off with her father on their voyage north to buy furs. Having no experience with which to compare the event, she assumed with a kind of contentment that Warin was probably better than most, if women's looks at him were anything to go by. But although the boat returned three months later with walrus ivory, unicorn's horn, furs and Warin, her father had been lost overboard in the icy waters of the North Sea and, by November of last year, 1087, Rhoese and Eric knew themselves to be orphans. And she was pregnant, having just passed her twenty-second birthday.

'You all right, love?' Eric said, holding her arm.

'Yes. Just remembering, that's all.'

'Don't.'

'I must.'

'Was it that woman with the howling bairn this morning?'

'No, I think not.'

'Then what?'

A squall of rain hit the thatch and burst through the door, flinging it hard against the wall and bending the flames over the logs with a sudden ferocity. 'Shut the door!' Hilda yelled as more men entered, unsure of the kind of welcome they were getting.

The effect of her father's death was worse than anything Rhoese had personally suffered until then, her mother Eve having died when Eric was born. Without her adored father, she saw her world turn slowly upside down, for she had awaited his return before telling anyone her secret. He was to have been the first. But the shock of losing him so abruptly and with no very plausible explanation made her ill, and she lost the foetus one terrible night with no one to help except Hilda and Els, the only ones except the chaplain to be told the truth. Eric had discovered it for himself.

Warin's sympathy over her grief was correct but barely adequate, and nowhere near enough for her to be able to tell him about the second cause of her anguish, especially when his attentions had already begun to veer noticeably towards Ketti on the pretext that she had lost most by Gamal's death.

Hurt, unwell and desperately unhappy, Rhoese began to spend more and more of her time here at Toft Green, in the hope that Warin would come and help to prepare it for their joint occupation. But that had no effect. Then one day she found him and Ketti lying together. Warin's defence—that he was merely offering Ketti some comfort—was unconvincing, and the outrage of his betrayal so soon after the other tragedies broke Rhoese's heart. There was no blazing row, no confrontation, simply a silent and hopeless withdrawal to her own house on Toft Green, the energy to fight for what had almost been hers having gone the same way as her happiness, her well-being, and her aspirations.

Hardly had she and Eric removed the remainder of their belongings than Warin moved in with Ketti, taking his aged father to join Ketti's cantankerous mother and the twelve-year-old son Thorn by her first marriage. The change-over was complete, and Rhoese redirected rents and dues from her Yorkshire properties to herself and Eric for the maintenance of an independent household.

Immediately, Ketti's hopes for a comfortable widowhood diminished at this withdrawal of supplies, and she protested. But Rhoese saw no reason to contribute her profits when Warin had taken over Lord Gamal's mercantile business, his large warehouses along the Ouse wharf, his two ships, his wife and the house on Bootham next to the expanding new abbey of St Mary.

In the ten hectic months since her father's death, Rhoese had erected a protective shell of ice around her damaged heart, keeping it cold with thoughts of revenge that, as yet, had done nothing to salve the deep wounds of rejection. Now, there was no man she could trust with her love except her brother, whose blindness from birth seemed not to matter when he had so many other rare qualities. He had already expressed a wish to join the monks at St Mary's, and Rhoese had sent a hefty donation for the new buildings, the foundation-stone of which was to be laid by the new king himself on the morrow. They now awaited a message from Abbot Stephen to say whether he would accept Eric as a handicapped novice.

He squeezed her arm gently. 'Go and prepare, love. We have guests to supper, and I'll play the harp for you afterwards, if you wish it.'

'And are you going to sup naked?' she replied. 'As an extra entertainment?'

'Neal!' he called across the fire. 'The lady has a suggestion.'

Judhael de Brionne's desire to know more about Rhoese had not even begun to be satisfied by his friend Ranulf's disclosure concerning the stepmother's tenancy problems. It was about the woman herself that he needed to know, and in characteristic style had soon decided that he could find out for himself, in private, more than he could be told by well-meaning friends eager to win wagers.

Alone, an hour after curfew, he rode through York's puddled streets to where the south-west corner of the high city wall enclosed Toft Green, where dark outlines of thatched huts within a stockade clustered around the great hall, with the scent of wood smoke carried on the blustering wind. Under cover of dark-

ness he waited in the hope that, sooner or later, someone would show themselves and tell him more about
how a Yorkshire noblewoman ruled the roost.

He did not have long to wait for a door at the back
of the hall to open, emitting the soft glow of firelight,
the strains of a harpist's song, and a woman's figure
silhouetted against the interior. Jude urged his stallion
forward a few paces so that he could watch her cross
to one of the smaller buildings and, now that the rain
had ceased, to leave the door ajar, presumably to shed
some light on the inside.

In a few moments she had emerged again, this time
carrying something beneath one arm and closing the
door stealthily behind her before slipping along the
side of the hut towards the trees at the end of the
croft, diving into their deep cover like a stoat sure of
its direction. Jude's heels touched the stallion's flanks
to direct him along the track until a gap in the wooden
stockade allowed them through. Heading for the same
trees, they picked a way silently over damp leaves,
showering both man and horse with droplets from the
branches.

The horse snorted indignantly, and the noise re-
sounded through the quiet woodland, sending the pursued woman skittering aside with a yelp of alarm,
then with a burst of speed that Jude was trained to
anticipate. The shadows were black and unhelpful,
but Jude's eyes were keen and used to seeking in the
dark, nor did the stallion have any difficulty in following the fleeing woman's crashing leaps that more
than once brought her down by clothes caught on tan-
gles of undergrowth and low branches.

With wildly fumbling fingers she tore herself free at last, only to find her path blocked by the huge snorting horse and its stamping hooves, then, as she dodged away, by its great hindquarters. A hand came out of the darkness to seize her, and at that same moment she hurled the bundle away into the under-growth with all her strength, yelping with terror at the restraining arms that pulled her backwards and held her, squirming and protesting. There was fear in her voice, and pleading. 'Let me go…please! I am the Lady—'

'Lady Rhoese of York. Yes, I know who you are,' Jude whispered in her ear. 'And you are breaking the curfew, which is worth a night's imprisonment, as I expect you know. Now, my lady, do I detect a change in your former manner, perhaps? Are you so dismissive now of inquisitive Normans?'

'You!' she snarled, twisting inside the cage of his arms. 'What are *you* doing here after curfew, sir? Let me *go*, damn you!'

'My, how your heart is beating.' His hand had delved under her cloak, moving upwards over her rib-cage to encircle one breast, his thumb monitoring the frantic thudding beneath her kirtle, an offence as serious as breaking the curfew.

'No…no!' she protested. 'No man may hold a woman so. Let go!'

'So tell me what you're doing out at this time of the night and who you're going to meet. A lover, is it?' His hand stilled, but did not withdraw.

'You have no right to know. My business is my own.'

'Not at this time of the night, lady. Tell me.'

Her hands could not prise his arms away. 'If you must know, I was on my way to St Martin's Church,' she said, angrily, 'to speak to Father Leofric. His tithes are due today.'

'And it couldn't wait until tomorrow? The priest is hardly going to starve for want of a tenth part of your dues, is he?'

Rhoese was silent. Her visit had nothing to do with the tithes, but she could not tell this Norman the real purpose when it was his earlier snooping that had prompted it.

'All right,' he said, turning her round to face him, 'if you won't tell me more, you can explain yourself to the sheriff tomorrow, if you prefer. Curfew-breaking is serious, and you should be setting an example.'

'Look…no…please! There's no need for that.' Her hands pushed against his chest, registering the soft wool of his cloak and the lower edge of the cloak-pin on his shoulder. Unable to see much of him, she could feel his breath on her eyelids as he spoke, and the withdrawal of his hand left a cool imprint below her breast. Now, all the fears and forebodings generated by his earlier interest, and in the dues she was receiving as he watched, surged back like night-demons, warning her not to antagonise him further. The Normans were a powerful force, and an appearance before the Norman sheriff could easily undo all her attempts to stay out of the public eye. The man must be appeased.

'No?' he said, softly. 'Then you have another suggestion?'

'Hospitality?' she offered. 'You could come into the hall and hear my brother play. He's a fine harpist. I can offer you mead, or ale?'

'And poison me, no doubt?'

'No, indeed. That's not what I meant. My chaplain himself will pour your drink, if that's what you fear.'

'Anything else, lady? Have you anything else to offer me?'

Rhoese froze, aware in every fibre of her being the direction his questioning was taking, and preparing herself to feel the insult and the helplessness of her situation, yet unable to prevent the sudden flare of excitement as she recalled how he had stood before her in the yard, his eyes beating hers down, challenging her attempts to dismiss him. She had felt that same excitement then, and had tried to counter it with a nonchalance that did not exist. She felt it again now and could find no sharp answer this time, not even when he moved her slowly backwards to press her against the broad trunk of an oak.

In the dark, excuses flitted across her mind like bats too fast to see. Then it was too late even for protests, and the shell of aloofness she had nurtured during the last ten months weakened under the tender-hard pressure of his body. She felt the muscles of his thighs through the fine fabric of their clothes, his soldier's arms bending her into him, the assuredness with which he handled her. His expertise showed in the way he angled her head into his shoulder and held it there with the most careful imprisonment, signalling that there would be no hastily snatched uncultured performance, even though the setting could have been improved upon. Later, Rhoese tried to excuse her lack of resistance as being useless against such a confinement, telling herself that she could not have evaded his mouth, even though she could.

There were no thoughts, only the warm insistent pressure of his lips slanting across hers that she knew was not meant for her delight but for his alone. His arms across her shoulders tightened, his grip on the nape of her neck was merciless, forbidding her mind to wander, compelling her to heed what she was forfeiting and reminding her that his was the conquering side, not hers.

Snatching at fleeting protests and thoughts of maltreatment, she tried to remain indignantly unresponsive, but soon realised that any reaction from her, either for or against, would have been swamped by the fierceness of his lust. Like a man starved of lovemaking, which she knew could not be the case, he explored her mouth from every angle with breathtaking skill and, when he paused, it was only to cover her throat with his kisses before returning with renewed passion to her mouth again. Warin, her only real comparison, had been eager and vigorous, but never with this man's masterly accomplishment, and though Rhoese would have preferred to rate him as no more than a clumsy molester of helpless women, she was far too moved to label him so when her legs were already turning to water.

She felt a hardness press against her belly, her own answering leap of fear and excitement, and the keen

contradictory betrayal of her shaky emotions. How
had she allowed this to happen? And why? 'Stop!'
she called to him. Her head was held back while he
tasted a path towards her ear. 'Please…no more…you
must stop. You have forgotten yourself, sir. I am an
English noblewoman and this has gone far beyond
talk of offerings. Let me go home now.'

He was breathing heavily against her skin, his
shuddering sigh barely acknowledging her protest.
Yet, even now, one hand had begun its own well-
informed journey on to her left breast, hurrying
Rhoese even further towards a warning. Grabbing his
wrist, she tried to pull him away, but her hand was
ignored and, as her cries were silenced by his mouth,
she understood that it would be he who called a halt,
and that this had less to do with the offence of being
out after curfew than with her discourtesy to him in
the yard.

This time, the beguiling movement of his lips over
hers was just enough to keep her mind teetering on
the brink of bliss while his hand like thistledown explored her in studied disregard of her command. Far
from forgetting himself, he was very much in control.
'Must?' he whispered. 'Are you still telling me what
I must and must not do, lady?' The stroking continued, stealing her protests away like a wind-torn web,
weakening her lungs so that she could not answer
him. 'Now I think we are beginning to understand
one another at last,' he said. 'Would you not agree?'

His question was easy enough to answer, for he'd
shown her in no uncertain terms what he wanted. That
much she could hardly fail to understand. Less sure

by far was her own understanding of herself, for now the unresponsiveness she had believed was hers to command had begun to desert her. She *was* responding, despite everything she could do to hold herself apart, to keep her mind level and cool. He would know. He was expert at this. Yes, he would surely know.

No, don't let him know. Pull away, before it's too late.

She pushed at him, viciously, heedless of the damage, and with the desertion of his caress and the sudden halt to her arousal, an anger took its place with a carelessness that shocked even Rhoese. 'You mistake, sir!' she snarled. 'It would take more of a man than you'll ever be to understand my contempt for your kind. I would find it easier to understand the mind of a toad. Presumably you have had your amusement at my expense, so now you can—'

His hand over her mouth cut off the rest of her tirade. 'Do not start again, my lady, if you please. There are plenty of dark hours left for my amusement, as you put it, and your unwillingness is of no consequence to me. If you value your noble chastity so highly, you had better learn to curb your tongue. I thought I'd made that clear. Shall I show you again who is master?'

Norman cur. Low-born scum. 'No,' she whispered. 'Leave me be. I can find my own way home. Just leave me.' There was the parcel to retrieve from the undergrowth, and her anger boiled not least because the whole episode had apparently been engineered to chasten her and to amuse this arrogant Norman who would now laugh about it, share the experience with his friends, itemising the points of interest, enjoying her humiliation. Most of all, her anger was inwardly directed towards herself for allowing this to happen without making any attempt to fight back or to injure him. Weak, stupid woman. So much for her scorn of men. Deeply ashamed, she lashed out at him with a delayed but futile attack upon his wide shoulders, hammering at him in a burst of rage.

'She-cat!' he laughed. Even in the darkness he caught her wrists. 'Come, lady. It's time you were locked up safely for the night.' He stepped away, still holding her securely.

'Locked up? No!' she cried, pulling. 'That's not what you agreed.'

'Hush, woman. I know what I agreed. I'm taking you home to your bower back there. You need not be concerned; I shall trespass no further on your domain, but nor is this the last you'll be seeing of me, so don't think it.' He hooked a hand beneath her armpit and led her towards the waiting stallion.

How would she know him? Chain-mailed and steel helmeted, they all looked more or less alike. Would he be in civilian dress or in war-gear? 'Your name, sir. Who are you?' she said.

'You'll discover that tomorrow, in the daylight.'

'I doubt it. You'll not see me tomorrow if I can help it.'

'You think not? Well, I know different, my lady. Take it from me, we shall meet again tomorrow.'

There seemed to be nothing to say to that, for the

last thing she wanted was to prolong a pointless discussion.

Without disturbing even the sharp-eared hounds, Jude returned her safely to the door of her bower, opening it for her before she could reach it, though his arm detained her until he had taken his proper leave. 'Until tomorrow, my lady,' he said with a slight bow. 'Do not venture out after curfew again.'

'No indeed,' she snapped. 'Who knows what ruffians one might meet?'

'Exactly,' he countered. 'York is a violent city. Sleep well.' In one fluid movement, he mounted the stallion and swung away, cantering off into the shadows in the direction they had come, leaving Rhoese shaken and puzzled, her body still tingling from his daring treatment. She was also concerned for the package she had intended for Father Leofric that would not benefit from spending a night in wet undergrowth, though she was not inclined to venture out again into the woodland that night. Turning in sudden fury, she aimed a savage kick at the innocent door, wincing with pain of a different kind as she hobbled into the dark warmth of her bower.

Dawn came ever later during those early autumn days, and the household was up and about before it was light enough for Rhoese to enter the woodland to retrieve the linen-wrapped bundle from its damp bed of leaves. To her relief, it was intact and undamaged. Last night, with the fear of a sudden interest in her ownership of an apparently thriving estate, she had felt the need to take this priceless treasure to a safer place. Father Leofric was the obvious one to understand the worth of a leather-bound, gem-studded gospel-book, its pages covered with a Celtic script and intricate patterns lovingly worked by skilled nuns in the last century. There was only one such nunnery where nuns' scholarship rivalled that of monks. It was Barking, in Essex, many miles away from York, but no ordinary citizen ever owned such a thing meant for the glory of God and for the use exclusively of holy men and women. And royalty. If it was ever found in her possession, she would have to offer a very convincing explanation of why it was in her keeping and, more to the point, why she had not delivered it immediately to the proper authorities. The brief joy she had derived from owning such a thing had long since been drowned by the fear of its discovery. She held the bundle close to her body as if it were a child.

Stooping to examine the ground, she noted the huge hoof-prints. Footprints, too. There was the oak. There was the slippery heel-print where she had tried to keep her balance. And there, when she closed her eyes, was the shockingly intimate and unlawful pressure of him against her, his hands roaming where they should never have been and which she should be trying to forget instead of remembering. An insistent pulse beat in her throat as the memory of his mouth reached her, catching at her breath and holding it until the tremor passed. *'Men,'* she whispered. *'Treacherous men.'*

Chapter Two

Ketti's House, Bootham, York

The sheriff's man reached Gamal's widow just before dusk at her large house in the area near St Mary's Abbey. He would have to deliver his message with some brevity if he wanted to reach home before the city gate closed at sunset.

With water forming a large puddle on the wooden floor around his feet, he delivered his most unwelcome news, if not with enjoyment, at least with a distinct absence of sympathy. Everyone in York knew of the woman's faithlessness. He stared the couple down with pale protruding eyes and wiped drips off the end of his nose with his wrist. 'If I may say so,' he replied to their protests, 'the news cannot be much of a surprise to you when my master the sheriff warned you during the summer that the consequences of ignoring the king's summons for knight-service would be the confiscation of property.'

'In the summer,' the woman called Ketti yapped, stumbling over the Norman-French, 'I was a newly grieving widow. I had other things on my mind.' Immediately, she wished she had a better grasp of the language when the sheriff's man glanced sideways at the strapping young man by her side, coolly assessing his bedworthiness by a pause at the bulge below his pouch.

'Yes,' he said, bringing his eyes slowly back to her angry blush. 'In scarce one month you must indeed have been grief-stricken, lady.' He cast an eye around the fine dwelling while Ketti and the young man, who had once intended to become her son-in-law instead of her lover, faced each other like a couple of rival mastiffs, each of them thinking how best to savage the other.

'It's Michaelmas,' Warin pointed out as if it would make some difference. 'The end of Holy Month. Where are we to go? This is our home.'

'That's something you should have thought of earlier,' said the sheriff's man, omitting the respectful 'sir' that an older man would have warranted. 'My lord the sheriff has instructed me to tell you that this land has been donated to the new abbey of St Mary for their extensions. The house and all the outbuildings will be demolished once the king returns to London, and you will have to find somewhere else to live. You will be sent signed confirmation of this in due course.'

Warin, bold, brawny, and not inclined to negotiate if it threatened to take longer than his limited attention span, would have liked to throw the impudent messenger out on his head, but even he could see the danger in that. He could also see, perhaps not for the first time, that he might have been a mite too hasty in his change of allegiance from daughter to step-mother, now that the latter was not as secure as he had thought.

Ketti swung her white veil over one shoulder. 'And I've already told you, whatever your name is, that my husband *died* last winter. He was in no position to send knights for the king's service.'

'But no message was sent. No excuse. No fine or relief in lieu of men. As you know, lady, a thegn holds his estate from the king in return for properly equipped knights whenever the king should need them. And the king *has* needed them sorely in this first year of his reign. His brother and uncles defied him. He needed all the men he could get. Any thegn who fails in this duty must forfeit everything to the king. That's always been the law and you must have known it. Now the monks need this land for their new building plan, and you will have to—'

'*Bugger* the new building plan!' Warin bellowed, unable to contain his anger any longer. It was bad enough to have made a wrong decision, but to have this pompous little toad-face telling him what they had ignored in the hope that it would go away was too much to suffer politely. The time for civilities had passed. His healthy outdoor complexion darkened with fury and his fair curls stuck wetly around his face. 'We've had your building plans up to *here* in York,' he blustered, levelling his fingers to his brow, 'and we're sick to death of them! You've raided our fair city and razed it to the ground, wrecked our homes and livelihoods, dammed the bloody river to make a moat for your bloody castles—'

'Warin…stop…shh!' Ketti warned, placing a hand on his arm.

But he shook it off. 'We've had to rebuild our warehouses, relocate our businesses, give up our orchards and grazing, see our houses engulfed in your stockades, see them trampled underfoot, and you dare to tell us that we can't live here now? We've built this place with hard-earned sweat on *our* land, and there's nobody…*nobody*,' he yelled to the man's damp receding back, 'going to get us out. Tell that,' he called across the courtyard, gesturing rudely, 'to your lord the sheriff, whatever his bloody name is.'

His return to Ketti was nothing like the hero's welcome he thought he deserved. 'You *idiot*!' she screeched, resorting at last to English. 'What good d'ye think *that*'ll do. Eh? He'll go straight back and tell the sheriff, the sheriff will tell the abbot, the abbot will tell the king, and before you know it there'll be a crowd of his strong-arm men here to tip us out into the street. You couldn't have waited for the king to go back home before you shot your mouth off, could you?' Her plain, sharp-nosed, thin-lipped face was blotchy with anger, and her fair-lashed pale eyes bulged more than ever in the stare of scalding reproof that Warin had already grown tired of.

The king, she was certain, had bided his time in this matter, waiting until he was up here in York at the end of the first difficult year of his reign. Feeling that some show of benevolence was appropriate, he had granted permission for the monks of St Mary's to extend their new abbey next to the church of St Olaf, and had granted them properties to sustain them with tithes due four times a year. He had come all the way up here to Northumbria with an impressively in-flated retinue to lay the foundation-stone and to show them how bounteous he could be, when he wanted to. And like sheep, the rest of the Norman landowners in Yorkshire had followed suit, donating land to the new abbey so that it would be said in years to come how they cared about the spiritual life as well as the tem-poral one. Liars. It was their own insurance they paid into, for their own quicker passage through purgatory.

Craftily, the king had let the monks have Bootham, the stretch of land beyond the minster next to the new abbey grounds where booths and stalls were set, and where the late Gamal of York's house stood. Now he could confiscate it for the best of reasons.

Ketti's screeching assault stopped Warin in his tracks, shocking him into a counter-attack. 'Well, what did you expect me to do? Stand here and be spoken to like a child who's been scrumping apples?' he yelled back at her. 'Don't be so daft, woman. He's not going to do anything before the king leaves for London.'

'Even so, you fool, you might have thought up a better way of handling the matter than by insults. Where d'ye think that will get us? You'll have to go to them and find out how we can get ourselves out of it.'

'It's no good *me* going to speak to anyone,' he snapped. 'I'm not the owner. You are. *You* go.'

'What good will it do for me to go?' said Ketti,

spreading her hands so that the tips of her wide sleeves skimmed the floor. She was not minded to do her own dirty work if someone else could be found to do it for her. 'So what are *you* doing here?' She waved a hand with some drama. 'If you want a home with me, go and fight for it. You wrestle with your mates like a prize bull; go and wrestle with the sheriff for a change.' She turned away, glaring at the smirking face of her twelve-year-old son Thorn. 'Get out!' she snapped. 'This is private.'

'Ketti.' Warin's voice dropped to a wheedling pitch, warming her back. 'Ketti, my love. We shouldn't quarrel over this.' He took her by the shoulders and pulled her back against him, sliding his great working hands over her breasts and kneading gently, knowing how that was guaranteed to soften her.

Her hands came up to cover his. 'Get off,' she whispered, pressing herself backwards into him.

Warin was careful to conceal his smile. It had worked already. 'No,' he said, bending to her veil-covered ear. 'You're so lovely, Ketti.' Her breasts were, in fact, the only lovely part of her, and not even the self-seeking Warin could pretend that she had either a face or a nature to match. 'There's no problem,' he whispered. 'We'll go and move in with Rhoese. She's still your ward. She's obliged to help.'

Her hands snatched his away and threw them aside as she whirled to look at him, her face suddenly hard with jealousy. 'You'd like that, wouldn't you?' she said. 'To live with *her*. My stepdaughter. Still hankering after her, aren't you?'

Still puzzled by his faulty timing, Warin's blue

eyes opened like a child's, though behind his façade
of innocence was a frantic attempt to backtrack. He
caught at her hands, holding her still. 'No, sweetheart.
Not to *live* with her, of course not,' he blustered.

'What, then?'

'Look, she's got her own place at Toft Green. She
moved out of your home, didn't she? Well, what d'ye
think she'd do if we said we had to move into hers
because we have nowhere else? Eh?' He shook her
hands to make her reply.

But Ketti's face was still hard. 'You think she'd
move out of Toft Green, don't you? Rubbish. She
won't. She's still crazy for you. She only moved away
because she couldn't bear the sight of you with me.
She'd let you into her bed every time my back was
turned. No, my lad. I'm not having that.' There was
a finality in her voice that Warin knew better than to
challenge.

'Well, then,' he said, 'we'll try sending her to the
king to see if *she* can negotiate another patch of land
for this one. Once she sees the threat of us moving
into her house, she'll fall over herself to be helpful.'

In that one respect, he was a better judge of the
situation than Ketti, though the flutter of pride and
excitement he felt at her jealous suppositions was
sadly misplaced. Rhoese would not have let him into
her bed if he'd been the last man alive in England.

By dawn next morning, the news had been delivered to Rhoese at Toft Green that her stepmother had
been deprived of everything she had inherited from
the Lord Gamal. The steward who delivered the mes-

sage had been with the family for as long as Rhoese
could recall and was almost in tears. 'Go and collect
your things,' she told him. 'You can live here with
us.'

The man knelt and kissed her hand. 'My lady,' he
stammered. 'My wife…may I…?'

'Of course. Bring your wife.'

After he had gone, Eric voiced his doubts. 'Was
that wise?' he said. 'To take him so soon? Him
alone?'

'After that woman took what was mine?' she replied. 'It may not have been too subtle, but it was
vengeful. And if they think *they*'re going to come and
move in here, they're mistaken. They're not.'

Eric sought her hand and took her from the end of
the hall out into the croft that was fenced with a wattle
hurdle to contain pot-herbs and medicinal plants. The
greenery dripped with diamonds and rustled with the
sounds of recovery after the heavy rain. 'Rosie,' he
said. 'Whatever you think of her, she's our kins-
woman and we cannot refuse to help. You know that.
She's also your legal guardian.'

Together, they leaned on the whitewashed wall of
the house beneath the steaming overhang, and Rhoese
knew a sense of despair yet again at the constant neg-
ativity of the Danish woman's influence upon her life.
Ketti had been married to Lord Gamal for only five
years with no apparent advantage to anyone except
herself and her family. Her son Thorn was well
named, and the old hag who was Ketti's mother rivalled the yard cockerel with her cackling. They

could not be allowed to disturb the peace of Toft Green.

'Yes, I know it. And she knows it too. That's what she's trading on. But the problem is hers, Eric. Why doesn't she get her Danish kin to help?'

'She knows that you know the archbishop, love. She's hoping you'll go and speak to him, I suppose. You could, if you wanted to.'

'I don't want to. Let her go and live with the cows.'

'Rosie!' he laughed. 'That's wicked! Go and see Archbishop Thomas. He and Father were friends. He'll be able to help, somehow.'

'Today's the stone-laying ceremony with the king. He'll be busy.'

'Afterwards, then. When the king's gone off hunting.'

She sighed. 'I really don't see why I should.'

'Yes, you do, love. I shall probably be safe at the abbey in a week or two, but you don't want to be landed with *her*, of all people. Or Warin.'

'He'll not put a foot in my house,' she said, angrily. 'I'll go.'

'When?'

'Later on, after the stone-laying. I may see Abbot Stephen, too.' She linked an arm through his and snuggled against him. 'I wish you would not leave me, love,' she said. 'I know you want to, but I shall miss you so sorely.'

'I think it's for the best. I can do no good here. I can't inherit. I can't protect you. I can't seek a wife. I can't fight for the king. I'm a liability. Best if I go and play my harp to the monks and do a bit of praying for souls. I can do that.'

'But you're my adviser. My counsellor. Who will I turn to?'

'We've had all this out before, love. It's been decided.'

'Abbot Stephen may not want you, after all.'

He smiled at her teasing. 'Then I'll *have* to stay with you, won't I? But don't you dare go and tell him of all my bad habits, just to put him off.'

'I will,' she said, kissing his cheek. 'I will. That's what I'll do. But this business worries me, Eric. The last thing I wanted to do while the new king was up here in York was to show myself. You know what he thinks about women who hold land. His reputation is every bit as bad as his father's.'

'Then find the archbishop, love. He's a Norman, but at least he knows you and our family. He'll listen to you.'

The crowds that packed into the city's narrow streets were thicker than ever that day, and as Rhoese and Els pressed forward against the flow, a seething mass of bodies surged through the arch in the wall, back towards the minster. The former king, William the Bastard, had visited York only to demolish it; his son had decided to give something, for a change, and those who had come to watch this phenomenon supposed that he must therefore be of a different mould from his brutal parent.

With a growing panic at the possible consequences of any delay, Rhoese had dressed in her best linen kirtle, dyed with damsons, over which a wide-sleeved gown reached to her knees, its borders decorated with a tablet-woven braid. The ends of her long plaits had been twisted with gold threads, and a fine white linen head-rail was kept in place by a gold circlet studded with amethysts, sitting low on her brow. Her last-minute check in the bronze mirror had been perfunctory, to say the least, for she found no pleasure in the reflection nowadays, nor were there smiles of recognition that had once sent back secret messages of love. Instead, she had pulled down her kirtle sleeves well over her wrists, adjusted the leather pouch at her girdle and hustled Els out of the door.

Only a few minutes ago, the possibility of a quiet word with the Norman archbishop had seemed like a reasonable course of action, but her doubts grew into real obstacles as they approached the minster garth where the great white cathedral reared above the roof-tops like a sleeping lion covered by cobwebs of scaffolding. Beyond it, the timber-and-thatch palace that was usually accessible to everyone was almost engulfed by a sea of fluttering pennants, tents, makeshift kitchens and stables, and armies of soldiers and monks who strode about or stood in groups, their gowns flapping in the breeze. Because the king was staying there, the archbishop's palace was being heavily guarded.

Two long lances crossed in front of them. 'Can't go in there,' one soldier said, looking Rhoese up and down. 'Not unless you've got something to give to the monks.' He winked at his companion.

Quickly, she seized her chance. 'I have land,' she said. 'Where do I go to make my donation?'

The man hesitated. 'You got the documents, then?'

'Of course I have, man,' she snapped, 'but I'd be a fool to bring them out in a crowd like this. The clerks have records. Just tell me where they are and have done with your questions.'

The lances were withdrawn. 'Over there, lady.' The soldier pointed to the largest leather tent outside which stood a table covered with rolls of parchment. A tonsured cleric sat behind it and by his side stood a tall Norman soldier who pointed to something on the parchment before them. He straightened and looked directly across at Rhoese as if he was expecting her, his head easily topping the men and horses passing in between.

She recognised him immediately, even though his head was now completely encased in a shining steel helmet, the nose guard of which hid the centre of his face. Small shining steel rings enmeshed his upper body down to his knees, split up the centre of the skirt for riding. Leather straps and silver buckles held a sword low on his left hip. A brawny young squire fed his huge bay stallion something sweet from his hand, and Rhoese was both puzzled and annoyed to see them there when she had been so sure of escaping his attention, after last night. The clerk lifted his head to look at the two women, then bent it again to his scroll, and they had no choice but to approach in the full critical stare of the man who had acquainted himself with her so forcefully. Hours later, she was to recall how that short walk was like pushing through deep sand, and how breathless she was on arrival.

Deliberately, she avoided looking at him, but spoke in English directly to the clerk instead. 'Master Clerk, I wish to speak with my lord the archbishop. Would you direct me to him, please?'

The cleric looked up at her, allowing the roll of parchment to spring back over his hands. He caught it and set it aside. 'You are?' he said.

'The Lady Rhoese of York,' she said. 'Daughter of the late Lord Gamal.'

'Speak in French,' said the Norman. ''Tis the language of the court, as you both well know.'

The cleric seemed surprised, but merely glanced at him before rising respectfully to his feet. 'Lady Rhoese, we were just looking at your—' He stopped abruptly at the Norman's signal.

'At my what?' she said. 'My estates? Is that what you have there? The survey taken two years ago of the Yorkshire lands? And who wants to know what I hold? Meddling Normans and their like?' Her glance at the tall Norman was unmistakeably accusing, but it was no match for a thirty-year-old captain in the king's service used to commanding men twice his age, and the fierce message from beneath the level steel brow of his helm took only seconds to make its impact. She had better say no more along those lines, it said. Remember last night.

The brown creased skin of the cleric's face relaxed into soft folds like a well-used pouch and his hands slid furtively past each other into the sleeves of his faded black habit. 'Yes, my lady,' he said. 'I have it here because the king himself needs to see it.'

Rhoese felt the blood in her veins freeze as a chill wind blew across the crowded field. 'Mine?' she whispered. '*My* property? Are you sure?'

'Quite sure. In fact, his Grace is with Archbishop Thomas at this very moment. Your arrival will be of some interest to them, I should think.' He gathered the scrolls up like a bundle of firewood and clamped them under one arm. 'I shall take these to him and tell him you're here. It will save some time. Would you mind waiting with Judhael de Brionne?' he said, indicating the soldier. 'He'll escort you, m'lady.' Half-smiling at her in apology for the lack of choice, he turned away and disappeared, leaving Rhoese more puzzled than ever and wishing she had not come.

The Norman had hardly taken his eyes off her. 'I understand you've been told of the confiscation of your late father's estate,' he said, matter of factly. 'Is that why you're here? To plead for reinstatement?'

Briefly, it occurred to her that this man could hardly have cared less whether she had heard or not, otherwise he would not have risked a mention of it so casually, moments before she was to meet the king, and again her anger flared keenly at the incessant and callous theft of English land and property into Norman coffers. 'It's a game to you, isn't it?' she hissed at him. 'To see who can take most, fastest, every last acre of it, no matter how many generations have held it. Just like your forebears the Northmen. No, Norman, I'm not here to plead for reinstatement. I'd not waste my breath so foolishly.' Her brazen stare swung away with her last words, conveying her despair as well as her consternation at seeing him again so soon, face to face.

'No,' he said, flatly. 'No game, I assure you. I was about to suggest that, if you had come to plead, you'd be wasting your time as well as your breath. Once his Grace has set his mind on something, he doesn't budge. But I see you need no advice from me on that subject. You northerners are fierce protectors of property, are you not?'

'Yes, and despite what I said yesterday, you've managed to find out what I am owed, who from, and for what. Haven't you? Well, it will be interesting to see how long it remains in my name now. You must be well pleased with your spying.'

'If you think the king is interested in you as a result of anything that I saw yesterday, lady, then think again,' he said, harshly. 'There is only one part of it so far that interests me.'

Holding her anger back on so tight a rein would normally have made her more aware of the precise implications of every word he said. This time, however, it was only his reference to the king's interest that caught her breath and held it like a hard ball of fear in her throat, and though she opened her mouth to speak, nothing came. Before she could loosen her lungs, the cleric reappeared, beckoning to her and Els to come forward, and they were led by him through groups of curious men across to the archbishop's thatched hall.

It was now almost unrecognisable, thronged with heavily mailed guards and their squires, monks and high ecclesiastics still in their jewelled vestments, scribes and messengers in the royal livery, nothing like the place she had visited with her father when he had been greeted as a friend. Her original idea to speak to Archbishop Thomas before he left with the king was already losing any appeal it had once had.

The man called Judhael de Brionne was close behind her, and there was to be no turning back. 'Go on,' he whispered, as if challenging her to dispense the same aggressiveness she had shown to him. But at first sight it looked as if such an attitude would be irrelevant, confronted as she was by such an unexpected sea of faces and a crowd of male bodies in a hall ten times the size of her own. Between every wooden pillar and alcove, men of all ages stood around in varying degrees of involvement, some clearly bored and restless, other attentive and hovering like hawks above rolls of parchment on the table before the archbishop, diving into the heaps to scavenge for information. Sprawled across a chair at the far end was a man she knew to be only twenty-eight years old and totally devoid of either charm or grace. William the Second of England. His hand fondled the thigh of a slender young lad who stood next to him, whispering into his ear and giggling.

At the entry of Rhoese and Els, the buzz of conversation stopped, making their long walk down the hall more like an hour's trek at the side of the Norman, while the inane grins and loud comments that she knew were meant for him fell upon her ears also. 'Well done, Jude,' one of them called. 'Keep your armour on, Jude,' another said. 'You'll need it.'

Normally, she would have insisted on fierce reprisals for this lack of respect, but the knight would allow her no time to respond, and she knew that she would not leave here any the richer for having met the king, or the archbishop. Furthermore, each step she took gave her a better understanding of why it was being said by the English that this new royal court was a disgrace, inclined to every kind of vice and corruption. In the shadows, men stood close together, openly embracing.

Her ears burned more hotly than her cheeks as she and Els sank into a low curtsy before the king, while any hope of being treated fairly evaporated like a pond in the height of summer. This was exactly what she had hoped to avoid for so long, and now she knew her time was up.

The natural light in the hall came from square holes set high up in the walls kept open by wooden shutters on pulleys. Extra lamps were perched on wooden beams nearest the king, and it was by this light that she now saw the man with whom she had hoped to speak in private: Archbishop Thomas of York. By his side stood a woman, except for herself and Els the only other female in this vast hall.

'You!' Rhoese whispered. It was Ketti, her stepmother, with not even a maid to accompany her. Deep inside, a part of her hardened still further at the realisation that no good could come of this either, while bewilderment, despair and foreboding returned to wipe out whatever words she had been preparing.

Even after one year, the new king had gained a reputation for getting to the point with a suddenness

that left people hardly knowing to what they had
agreed. It was no different for Rhoese, nor was she
helped by the deeply unpleasant rasping voice that
needed all her concentration to understand it. 'Lord
Gamal's daughter,' he barked, erupting from the chair
like an unleashed hound and coming to stand before
her. He was stocky and belligerent, bull-necked and
florid.

'Yes, your Grace,' she said. His eyes were odd, one
flecked with brown, the other bluish-green. Quickly,
she looked away.

'Well, I've called in your father's estate, so that's
that. If I cannot rely on my tenants to provide men
when I need them, I'll give my property to men who
can.' He looked around him, well content with his
summing up. 'He didn't even send out three merchant
ships last year at his own expense, so I'm told, and
that's another failure,' he said, looking this time directly at Ketti.

Against all protocol, Rhoese interrupted him before
being invited. 'But your Grace…my father died…lost
overboard. Surely these are extenuating circumstances?'

'Eh?' the king bellowed, visibly reddening. 'Extenuating *what*?'

The hall fell ominously silent.

'Circumstances, sire,' she said.

There was a sound and a slight movement from one
side, and the archbishop moved forward into a pool
of light where a fitful ray of sunshine caught the gold
panel on his chasuble. 'Too late to go down that road,
my lady,' he said quietly into her ear. 'The Lady Ketti

has already explained that to his Grace. You are here to help *her* at this difficult time. She's going to need a home, you see. Isn't she?' He held out his ring for her to kiss.

Archbishop Thomas had known her father well. The York merchant had brought back rarities, furs, falcons, walrus-ivory and wine for the Norman churchman's pleasure, and they had trusted each other. No doubt the archbishop believed he was returning the favour by helping Gamal's widow after the confiscation of her livelihood. Yes, she *was* going to need a home. Rhoese's.

She looked across at her stepmother dressed modestly in grey with not a jewel in sight, her mean little face the very picture of pathetic humility, her hands clasped tightly around a rosary of jet and bone which Rhoese knew not to be her best. Cleverly, the woman had got to the archbishop first to remind him of the wealth of her ward Rhoese, and how her stepdaughter had recently refused her friendship when she, Ketti, needed it most. Their eyes met, and Rhoese read the blazing malice and jealousy behind the mask of pity. 'My stepmother has a large family of her own, my lord,' said Rhoese, hearing the heartlessness of her reply fall upon the silent hall.

'They're in Denmark, woman,' barked the king. 'And what's more, it's high time *you* were married.'

Rhoese frowned, unsure of the exact nature of his pronouncement. She felt the strong clasp of Els's hand, then she turned to look behind her for the knight to see whether he had left her to her own devices and was unaccountably relieved to see that he was at her back, less than a pace away. Her eyes travelled upwards over the steel links to his eyes and found that they were fixed on her with an expression she could not interpret. Still baffled, she turned next to the archbishop whose kindly face was, for a Norman, usually easy to read. *'What?'* she whispered.

'His Grace is telling you that he wishes you to be married, my lady.'

'But I don't want...I haven't...no! This is *your* doing!' she said to Ketti, furiously. 'How *could* you? You know full well that I have no intention of marrying. Your Grace, marriage is not for me, I thank you.'

To her utter humiliation, the king appeared to be enjoying the dispute as if it were an entertainment for his delight, and his bellow of laughter was so unexpectedly loud that Rhoese stepped back, causing her to trip over the Norman knight's foot. Instantly, her elbow was supported by his large hand, her back by his body, holding her upright until she could find both feet again.

The king squeaked as he replied to her, 'I hadn't thought...ugh...hadn't thought of marrying you *myself*, woman,' he laughed. 'Did you think...oh, my God...that I was offering you...?'

'No, your Grace, I didn't.'

'Well, thank God for that,' he blasphemed, impervious to the disapproval on the archbishop's face. 'I was trying to tell you that you won't need *your* house in York when you'll have one with a Norman. I've had a good—'

'A *Norman*?' Rhoese snarled, glaring at the king.

His laughter stopped as abruptly as it had begun and his face reddened again to a tone deeper than his pale red hair. 'Yes,' he snapped with a sudden anger. 'A Norman. What have you against *that* idea? Is a Norman not good enough for you? Or is not *any* man good enough to fill the role of husband? Eh? Is that why you're still unmarried? What age are you?'

'Almost twenty-three, sire, I think.'

'God! You should have had a brace of bairns by now, woman.'

He could not have known it, but that was probably the most hurtful remark he could have made, but to make it in public before a hostile crowd, and before her vindictive stepmother who had stolen the man she was to have married, made it doubly harrowing. Rhoese paled, swaying with the pain, and once more the hand came to steady her beneath one elbow.

The king noticed nothing. 'Well, as I said, I've had some good offers for you from my loyal vassals, lady, and you have your stepmother to thank for releasing you from her wardship. She was quite reluctant to let you go, were you not, lady?' He looked across at Ketti, who bowed her covered head demurely, hiding the triumph in her eyes. 'Yes, so she was. And anyway, no women in my reign will hold land in their own right. I'll not have it. It's against God's laws, isn't it, my lord Thomas?'

The archbishop bowed. 'Indeed so, sire,' he said. 'I'm sure Lady Rhoese will see your reasoning, once she gets used to the idea. English women, I believe, are not used to having their husbands chosen for them. Is that not so, m'lady?'

She had nothing to lose now except her life, and it was only the thought of Eric, her brother, that made her worth anything to anyone as a person rather than as a commodity. 'English women *are* used to having their husbands chosen for them,' she replied stoutly, looking directly at Ketti, 'but they are invariably given some say in the matter. A woman has the right to say no, if she doesn't approve.'

'Not in my reign she doesn't,' said the king, loudly. 'And it's time this matter was settled. I'm getting bored with it, and I've been ready to go hunting since we got back from the ceremony. I'll have no more argument. Lord Gamal's widow and her household can have the place at Toft Green and you'll have the husband I've decided on. So there.'

Shaking her head in despair, Rhoese saw that to try to reason with this man would be pointless. He was unpredictable, and closed to any argument a woman could put forward. His sense of humour was grotesque in the extreme, and his insensitivity was too humiliating to be suffered by prolonging the discussion. Again, she turned to the knight behind her for one last glimmer of understanding from someone, anyone, but he was looking across to the other side of the hall where there was a jostling and a shoving accompanied by bawdy shouts and hoots of laughter. A man was emerging, summoned by the king's beckoning hand.

'Come on over, Ralph!' he called, roughly. 'It's your bid I've accepted. She's yours, and her estate. It's quite a fair size. I don't know what the rest of her is like; you'll have to find that out for yourself.

Eh?' The laughter he generated by these coarse remarks brought hot waves of shame to her cheeks and
a suffocating fear that rose into her throat like a sickness. Vaguely, she felt a firm grip around her upper
arm, pulling her hard against a chain-mail chest, and
when she looked for the source of her support, she
found that the knight was still not looking at her but
at the man who was being almost pushed forward to
where they stood.

'Come closer,' said the king to Rhoese, 'and meet
your future husband. He's a good fighter, is Ralph.
None better. A loyal vassal. He deserves a reward.
Here, Ralph de Lessay, put this in your bed to warm
it, man. This should get you a few heirs, if you know
how to go about it.'

There was a roar of laughter and applause so loud
that none of Rhoese's protests were heard, yet still
the grip on her arm was maintained as if the knight
had forgotten to release her. Nor had he laughed.

'Let her go, Judhael de Brionne,' the king commanded. 'It's your turn next. This one's for de Lessay. Let go, man.'

The grip slowly relaxed, casting Rhoese adrift into
a sea of grinning faces and clapping hands through
which she could still make out her stepmother's jubilant expression. Turning her back on it, she came
face to face with a man of more than middle age, a
deliberate move on the king's part to get another lu-
crative offer for her when this husband died, making
her an even richer prize than she was now. It was a
favourite artifice.

Ralph de Lessay, it seemed, had as little grace as

the king and as much excitability, for he grabbed Rhoese unceremoniously by the shoulders before she could stop him, pulling her hard into his sweating face for a mouth-stopping slobbering kiss that left a trail of spittle to drool down her chin. His soldier's grip hurt her intensely.

She brought up her arms to push, to wipe her face with her sleeve, to keep him at arm's length. Gasping for air, she sobbed to the king, 'No, sire! *No!* This is unworthy. This is *not* the way the daughter of a king's thegn should be treated. Please, let me go home, I beg you.'

The king's face straightened into a sober block of recognition like a child who had suddenly become aware of a misdemeanour. 'Yes,' he said, tightening his mouth. 'That's enough. Take her home, de Brionne. It's time we were away on that hunt.' With a sudden about-face, he turned and strode through the hall, knowing that the crowd would part for him like the Red Sea, and soon the place was emptying except for the clerks, the archbishop and his assistants and those most involved with the whole disgraceful incident.

Thoroughly shaken, Rhoese was the first to find a voice, determined not to give Ketti any pleasure by an exchange of incivilities that she would win, hands down. From the archbishop, however, she hoped for something that might still lend a grain of dignity to the proceedings, something that might allow her to walk away from this nightmare with her head held high. A blessing, perhaps? A word of comfort that would remind her of some small benefit? 'My lord?'

she whispered. 'Am I…is he…? Oh, my lord, is this truly happening to me? Can he *do* this?'

He had seen it before and he knew that William Rufus could do exactly what he pleased with any remaining English property, especially a woman's. 'Yes,' he said, scowling at the stupidly grinning face of the man who had won her, 'he can. And may I suggest to you, de Lessay, that you get a grip on yourself and behave with some dignity towards this woman who is to be your wife. Go and bathe, man. You stink like a fishmonger.'

Taken aback at the unflattering comparison, Ralph de Lessay's shoulders slumped as he turned obediently away, and Rhoese saw how the bald patch on his head was scabby and brown where the summer sun had blistered it. At the same time she had to resist the temptation to hug the archbishop for saying what she herself would like to have said.

To Judhael de Brionne, the archbishop said, 'Take the Lady Rhoese home, Jude. There's nothing to be gained from hanging about here. The marriage will be in York before our return to London, I'm sure. His Grace doesn't like delays.'

Ralph de Lessay, euphoric after his success, seemed to have second thoughts about the mode of Rhoese's return to her home. 'Wait!' he called, coming back to them. 'I'll take her myself. I've a mind to see…'

Swiftly, Judhael de Brionne caught him by his mail beneath the chin, almost lifting him off the ground with one hand and hurling him backwards into the king's chair with such force that the man and chair went crashing over into the rushes. 'You've seen enough, short-arse!' Jude snarled. 'Do as the archbishop says and take a bath. You *stink*!' Without waiting to see the man recover, he placed a hand under Rhoese's armpit and walked her at an urgent pace out of the hall and into the bright light of day, with Els almost running to keep up. Neither of them even glanced in Ketti's direction, so missed her change of expression from satisfaction to admiration.

'Let go!' Rhoese said, swinging her arm up. 'We can take ourselves home.' Over their shoulders, men watched for the inevitable scene.

He caught her around the waist, ignoring her yelp of protest. 'Yes, lady, I know you can. And the sooner we get away from this place the better. Come on!' He swooped to gather her knees over his arm, then hoisted her high on to the stallion held by his squire, dumping her without ceremony behind the high saddle to which she was bound to cling to avoid falling off. From that height it was difficult for her not to look at him, and through her confusion and anger, she noted every detail as if to compare it with the scruffy and disgusting knight who had insulted her so publicly. Under English law, he would have been punished for that. Here before her was a tall confident knight whose hands had supported her, whose appearance was immaculate from gleaming helm to polished spurs, whose stern expression told her he was not one to cross, unless she was prepared to be hurt. Formidable was the word that sprang to her mind.

'You'll ride pillion with me,' he said. His look took in the beauty of her full mouth and the perfect flushed

bloom of her cheeks before returning to her eyes, settling into their anguished velvet brownness with a
slow blink. He would know exactly what to do with
her, his look said, unlike that boor he had knocked
flat.

Her mind stopped working, and for once she found
nothing to say to him. But as he leapt into the saddle
as if vaulting over a gate, swinging one leg over the
horse's neck, she could not help the shiver of unwilling pride that, after that degrading scene of a few
moments ago, she was riding high behind a man with
some sense of how she must be feeling, even if his
way of responding to it was less than gentle.

Over the knight's broad shoulder she saw that Els
was similarly seated behind the squire on a chestnut
gelding and that her arms had already encircled the
young man's waist. As Rhoese felt the horse move
away, she clung with one hand to the cantle until the
knight's hand came round to find it and take it to the
belt at his waist. 'Hold on to that,' he said over his
shoulder, 'and stay close.'

'Why would I want to stay close to you?' she said
under her breath.

'Because it's easier on the horse,' he replied, as if
she should have known.

It had not taken the knight, Judhael de Brionne,
long to reach a conclusion about how best to win this
woman, though it had already begun to look as if bets
could be lost to those who had put money on his
success. The matter that Ranulf Flambard had men-
tioned yesterday had accelerated far more suddenly

than any of them had anticipated, and now she was almost out of bounds before the game had begun. And yes, she had been correct in her assessment: it *was* a game to take from the English whatever was available, both a game *and* a business at which he had already benefited. It had been all the more satisfactory for being quite difficult, English laws having been designed to cover every small point regarding possession of property *and* women. Nevertheless, since the first William's death, his son had shown himself to be less particular about keeping the English laws intact. This afternoon's fiasco was an example of how happy he was to bend any rule that would put more money into his treasury, whether it was fairly done or not. Like his father, William Rufus had no qualms about going back on his word if another bidder made him a better offer. Ralph de Lessay must be displaced.

Jude felt the touch of Rhoese's shoulder on his back and her little thumb stuck into his belt. The king had been his usual unpredictable self, dragging de Lessay out of the crowd in the excitement of the moment as one more spontaneous and bountiful gesture of the day. As if the woman had not been embarrassed enough. It had not been well done. He had felt her sway with consternation. Her body was soft, and though she was showing the world her indomitable spirit by spitting fire at every man in sight, he had seen the pain behind her eyes and felt the shockwaves as the king's demands had shaken her. Man or woman, it made no difference to William Rufus. He used them both the same.

Ranulf Flambard had been eager to hear how Jude

would go about winning the body, if not the heart, of York's unassailable beauty. Ranulf had offered what he believed were helpful suggestions, none of them particularly original and most of them quite missing the point that she was obviously immune to that kind of approach. Jude knew better than that; any woman with such a chip on her shoulder for whatever reason required a different kind of handling. She was not for the faint-hearted, and certainly not for a seasoned hard-bitten campaigner like de Lessay who hauled on his reins as if he was pulling a boat in.

But things had moved ahead with unsettling haste, and what had started out as a game meant to last a week or two, as such games usually did, had now grown into something more serious. Not just that she was to be married at the king's discretion: that happened all the time. Not because she was wealthy, either, or because she had made an enemy of that weasel-faced stepmother. No, there was something more to it than that, something that had disturbed Jude since he had first seen her counting her rents. She was vulnerable, exquisitely beautiful, tempestuous yet with a hint of scaredness, and not quite as ice cold as she would like to be thought. He had seen the look used on him that men used on women, and though it had been quite unconscious, he was experienced enough to recognise it. Until now, he had only toyed with thoughts of marriage, laughing at his father's urgings to find himself a wife and enjoying his reputation as a breaker of women's hearts, both married and single. The possibility of taking an Englishwoman to his bed permanently had never been more than a passing thought during his eight years here in England. Until now.

But this one presented more than a challenge; more like a crusade to discover the cause of all that anger, to channel it into the positive energy of loving. Too bad that oaf had tried to kiss her with that great broken-toothed mouth of his. Now he, Jude, would have to show her how it ought to have been while she was still weakened, and then he would have to find the best way of removing de Lessay from the position into which he had just been hurled by the king.

The ride through York's crowded streets would have taken only minutes if there had been more than one bridge across the river, for the minster garth and Toft Green, not so far distant as the crow flies, were on opposite banks. To Rhoese, with her mind in complete turmoil once more, the journey was a total blank. Normally, she would have enjoyed seeing the traffic of pilgrims and merchants, foreign faces and strange dress, traders and their stalls, women calling greetings; but not on this day and not from a seat behind a Norman, of all people, those most feared and hated of all strangers, as foreigners were known. Even after twenty-two years, they were nowhere near being accepted, nor did it appear that they were making any effort to be. And now, it looked as if she would be tied to one for ever, bought and sold, betrayed by the stepmother who not only wanted to possess her home, but also wanted her to disappear.

They crossed the wooden bridge over the River Ouse where her late father's ships were tied up along the wharves, giving up their precious cargoes from the northern ports. Few merchants would set sail this late in the year; fewer still could understand why Gamal had chosen to do so, to his cost. Rhoese wondered if Warin would be there and whether he might look up and see her riding behind this taciturn Norman knight. There was no sign of him, however, and then they were on Micklegate, literally 'the big street' in Old Norse, and almost home. Then she would have to tell them how all their worst fears had materialised in the time it took to say a Pater Noster.

Dismounting, the squire opened the gate at Toft Green and let them through into the deserted court-yard where only a dignified line of geese waddled away from the hooves. 'Take the girl in,' said Jude to his squire. 'Tell them we're coming.'

Rhoese would have preferred not to rely on this man's say-so, but it was a long way for her to drop without assistance and she was left sitting alone on the horse's rump as the knight led both horses across to the stable and tied the reins to the ring on the wall. Then he came to her to place his hands upon her waist, and she had no option but to lean forward and be caught in his arms like a child. Without a word, he carried her straight into the dark stable where the warm aroma of dung, hay and horseflesh mingled sweetly and where he stood her carefully upright against the timber wall with the bulk of his body clos-ing her in.

She wanted to remonstrate, but this confrontation seemed as unreal to her as the previous one and noth-ing made sense any more; nothing and no one. In one quick pull he removed his helm and placed it on a sack of oats, pulling back the mailed leather-lined coif from his head to reveal a layer of thick dark hair that stuck like silk to his skull. Once again, he was the man with whom she had had words yesterday, and now she knew for sure that this was a continuation of that, where he was about to settle the score with the last word.

She placed her hands flat on his steel-linked chest, but he pushed them away with one quick flick of his wrists and, picking up the hem of her long sleeve, used it to wipe her chin of de Lessay's odour that still clung there. He held her face, watching her eyes show confusion and anger before they clouded with defence. And a warning. 'Oh, no, Norman,' she whispered, pushing at him again. 'Oh, no, you're out of your depth here. I do not owe your kind any thanks for this day's work, nor am I ready for another mauling. There is no man I want near me—'

He did not wait to hear the rest, for none of it was relevant to him and there was no time to explain. Catching her wrists, he held them behind her back as he pressed her against the wall, and though her intention had been to writhe, to scratch at his eyes, kick and scream, the invasion of his mouth held her completely immobile, draining the energy from every limb. Concentrating all her awareness into that moment of tantalising sweetness, she was suspended like a star in space and time, forgetting to fight or to think about objections or the futility of it all. Something at the back of her mind flared like a dying flame in a draught of pure air, blazing briefly to illuminate a gem, something precious and sublime, just beyond her reach. Then it was gone, and his lips were releasing her, hovering warm and firm over hers with just enough space for words. 'You are wrong, woman,' he whispered. 'It is not I who am out of my depth. Is it? And I shall get closer than that, believe me.'

Her eyes opened and her body sprang into action without her bidding it, pushing, twisting, panting with the effort. Then, as he made no move to release her, she was obliged to wait and to watch his eyes, knowing by their direction that he had not finished with her and that she would be made to wait until he had. And though his arrogance both angered and unnerved her, the taste of him was still seeping through her senses, lingering and enthralling her, holding her in readiness. Again she felt his mastery as her eyes closed, and what she thought she knew about a man's kiss was wiped out at the next touch of his lips, like finding a superb wine after knowing only stale water.

But it was too sweet to be borne for long after the dreadful events of the afternoon, and her heart pleaded for some respite from the surfeit of emotions. She tore her mouth away with a hoarse cry of anguish. 'Let me be…no…please…go away. Leave me! *Leave* me!'

At once, he released her, catching her elbows as he had before when the ground had lurched beneath her feet, waiting for the inevitable questions and reproof, feeling the trembling anger through her arms.

'Who *are* you?' she said. 'Do you insult Norman women so freely, sir?'

'Judhael de Brionne,' he said, adjusting the linen head-rail over her hair. 'I am Count Alan of Richmond's vassal, and I came with him in the king's retinue. And I don't think it would help matters for you to know what I do with Norman women, my lady. More to the point is that you should see how some Normans are more skilled than others. You may have been sold to de Lessay for the moment, but that will have to change.'

'I can scarce believe I'm having this conversation,' she said, intending to cow him with her wide blazing eyes. 'You are telling me, are you, that as well as being married to that…that *boor*, you want me to take you as a lover? Is that it?'

He placed a hand on the wall behind her and lowered his face to hers so close that she could see only his eyes making inroads into hers, reading far more than she wanted to reveal. 'No, my lady, that is not it. I am telling you as clearly as I know how that you will be mine. Understand? Mine.'

'Ah, so it *is* the property. You saw it. You wanted it, and now you see a way to get it. Well, that didn't take too much effort on your part, did it? So now all you have to do is to offer the king more, which he'll not refuse, of course, and then you can add my estates to those you hold from Count Alan. Well done. But if you think you'll get any co-operation from me, knight, then you'll be wrong. You won't.'

His nose almost touched hers, so close did he look into her heart. 'I don't need your co-operation, Rhoese of York. I thought I'd already demonstrated that. And I also believe that your protests are a mite too strident to be sincere. Would you like me to show you what I mean?'

'No,' she whispered. 'No…no, don't. You do not know…'

'No, there's quite a lot I don't know that I intend to find out. But you had better know this, my lady, that you are on the losing side. Your snarling and snapping and keeping yourself chaste will get you nowhere. What I set out to take, I get. Now, I shall take you in and I shall return tomorrow to escort you back to the king. He'll want you to make your mark before witnesses, I expect. But I shall have spoken to him by that time.'

'You're very sure of yourself, knight. What if he refuses?'

He smiled and levered himself off the wall. 'You can begin by using my name. I'm known as Jude.'

'And I'm known as the daughter of Lord Gamal,' she replied sharply, 'and I'm capable of making my own plans. English women are not so biddable as your Norman dames.'

'We'll see,' he said, still smiling. 'Come, show me your hall.' He held out a hand, closing his strong fingers around hers and leading her out into the light. And this time Rhoese saw no point in depriving him of the last word.

Chapter Three

So, the squabbling over possession of her estate had already begun before the decree was barely out of the king's mouth, and Rhoese's short-lived attempts to maintain her independence had gone for nothing. It would never have happened before the Normans came. There had been laws to protect women's rights then, she told her brother.

'It's no good chastising yourself, love,' Eric said. 'It would have happened eventually, one way or the other, whether you'd shown yourself or not. The king had already trawled through the records to see who owned what. It was only a matter of time.'

'I know,' said Rhoese, pulling a fistful of brown seed-heads off the sorrel, 'but if that woman hadn't got to Archbishop Thomas before me with her offer of a wealthy ward, then I might have stood a chance. She's capable of anything, Eric. And the new king is a *monster*. How *dare* he treat me like a cow for sale to the highest bidder and allow his man to handle me so coarsely? I was never so humiliated in my life. Never.' They sat side by side on the low remains of a Roman wall that ran along one side of the croft where nettles, sorrel and dock hung heavily with seeds between the stones. She had given the news to Hilda, Bran and Neal, to Brother Alaric and the household servants, watching the silent shock on their faces turn to consternation and fear for their own positions about which she was unable to comfort them. Not since her father's death had she felt so helpless or so fearful for her future.

But underscoring everything else in her mind was the way in which the Norman, Judhael de Brionne, had seen Toft Green during his visit to York and had instantly decided to acquire it, despite the king's first choice of recipient. He had told her so, knowing that his kiss would be far more to her taste than de Lessay's bungling attempt, and that she would file it away amongst 'things to be savoured again' in the dark privacy of her bower. And, like a fool, she was already doing it, regardless of her determination never to let a man into her dreams.

He had entered her hall, impressing those within by his civility, his courteous greetings to Eric. And to Neal, who could almost guess the result of Rhoese's visit to the king, if her angry expression was anything to go by.

'So there's to be a higher bid, you think?' said Eric. 'That man?'

Instead of an answer, she took his hand and held it on her lap. 'I'm going to speak to Father Leofric,' she said, 'at St Martin's. I can't just leave it like this, love. I'm not going to let them walk all over us and let that woman take over my house without putting up a fight for it. She's taken everything I had, so far, and I'll be damned if she's going to get this so easily.'

'I can't see that *he*'ll be able to do much to help. An English priest.'

'It's worth a try. I'll be back before supper.'

'You're taking Els with you?'

'No.' She smiled for the first time. 'She prefers to gawp at you.'

He stood up to go with her. 'Then I'd better not deprive her of that pleasure before I join the monks. What's that man's name? Judhael Debrion?'

'Yes, love. Something like that.' Jude, he had told her. *Jude.* She held a hand to her mouth and pressed gently, feeling the warm skin with her lips and the quick surge of something vibrant within her belly. 'The house martins have almost gone,' she said, 'so we shall not have their protection from thunderstorms now. Come into the hall, love. Mind that bucket on your left.'

Whilst not expecting a miracle from Father Leofric, Rhoese felt that he might have been the one to offer her something more positive than Brother Alaric, her chaplain, whose position in her household was principally to lend an air of respectability to her masterless menage, and to keep the accounts. She had, in fact, already put the idea to Brother Alaric that the best way for her to avoid the king's command would be to enter a nunnery, but his response had been guarded rather than sympathetic, and he had advised her to ask Father Leofric what he thought about it. Whether the chaplain had an inkling of what the priest's reaction would be was debatable but, if so, he had the wit to keep it from showing when Rhoese returned to Toft Green an hour before supper.

He laid down his quill as her shadow fell across his doorway, rising to his sandaled feet to invite her into his hut. A flurry of leaves swirled round the threshold and rattled away as the chaplain drew up a stool to the door where they could be seen, careful for her reputation.

'He's shocked,' she said. 'Very shocked.'

He made a small sound of agreement. 'Understandable. What's his answer to the convent idea? Concerned about Eric, is he?'

That, indeed, had been a consideration. For Rhoese to commit herself to taking the veil before they knew whether Eric had been accepted at St Mary's was to tempt fate. The last thing any of them wanted was for him to be left to rejoin Ketti's household, and Father Leofric's admiration for Eric was less well disguised than he believed it to be.

'Yes,' she said. 'Naturally. He thinks that running off to a nunnery immediately would leave Eric in a difficult position, but he also knows the man the king is selling me to. He's one of the worst types. A real ruffian, he says.'

'He told you *that*? That can hardly have put your mind at rest.'

'I wish I hadn't gone now. The only helpful thing he said was that he'd try to find a way of getting me out of it, but for the life of me I don't know what he means.' It was not the only thing Father Leofric had suggested. The lie had been for modesty's sake and because she could not repeat to her chaplain exactly what the parish priest had suggested to her, in private. His words still rang in her ears.

'My Lady Rhoese,' Father Leofric had said to her, not unkindly, 'I can see a way forward in this. Will you take a beaker of mead with me?'

He was not physically unattractive, on the young side of middle age, spare and smiling—too smiling?—busy with his hands, which should have been hidden and still. Rhoese did not want the mead, but took it anyway and thanked him, wondering about the way forward.

'Now,' he said, seating himself just a little too close to her, 'I'm not a man to mince words, as you know, and my thinking is that, if the king were to be told that you are already married, in secret, you understand, then he'd have to release you from this humiliating sale you've told me of. We really cannot allow that to happen. Can we?' His hand touched hers and withdrew, but that one gesture alerted her to the direction of his mind.

Even so, she pretended. 'But, Father, you know I'm not married, nor do I even have a contract to marry.'

He smiled at what he took to be her coyness. 'What? Even though I put it to you three months ago that your pain might be eased by accepting my protection? I take it only you know of what transpired then?'

'Yes, Father.' She placed the mead on the chest and tucked her hands away into the wide sleeve openings. 'I've told no one of your offer. It was thoughtful of you, but as I said then, I doubt whether becoming your concubine would really solve anything. And if you're now offering me marriage, well…no…I think I must decline. Please don't misunderstand. I am honoured but…well, it's not for me.'

'I see,' said Father Leofric. 'So you'd rather marry a Norman?'

'I'd rather not marry at all, Father.'

'I'd look after you well, my lady. And your handicapped brother, too.'

It was the handicapped brother she feared for more than herself. In her eyes, Eric was open and unwary of any vice, loving everyone, innocent and blind to the thoughts of men as well as to the lingering glances over his fine body. She had never managed to convince him that showing it off so much had its dangers, nor did she know how to insist without replacing the love of his fellow men with fear of them.

'Yes, I know,' she said.

'And there are things said about Ralph de Lessay that—'

'That I don't think I need to know, thank you, Father.'

'That you should know, my lady. He's been accused of rape more than once, and he had a wife who died in very suspicious circumstances. He's a well-known—'

'No! Thank you, Father Leofric.' Rhoese stood and headed for the door even before the priest could elaborate on the last unpleasant aspect of Ralph de Lessay's character. 'You've always been helpful and kind, and I'm truly grateful, but I have to find a solution of another sort, one way or the other.'

She had tried to smile at him before she left, fearing that her refusal might be seen as madness when the alternative was so much more unacceptable. Nevertheless, she could not deliberately put Eric at risk, though had she but known it, her brother was perfectly capable of looking after himself with Neal as his guide. Between them they had discussed every aspect of men's needs and digressions, as well as women's, and the only thing Eric now lacked was more detailed experience. Which, he had assured Neal, they would both get when the time was right.

Rhoese had known for some time of Father Leofric's wish for her to become his concubine. Now he was suggesting that, if they were to claim to be already man and wife, her escape from the king's command would be automatic. Priestly marriages might not be encouraged nowadays, but Archbishop Thomas himself was a married man and he would not advocate annulling one that had already taken place. What was more, she was fully aware that in describing to her the crimes of Ralph de Lessay, the priest was trying a last potent line of persuasion. Nevertheless, she had returned without having learned anything useful except a distinct impression that Father Leofric's interest in her was secondary to his interest in her brother. Though not unique, it was a disturbing development. Eric would be safe enough with Neal, but this attraction had the effect of sidetracking the real issue. She was glad, in the circumstances, that she had decided against taking the valuable gospel-book to the priest in broad daylight.

*   *   *

For reasons she was not willing to admit to herself, Rhoese went early to her bower after supper, for it was almost dark and her mind was in total disorder, tossing her thoughts between bouts of determination and despair while searching every angle of the multiple problem. There was the merchant Murdac who had also asked her more than once to marry him. He also had been a friend of her father's, a steadfast, dull but wealthy man who could have given her far more than Father Leofric if only her heart had not been set against giving herself in return, as she had once been foolish enough to do.

The scene in the archbishop's palace was before her like a recurring nightmare; that dreadful man de Lessay's grip upon her arms, his disgusting face, his reeking breath. She would have to suffer it nightly unless…unless what? He had been hurled backwards, crashing like a skittle into the king's chair. The Norman was to bid higher for her as if she were a prime heifer, so greedy was he for what he had seen.

She sat on her clothes-chest to unravel the gold braids from her plaits, placing a brief caress upon the neck of Eric's hound as he rolled his dark eyes towards her. He slept in her bower each night and returned to him each morning, and she felt as safe with the waist-high wolfhound as if he'd been an armed guard. He lifted his massive grey head, pricking his ears and looking towards the door.

'It's Els,' she told him, 'bringing my warm milk.'

His ears dropped and pricked again while his tail whacked a slow thud upon the boards. Then he rose, lowering his nose to the bottom of the door, snuffling, ignoring Rhoese's command to get out of the way. His tail swung madly as the door opened and a tall broad figure filled the frame, blocking out the last of the waning light. The lamp wicks fluttered in the sconce. 'Hello, boy,' he whispered. 'You still know me, eh?'

Rhoese was on her feet, dropping the gold braid and picking up a small three-legged stool like a weapon. 'Get out!' she said. 'Get out, or I'll shout for help and have you thrown into the cesspit. I mean it, Warin. You don't put one foot in my house.'

'Ah, but I do, Rhoese. Mistress Rose of... hic...York. I do. See?' He was inside and the door was closing behind him, and the hound who had known him all his life came back to flop beside the curtained bed, his job done. Warin was extremely drunk, but not too far gone to stand still as the stool flew across the room and hit the door. He kicked the stool aside. 'I'm destined,' he said, grunting, 'to live with women who throw things. I thought you'd have...hic...got over it by now.'

'Get *out*!' Rhoese yelled, hoping someone would hear her. But in the hall Eric was singing and playing his harp, and no one would, and that was why Els was taking her time over warming the milk. Even if Warin had been sober, she would not have wanted him near her; drunk, he was doubly offensive. He was also twice as dangerous. 'Warin,' she said, trying to sound reasonable, 'where have you come from? Have you not been home?' She knew he had not; Ketti would not have allowed him in, in that state.

'Been out on business, darling.'

'Don't call me that!'

'Since this morning. She sent you the message, then? Yes, I knew you'd want to help...forget the past...eh? Friends again?'

'You're not only drunk, Warin, but crazed, too. Get out of here and go home. I have nothing whatever to say to you, nor do I want to listen.'

He came into the centre of the room and wrapped an arm around the great post from which the beams radiated. The light fell upon his thick fair curls and broad brow, catching upon white eyebrows bleached by the summer sun and sea. She had once thought him comely and exciting: now his eyes were tired and bloodshot, and she was seeing the same signs her father had shown of a man worn down by a scolding, nagging, dissatisfied wife. It was no wonder he had preferred to go to sea in autumn rather than stay at home. But Rhoese could muster not a shred of pity for Warin.

'Rhoese,' he said, holding out a hand. 'Come here. Come to me. You know why I've come, don't you? I've been at the wharf all day, so I've not seen her...hic...can't bear to be with her any more. I got it all wrong, darling, all wrong. I want to come back. I want to be with you. You know you want me... don't you?'

She backed away, wondering how she could have been so wrong about this pathetic creature who had once been her world. He was gross, self-pitying and false. She despised him, utterly, for his unsoundness. 'Want you?' she said. '*Want* you? No, you great lumbering pot-head, I *don't* want you. Go back to your woman and sort out your problems between you, and don't come to me whining about how wrong you got it. You made your bed, go and lie on it. Go on…go. Get *out*!'

'Don't send me away,' he pleaded. 'That's so cruel. Don't you remember how we loved—'

'No!' she yelped. 'I don't. I remember how I trusted you and how quickly you betrayed me when I most needed you. I remember your promises to me, Warin. Broken, every one. Have you *any* idea of what I suffered then? Have you?'

'Rhoese…' he mouthed. His face registered a blankness that fought to make something of what she was telling him, something of which he was incapable of imagining. What was he supposed to answer?

'Have you?' she croaked, feeling again the sickness of despair in her stomach. 'Your promises of security, a family, undying love? Remember? And where were you when I needed you after my father was lost? With *her*, Ketti, comforting *her*, not me. Did it not once occur to you that I needed you then, Warin? Was it too uncomfortable for you, or had you already decided she had more to offer, after all? Eh? Coward! Stinking coward! Get out, Warin. You foul my room with your pathetic bleating. I needed a man, not a sheep. Now I need no one.'

Breathless, and fast running out of air, she felt her heart thudding with the pain that she had tried for so long to relegate to the back of her mind and which had now surged forward in fury at its release. 'Keep back!' she whispered, putting up a hand to ward him off and wishing desperately that Els would return. She screamed, loud and hoarse, setting off the hound's alarming deep-throated bark, as she had intended.

'No, Rhoese,' Warin said, catching at her wrist, 'don't scream. We can be lovers again, you know. Try to forget the past. It was a mistake. It'll not happen again, now we're together.'

She pulled and hit at his arm, very much afraid of what he could do. His breath wafted across her in hot waves, stinking and nauseous, making her retch. 'We're *not* together,' she screamed, 'you stupid idiot! You're with *her*, and I'm to be married. And if you want to know who set *that* up, then go and ask your beloved Ketti, the one with all the money. Remember? Yes,' she snarled at his astonished face. 'Married. To a Norman. One of the king's favoured ones.'

'The *king*?' he whispered, dropping her wrist. 'By his order?'

'By his order, yes. And I shall live in luxury in grand houses and castles and have everything I desire while you and that harpy can come and live here in this little hovel. There, Warin, isn't that what you wanted? Not me, but *this*!' She had to yell to be heard above the hound's continuous barking, but the sound of a man's shout had already reached her, adding a higher note to the cacophony.

Warin staggered at the news, his boyish face contorted with disappointment and incredulity. 'But…but you can't, Rhoese. You know I've always…always loved you…' The door crashed open to admit a swarm of dark male bodies that engulfed Warin like ants on a helpless spider, dragging him out into the night, scuffling, yelping, roaring. 'I love you…

Rhoese...you know I do...I'll always...get *off* me, damn you! I can walk!' His howls echoed down the croft to the men's pitiless shouts that Rhoese would have warned them to curb, if she had been there with them. Warin was a merchant now, and not without influence. There was no knowing what he might do next.

Neal returned first, followed by Brother Alaric, both of them hesitant and unsure of their ground in a lady's bower, now that the threat had gone. 'You all right, m'lady?' they said. 'Did he harm you?'

'No, I'm all right. Really. Has he gone?' She found she was shaking and, at the appearance of the others, felt a kind of hysterical laughter not far from the surface that might turn the event into farce at any moment.

They insisted that she and her two women should sleep in the big hall that night, yet it was many hours before sleep came, or any slight compensation for the disastrous day. Warin's untimely visit had deeply disturbed her, for it had been the first time they had spoken since his departure from her life, if not her thoughts, and his appearance had brought back to her all the agonies of loss and betrayal that twisted like a knife in her most secret parts. She could not have told him of her pregnancy, that being a loss not to be shared for the sake of making a point. He had forfeited any right to know of it, and now it was something for which she would never find a solace, much less be able to share with anyone. To hold his child in her arms was all she had wanted then, all those months ago, and still her womb ached with longing and readiness. But not for Warin. Not for any man.

Much less solace did she find in being wanted by five men for entirely the wrong reasons and by wanting none of them herself for any reason. Yet the one who was last in her thoughts before sleep came was the one in a dark stable, steel-clad and uncompromising, and very determined. Each time she woke, listening to the mice in the thatch, the owls, the low growl of Eric's hound, the same man returned to disturb her peace, a man who made Warin look like an uncouth schoolboy by comparison.

The sounds from beyond her curtained alcove closed her dreams and told her that the men were already up, even though there was but a glow of dawn in the overcast sky. The thatch pattered under heavy rain, and today was the first day of October, known to the English as Winterfylleth. It was the day on which she would be taken to the king to make her mark before witnesses. If she wanted to run to the nunnery at Clementhorpe, she had better do it now, the day before her twenty-third birthday.

With Els beside her, she went quickly across the yard to her bower, hurling herself through the door into the dry dimness where a faint smell of sour ale still hung like a bad memory. 'Open the shutters,' she said, lifting the lid of her chest. 'This place stinks.'

Els hastened to obey, but her initial yelp of fright was followed by another, then a louder shriek. 'Oh...oh, Mother of God!' she wailed. 'Oh, I stepped in it! Mistress...look!'

'Stepped in what?'

'Blood! Look over here.' Unable to describe the black lump on the boards, Els could only point and shake.

Rhoese hauled on the rope to pull up the shutter and catch its loop around the peg, letting in enough light to illuminate a large body sprawled on its back very much as they had last seen it yesterday under the king's chair. It was Ralph de Lessay, with the hilt of a dagger protruding from his chest just above the dark blood-stained tunic.

By the time Judhael de Brionne arrived with mounted men to escort Rhoese to her appointment, the rain had ceased and the courtyard had already begun to fill with concerned neighbours whose duty it was to police the actions of anyone living in their area, a district known in Yorkshire as a 'hundred'. Everyone, in effect, was responsible for the actions of everyone else, their concern in this particular case being to identify the murderer as quickly as possible. It did not help matters one whit that the dagger used to kill Ralph de Lessay had belonged to Eric until he had passed it on to his sister to wear whenever she needed it.

'It was hanging on the big post in the middle of my bower,' she told Brother Alaric as they watched four Norman soldiers carry the body into the hall. 'I keep my shears hanging there, too. And my spindles. But what was he doing in my bower, of all places? D'ye think he thought I was in there?'

That *was* what the chaplain and everyone else

thought, but he merely sighed and shook his dark head. 'It's not that that worries me, my lady, so much as this eternal problem of who to blame. You know what the Norman manner is of dealing with this situation, don't you?' At the shake of her head, he continued, 'Well, when a Norman is killed, they always assume an Englishman to be guilty until the men of the hundred can produce the culprit and the evidence. And until they do that, the hundred suffers a crippling fine. They're going to want to find the murderer as fast as they can or, if they can't, they'll grab anyone who can't defend himself. Did you hear anything in the night?'

'Only the usual noises. Nothing suspicious. What about Warin, Brother? D'ye think they'll question him about it?'

Brother Alaric snorted, then thought better about the pending laugh of derision. 'Warin,' he said, dismissively. 'And what do you think he'll have to say about where he was all night?' He looked at her face and saw the answer. 'Exactly. The Lady Ketti and her family will stand by him in this, never fear. They'll not pin anything on *him*, even if we all say where he was beforehand. Not a chance.'

'Then who?' she whispered, anxiously.

He looked up, watching the approach of the tall helmeted captain. 'That's what this character is going to want to know, if I'm not mistaken. I shall leave you to it, my lady.'

'No...stay!' But the chaplain was already out of earshot, to make way for the man she had called Jude before she fell asleep. She challenged him before he could speak. 'You're thinking it was my doing because he was in my bower with my brother's dagger in him. Well, it was not. I slept in here all night. My bower was empty.'

He removed his helmet while she was speaking, holding it in the crook of his arm like a roc's egg. His hair fell like a heap of spear-points over his head, as a child's does after its bath. His eyes were hard and difficult to read until they travelled quickly over the contours of her old kirtle before returning to her face. Then she knew full well the direction of his thoughts, in spite of what he told her. 'What I am thinking, my lady,' he said softly, 'is that it might have been more convenient for the men of this hundred if you *had* done it, because then it would have been in self-defence, most probably, wouldn't it? He was in your bower. At night. And your brother's dagger was used. Do you wish to change your plea? There are no punishments for a woman who kills a man about to rape her on her own property, as you know, though you'd have to prove you didn't invite him.'

'*Invite* him? Invite a *Norman*…that…that *creature*?' she blazed. 'You don't believe me, do you? Why not just say it? You don't believe me.'

He placed an arm across her back and manoeuvred her out of the end of the hall into the croft where a white goat stood bleating to be milked. The bower door stood open and deserted, the pathway mangled and muddied by a parade of heavy feet. He turned her round to stand against the wall, making her both resent and quiver at the touch of his hand on her arm.

In English law, no man may touch a woman's arm, unless she wanted it.

'Rhoese of York,' he said, 'it doesn't matter whether I believe you or not. What matters is who the men of your hundred arrest. Yes,' he said to the brown eyes that widened in surprise, 'I know enough about your laws and the Yorkshire hundred system. I've been in this country longer than you know. And you may not think they'll arrest you for this crime, but believe me, they will if they can't find anyone else to blame. They'll not want to be fined just to save your skin, or any of your household.'

Her mind raced around the possibilities, trying to keep away from the one that kept recurring in the form of vengeance, the vengeance that would sweeten her bitterness. Tell him about Warin. Tell him that he now knew of the king's plan to marry her to Ralph de Lessay, that he had found him, killed him, and dumped him in her bower. No, that made no sense, for a jury would believe all those who had heard him shout that he still loved her, and no lover would leave his victim's body in the bower of the one he professed to love. She could not blame it on Warin.

'I can't help that,' she said. 'I shall not say I killed a man in self-defence for that reason or any other, when it's untrue. I don't know what the man was doing there, but fortunately I don't have to imagine. I was sleeping in the hall, the doors were barred, the hounds were in there too, and there were men sleeping round the fire. I'd have fallen over at least ten of them.'

'You didn't visit the privy?'

'No, we have a bucket when it's raining, like everyone else.'

'Very well, I shall take the body back to the king and report what I know of the business. You must stay here until I return, and I suppose I'd better warn you that—'

'That he'll be none too pleased. Yes, I can believe it. Well, nor am I, come to that.'

He looked down at her, sharply. 'Not pleased, lady?'

'No,' she said, wearily. 'I didn't want to marry the man, any more than I want to marry anyone, Norman or English, but neither did I want him to be murdered, especially on my property. And if I or any of my household *had* murdered him, sir, do you really think we'd be stupid enough to leave him where he could be found by you, when we knew you'd be here first thing in the morning? *Do* you?'

'No,' he said. 'I don't.'

'Well, *that*'s a relief. Knowing that, I can take the king's anger in my stride. But tell me one more thing, sir, if you will. In spite of all your questions concerning my doings, could this…accident…be *your* way of getting your hands on my estate, as you said you would yesterday?'

His stern expression relaxed as he savoured the suggestion, then he leaned a hand on the whitewashed wall just above her head. 'I can understand your concern,' he said, bringing his face nearer to hers, 'but the answer must be no. If I'd needed to kill him, I'd not have done it this way, my lady. Not my way of doing things; nor my men's. No, you see, I outbid de

Lessay only an hour after the king returned from his hunting yesterday. He was merry, and happy to take more for you than de Lessay had offered.' He smiled. 'Quite a lot it was, but worth it, I'd say. And as for the question you're about to ask about where I was last night, I was at the palace of the archbishop, playing chess. In fact, I beat him.'

'I see.' Her heart hammered uncomfortably somewhere in her throat. So, it was as simple as that. Sold to a higher bidder.

'Yes, there was absolutely no need for me to get him out of the way. I'd already done it. Which still leaves the question of why he was here last night after he'd found out that you were not to be his. Obviously he departed this world a very disappointed man.'

'Go,' she said. 'Just go, and take your suspicions with you. I did not ask for any of this. All I ever wanted was to be left alone in peace. Is that too much to ask, sir? Take my land, if you're so intent on having it. Take the water-mills, the houses, all the things you so carefully looked up in the survey, but just leave me be. Marriage is not for me. I shall make you a poor wife and you'll regret the day you thought otherwise. Believe me.'

He watched her as if to enjoy the way she spoke rather than to hear what she was saying, and when she had finished, he picked up the end of her long plait and wound it round her neck like a halter before she realised what was happening. 'And if the time ever comes when I remind you of these so-called regrets, my lady,' he said, 'then you have my permission to say I told you so.' Holding her head by the soft rope of hair, he lowered his mouth to hers, reminding her again of that elusive and scintillating flame of sheer pleasure that danced just beyond her reach, as if to mock at all those times she had denied the idea of ever wanting a man.

Cursing herself for her weakness, she told herself to close her mind to it, that he could never be anything to her, that this was merely a show of his new lordship. It would mean nothing to him except to keep in practice. 'My heart is hard, sir,' she panted, on the verge of tears. 'You'll never soften it with kisses and such like. You may as well not try.'

He touched the corner of her mouth with his. 'Is it so, my lady?' he said. 'Then it's as well that the state of your heart is not my concern. Keep it as hard and ice-bound for as long as you like; it will not affect me one way or the other. But you come as part of the deal because I cannot get at it any other way, and since you have a fair enough body into the bargain, the sampling of it now and then will fortunately not be too much of a penalty for me. It's something *you*'ll have to put up with, lady. Besides, I need to spawn an heir, and I don't need a willing woman for that, only a healthy one.' He tipped his head, flicking his eyebrows in amusement at her mortification and the flare of hatred that followed. 'Ah, did you think otherwise? Surely not. We began our relationship with some plain-speaking, and I intend to go along with that. By all means let us understand each other from the beginning. It will save much time in the end, don't you agree? You are silent. Had you thought to break *my* heart as you've been used to doing?' His laugh was silently mocking. 'No! Not a chance of that. It's way beyond *your* reach, lady.'

'Fiend! Cur!' She took his thick wrist in her hand and tried to prise her plait out of his grasp. 'Let me go. I can put myself beyond *your* reach too, Norman. Don't think I shall let you walk into my life like this and take it over.'

His heavy fist was beneath her chin, easing it upwards so that she was obliged to look into his eyes, serious eyes that had quickly lost all signs of derision. 'You intend to take your life, lady? Is that what you're saying? You are not such a coward, surely?'

'If that's what I was saying, sir, it would be for pride's sake, not for cowardice. We English are not easily walked over, and northerners have a reputation for resistance. You must have heard how the Yorkists suffered for holding on longer than the rest to what is theirs. No, we don't hurl ourselves into the flames, but there are other means of evasion from men's brutality.'

'I have not offered you brutality, Rhoese of York. I can get what I want from a woman without that. You'll see. But thank you for the warning. I shall take precautions to see that it doesn't happen.'

Fool…*fool*…she berated herself for letting him rile her into blabbing like a child about her options. She could, if she'd kept quiet, have run out of Micklegate down to Clementhorpe, where a small group of nuns eked out a meagre living, tending the sick and relying on charity. But it would have meant leaving Eric to his own devices, and in retrospect she could not have done it. 'You can hardly tie me up,' she snapped, wrenching her head away.

He smiled. 'Hardly, I agree. Shall I need to? Eh?'

A heat spread from her shoulders up to her neck, and it was difficult for her to make an appropriate reply while his body was so close to hers. He must have known, with his obvious experience, that there would be no need for restraint. 'No,' she said, looking away. 'I am still mistress of this house.'

'Then make the most of it, lady, while I take your latest victim back to his lord. I shall return later.'

It had not, in fact, been anything like as easy to buy Rhoese of York last night as he'd made it sound. The king had *not* been happy even to discuss the deal, being already bored with the whole business and eager to move on to more relaxing delights in his private chamber. Jude had gently persisted, and for his pains had been forced to offer almost twice as much as de Lessay, and for that he was adamant that she was not going to escape him as she had from the others. He could afford it, but she need not expect to find much softness in him until she had learned who was master.

Even so, his spring into the saddle was light and, although his face was set just as grim as usual, to those men who knew him there was a spark of laughter in his eyes they'd seen many times before when a woman was in his sights. Laughter and determination.

He did not return later, as he had said, but sent men to guard the gates of Toft Green, which Rhoese at first assumed was to prevent her escape, until her bailiff, Bran, presented her with some disturbing news that added to the already troubled state of her mind.

His face was creased with concern. 'My lady,' he said, wiping his hands down his tunic, 'it doesn't look good.'

None of it looked good, but Rhoese was not sure which aspect was worst. 'The men, you mean? They don't know where to start looking?'

'By the sound o' things, they've already decided on that. They're talking about taking Eric and Neal in. They say your brother's the most likely culprit.'

'Eric? Because he's the easiest option, you mean? Because of his blindness? Is that it?'

'They say he could have done it to save you from rape. They know how close you are, my lady.'

'What utter nonsense, Bran. They must be out of their minds. He'd not have left the body there, for one thing, and anyway, how could a blind man have killed a trained soldier like de Les-say and then gone back to bed without a scratch and with no one hearing?'

'They say he could. He wrestles with Neal and wins. He knows where people are, and he has the second sight.'

'They say that about anyone who's different, don't they? But he and Neal slept in the hall. We all did. And you were nearby, weren't you, Bran?'

Bran's eyes shifted. 'Yes, my lady, but…'

'But what? Surely *you* don't believe it? Not Eric, or Neal?'

'No, no, of course not, but we should get them

away before the men start the hue and cry. They should hide.'

'There are guards on the gate, Bran. They wouldn't let men in.'

'Only two. That's not going to stop thirty or forty men.'

'Then we'd better get him away through the croft at the back. We'll take him to St Martin's, to Father Leofric. He'll be quite safe there and no one will know.'

'You could always ask help of that Norman who was here a while ago. What's his name, Jude of Brian? He'd post more men round—'

'No, Bran.' Rhoese's reply was decisive. 'I don't want Norman guards posted all round my demesne.' Which was not the real reason for her objection. 'We'll smuggle them out of the back through the trees. You'll help?'

'Of course, my lady.'

So Eric had to be told of his sister's forthcoming marriage, to Judhael de Brionne, after all, and then had to be sent to stay with Father Leofric with Neal and Brother Alaric for their safety, while the hue and cry of thirty men marched with torches to Toft Green as darkness fell, ready to take the young man in their midst. To their surprise, the guard at the gates of Toft Green had been increased from two to ten just before their arrival, which left a few unanswered questions about the reason for their sudden appearance. The men were forced to leave empty-handed, and the household at Toft Green slept easily that night, as did Eric and his guardians.

* * *

The next morning, the day on which she usually celebrated her birth, brought new developments, which made Rhoese wonder when she had been so wicked as to deserve it all. The first was a message from Abbot Stephen of St Mary's Abbey who had by that time heard of Eric's presumed guilt. Being a Norman himself, the abbot was not minded to give the young man the benefit of the doubt and in his message he regretted, in the most tortured and formal language imaginable, that he did not feel able to accept Eric as a novice. In the circumstances.

'And *that*,' said Rhoese, angrily, 'after I've given a hefty donation to his new buildings. Well, he doesn't know what he's missing, but I can't say I'm sorry. It means Eric will be able to stay with me.'

Needless to say, Els was beside herself with joy.

'Even so,' said Rhoese, 'he seems to think Eric is guilty already. I wonder if the king will agree with him. What are we to do, Els?' The maid did not have a ready answer.

Hard on the heels of the abbot's messenger came the burly merchant named Murdac, who had heard about the crime and Rhoese's problems. Earnestly, he offered Rhoese his home, his hearth and, of course by implication, his bed. He had influence with the king. He could rescue her if only she would allow it. He had pleaded with her on his knees.

But now there was something she dared not fight against, which had not existed only a few days ago, and she had to tell Murdac that, although his kindness was appreciated, it had come too late to be of any use. Murdac's umbrage came close to a display of temper that gave her a view of his character she had not suspected. It also confirmed her opinion that the male breed as a whole was unstable.

Nevertheless, there was one particularly impressive male whose heartless declaration of intent had so far shown no such traits of instability. His earlier support, she supposed, had been more a natural reaction than a show of tenderness; his fierce attack in the archbishop's palace upon de Lessay more like a soldier's anger at another's lack of discipline than that of a lover towards a rival. Openly, he had stated his lack of interest in obtaining either her approval or her heart, which should have given her some relief, but did not. He had agreed with her policy of plain-speaking and had done some of his own with brutal clarity, but this honesty had not contented her as much as she might have expected from a Norman opportunist. Yet when she asked herself why the hurt, why the dissatisfaction, she felt again the imprint of his hands upon her, the sensation of his warm seeking lips over hers, and that bright intangible promise of joy that had appeared in an instant and faded just as quickly.

Ideally, she concluded, she would have to make him become fond of her to be able to hurt him, revenge on the male species being her priority. To make him *love* her would cause him even greater damage and give her more satisfaction, but to turn his frightening coldness into anything like that would take too long and, perhaps, more skill than she possessed. She had never tried to make men want her. Not once had she bothered to flirt, nor did she understand the art of it. Besides, any effort on her part would now seem ridiculous after their last conversation and, worse still, would be totally opposed to her cynical views on the subject. No, the problem would be how to take his heart into her hands without the slightest betrayal of her principles, how to squeeze and hurt and break it as hers had been broken, and then to know the satisfaction of revenge for her own pain.

Lifting the lid of her wooden clothes-chest, she removed several layers before her fingers touched the firm leather-bound covers of her mother's old recipe book, its colour fading with age and use. The yellowed vellum pages were covered with closely written script, part English, part Latin and part runic, which she had almost forgotten how to decipher. No matter, there would be something in here.

It took her quite some time to collect exactly what she needed, it being autumn and past the time for flower-heads and new leaves. She did, however, find some roots of both the male fern and the wild carrot, some seeds of cumin and endive, the leaves of vervain, mallow, Our Lady's bedstraw and purslane and, for the next hour or so, she pounded the ingredients with her pestle into a greenish paste which she hoped would not be noticed in the ale in the dark earthenware beaker.

Chapter Four

A distant rumble of thunder caused the dark bay stallion to prick its ears and shift uneasily, giving Jude in the high-backed saddle another view of the scene. 'Steady,' he said, casting an eye across to the darkening trees. Two days ago, he had been a stranger here. Now, he had familiarised himself with the layout of the narrow back streets, the markets, wharves and churches, the ports in the great city walls, and had soon discovered the alternative route by which one could leave Toft Green without being seen. The guard he had sent to watch had not interfered with yesterday's escape of Rhoese's brother and her two guardians to the priest's house, though, for the young men's security, he had put a guard on that, too. Not for one moment did Jude believe the rumours of Eric's guilt. On the contrary, Eric had impressed him with his intelligence, his bearing and courtesy, and Jude had thought how useful it would be to have this ally amongst the strangely disjointed family.

From the trees, a mounted guard approached him at a fast trot, his steel hauberk reflecting the heavily clouded sky. 'Over behind the lady's demesne, sir,' he called. 'She's been taken. She's giving him a hard time, but he's a great bullock of a man and he's in a hurry.'

'Where's he going?' Jude called back, wheeling the stallion round on its hocks. 'Does he have a horse?' His spurs touched soft flanks, and already he was sitting into a canter.

'No, sir. They're heading for the old Roman site beyond the trees, just by the city wall. There are old huts on the wasteland. We can get through this way.'

'Hah!' said Jude. 'I thought it might not be too long before *he* showed up again. Come on. The king won't be happy if she gets away at this stage. And nor will I,' he added under his breath.

Beyond the trees was the waste ground where the low stone ruins of earlier Roman dwellings were scattered with abandoned huts, half-burnt from more recent Norman devastations. Old gnarled elders, banks of dying nettles and the white heads of seeding willow-herb swayed in the gusting wind, and a flock of scavenging crows clattered upwards out of their way. Jude halted and signalled to his men to stay back, crossing the waste ground on foot from tree to tree until he came to the dilapidated hut from which voices rose in argument. The wattle-and-daub walls were thin and in disrepair, and Jude soon found a small hole through which to peer into the dark interior, able to hear every word.

The man held a sack in one hand, the tousled state of Rhoese's hair showing that she had recently worn it over her head. Even in the dim light, her fury was plain to see, for her hand lashed out at Warin's face before he could duck, knocking his head to one side with its force.

'For pity's sake, Rhoese!' he roared. 'Leave be! And stop pretending. I'm not drunk now as I was the other night, and you can listen to me, for a change.' He held a hand to his face. 'You're getting to be as bad as *she* is.'

'Warin,' Rhoese scolded, 'when are you going to get it into your thick head that you can't come back? It's over and done with. I don't *want* you in my life. Can't you understand that I mean it?'

'No. I don't believe it. Ketti says you still want me.'

'And you'd rather believe *her*, idiot? Ketti is a scheming, grabbing, jealous, nagging shrew, and you know it. She even drove my father from home with her scolding, and he was a far better man than you, even on his weakest days. You thought you could get a better deal with her than with me, that's all, and it's as well that I found out what you're like sooner rather than later. I've had a narrow escape, and I'm not changing my mind.' She turned away, trying to find a way past him. 'Now let me out of here, Warin, and let me go home. Right now. Move!'

'But I've changed, Rhoese, believe me. I've learned my lesson. And now that I've got rid of that Norman cur from under your feet, you can tell the king you're betrothed to me. We'll be married. Eh?'

She was staring at him, wide-eyed. 'You? *You* killed him?'

'Well, of course I did. He was lurking at the end

of the croft as I went home, and I followed him to your bower. I know what he was after, but he was drunker than I was. He'd never have managed it.' He reached out for her, blocking her attempt to sidestep him. 'Come on, love. Let's put things straight now, shall we? I did it for you, you know.'

'You *fool*!' she said. 'You complete and utter pothead! You killed a Norman and you think you can get away with it? Don't you know they're after Eric for want of a better culprit? And I said nothing to implicate you because I thought even *you* wouldn't be stupid enough to leave a man dead on my floor.'

Warin looked pained. 'I didn't know about Eric. And anyway, it was supposed to look like self-defence. Attempted rape. You know what these Norman pigs are like.'

'Was it *really*?' she scoffed. 'And you think I could have neatly stabbed him, an old war-horse like that, and then gone quietly back to bed and not said a word to anyone? No hue and cry? Really, Warin. You make me sick with your stupidity. Get out of my way.'

But her attempt to reach the door failed as Warin caught her around the waist and swung her hard against the fragile wall of the hut, sending flakes of filling to the floor and cracking the wattle, making Jude jump back as the hut vibrated under the force of their tussle. It was time to put a stop to it before she was injured.

The shaky door fell with a crash as Jude strode through into the dim space, yanking Warin backwards with an arm across his throat and a well-placed knee in his buttocks. With a wrestler's twist, he threw the

man off-balance into the furthest wall, puncturing it
with the jab from Warin's elbow. Roaring with surprise and fury, Warin came up from a crouch and
hurled himself at Jude who dodged, sticking out a foot
to trip him and send him face down on to the rubble
floor. Size for size, the two men were evenly matched,
but Jude's training as a soldier gave him every advantage over Warin's lumbering brawn, and, as Warin
scrabbled to his feet again, he was caught by a felling
blow to the cheek that shook the corner of the hut
and held him in its angle, panting and dazed.

With one hand on Rhoese's arm, Jude restrained
her. 'Don't go to him,' he commanded.

Warin struggled to his feet and took a step forward,
his face smeared with blood. 'Norman bastard!' he
spluttered. 'What d'ye think you're doing? Me and
my woman were just about to have a—' The word
was cut off by a blow from Jude that took him backwards again, clutching at his head.

'Don't say it!' snapped Jude. 'I know exactly what
you have in mind, halfwit. Your voice drowned even
the thunder. Yes, you can stare. Half of York will
have heard your pathetic whining, as me and my men
have. And seven of us, including the lady, have witnessed your admission to murder, fool.'

'Rubbish!' Warin yelped. 'You don't think I was
serious, do you? I was trying to impress her, that's
all. I don't know anything about it. We're lovers.' He
pointed to Rhoese. 'Ask her yourself. We've been
lovers for well over a year. She was only being skit-
tish. You know what women are like, don't you?'

By the time Warin's excuses had finished, Jude was

looking at Rhoese and, for only a moment, was able to hold her eyes before a veil of lashes hid them, shadowed by a frown. So, it was true.

Warin saw his advantage and blundered on, searching in his pouch for a twisted gold braid that dangled from his fingers. 'See?' he said. 'Her love-token. Given me the night before last. That's what I was doing in her bower. Screwing her.'

Like a whip, Jude's hand slapped viciously against Warin's mouth. 'This,' he rasped, indicating Rhoese, 'is a lady. You wouldn't know that, but you'll keep your language proper, or I'll knock your lying teeth down your throat. I *know* what you were doing in the lady's bower the night Ralph de Lessay was murdered, because I have the whole neighbourhood to witness the way you were thrown out.'

'I *walked*!' Warin roared. 'And she's no lady, either. She's anybody's. She sent for me and I went, as they all do. Your Norman crony too. Ask her who was there this morning. Murdac the merchant. He came to see her, in private. Ask her what *he* wanted. Ask her what they all want. She's a witch. She feeds us love-potions. She's—'

Once again, Jude's patience snapped. 'She's *mine*,' he growled, grabbing Warin in both hands by the neck of his tunic and shaking him, 'you vindictive swine. Mine. Do you understand? She is not free, as you seem to think she is, to marry you or anyone. She's mine, clod-pate. You can go before the sheriff to explain yourself, and if you lose a hand or your sight, or your stupid life, you've only yourself to blame.' At a signal to the men who waited by the doorway,

Warin was dragged out of Rhoese's sight yet again to be roughly bound, tied to a horse, and led away still protesting that it was all her doing, that she had played him false and that he'd get no justice from the Norman sheriff.

Jude turned back into the hut and scooped up the length of gold braid which she had so recently unbound from her hair, holding it before her. 'Well, lady?' he said. 'What was this about?'

Rhoese was shaking, her voice weak and unconvincing. 'It's mine,' she said. 'From my plait. The night—'

'The night he came to your bower. Is that what you were going to say? Did you give it to him? *Did* you invite him?'

'Oh, God,' she whispered, 'not you too. No, of *course* I didn't. He came for no good reason except that my stepmother's fortunes had suddenly reversed and he thought he'd better play safe by coming back—' She stopped, aware of what she was admitting.

'By coming back to you. I see. So you *were* lovers. And where does Murdac the merchant fit into the picture? Is he another? The priest? Him, too?'

Her brown eyes opened wide at that, searching for a connection. 'It really can be nothing to you, sir, can it?' she said. 'If you choose to make your enquiries *after* you've bid for me and my estate, then you must take the consequences, however sordid they may appear.'

But now she was dealing with a different kind of individual who would not be so easily chastened by her sharp tongue. As he had done before, he braced his arms on each side of her, and she knew he would demand a better response than that. 'E-lab-or-ate,' he said, clearly. 'I want more than that. I want the truth.'

She found it difficult to communicate with any sense of reality to a man behind a steel nose-guard; the eyes in deep shadow she knew to be as hard as the fists that had sent Warin flying, and the mouth that had been so tender upon hers was set in a grim line that held nothing of that moment. 'Yes, Warin and I were to have married, but he's lived with my stepmother since my father's death,' she whispered, 'and I moved out at the same time. We have not spoken since then, I swear it. As for Murdac, he came to offer me marriage, but I told him it was too late. He was angry. Warin and I were lovers, but never Murdac. I'd not have accepted *him* at any price.'

'Why? Because you were already—'

'Because I want *no* man, sir,' she snarled. 'I have already said as much. Several times.'

'And the priest? Father Leofric?'

'What about him?'

'He's confessed to the murder. Was that for your sake, too?'

Again, her eyes searched underneath the steel helm for something that might help her to understand him but, angrily, she admitted defeat. 'If you'll take that damned contraption off your head,' she said in exasperation, 'I'll be able to talk to *you* instead of to a...a *fortification*! Now, be pleased to tell me,' she said as he obliged, 'what on earth you're talking about. Why should Father Leofric admit to something he couldn't possibly have done? When did he say so?'

The offending helm now hung like a cup from an old nail above their heads as he replied, 'A short time ago. He went to see Archbishop Thomas, who's keeping him in custody. Your brother and his guardians will be back home by now.'

'You knew, then?'

'That they were with the priest? Of course I knew, lass,' he said. 'So for whose sake is the confession, yours or your brother's?'

She shook her head, looking past him into the dark corner where Warin had crashed against the wall. She had never seen him beaten like that, and it had given her nothing like the pleasure she expected. 'I have the distinct impression,' she said, 'that you know more than I do about what's going on. I seem to be a pawn. You can all carry on the game without me and pick me up before you go. And if you want to believe anything Warin has just told you about my behaviour, then I cannot stop you, but I'll be damned if I'll try to justify myself against such malicious blather. I have better things to do on my feast—' Quickly, she pressed her lips together, but he had caught the word.

'Oh?' he said, lowering his head to hers. 'Your feast-day, is it?'

To be truthful, she had always celebrated this day because although her mother knew her birth to have been just after the feast of St Michael, she was not sure of the exact date. Her father had been worse, for he could never remember how old they were, so both she and Eric had gone through life being uncertain.

It was not so very unusual when deaths were recorded with more interest than precarious births. They had not expected Eric to live.

'Yes,' she said, in a low voice. 'It *was*. I've decided to ignore it this year.' As if in answer to her dark thoughts, a brilliant flash of lightning cut and flickered through the hut, bathing them both in white light, and the crash of thunder that followed was like a current that sent her lurching into Jude's arms with a yelp. He caught her, crushing her to him, his mouth closing over hers as the gods boomed angrily overhead. Neither of them heard the stallion's neigh and scream of fear, or the squire's shout of alarm, their minds being closed to every sense except the consuming rapture of a kiss so ravenous that neither of them could have said who needed it most. Her body melted, and her mouth fused with his as if the lightning had welded them into one, still simmering with heat.

This time, Jude's hunger for her overrode his tenderness, and he responded to her wordless cry with a ferocity that spilled over from his showdown with Warin, as if he was determined to wipe all others from her memory, to be the only one she would recall. This time, with overtures well past, they submerged themselves and each other in the dark thunderous privacy of the storm and, while torrential rain tore at the meagre shreds of the thatch, their long kiss was like a drug that neither of them knew how to discontinue. Nor did they want to.

Something, at last, must have responded to his soldierly discipline, for new questions surfaced against her mouth, waking her. 'Well, woman?' he said.

'What is it that draws men to you, then? *Are* you a witch? Do you feed them all love-potions?' These were not questions she could answer truthfully, for she *was* about to feed him a love-potion with the intention of making him suffer for it, eventually. But thankfully, he expected no reply, and his next questions took on an edge of unkindness as if to devalue the passion he had just uncovered. 'And are you satisfied now, Rhoese of York, to know that one man is dead and two more will have to suffer the ordeal, or mutilation, or execution? Does that please you, Lady Rhoese who cannot be won? Do you plan a similar fate for me, my beauty? Well, don't go to any trouble there. You'll find you've met your match. We are to marry this evening at the palace.'

Today? So soon? 'No,' she whispered, still shaken by the kiss and by her own contemptible lack of control. 'No, not today. Please. It's too soon.'

'For what?' he said, tasting her lips teasingly. 'Too soon to have a poison made up? Is that what you want? To add me to your list of victims?' He felt the panic rising in the tense bow of her body.

She struggled against him, smarting at his stinging accusation. 'I have no list, Norman. Why won't you believe me? I care nothing for any man, not even enough to wish death upon one. I cannot help what they do. Their fate is none of my doing, so why blame me for it?' It was on the tip of her tongue to say that she was sorry for it, but realised in the nick of time that regret for a man's pain was not a part of her strategy. But then, neither was she supposed to have felt the pain of his allegations when she had locked her heart against such weakness. Nor had she wanted to feel anything but coldness under his lips, and certainly not bliss. Yet, to her shame, she believed she had. 'Please,' she said, trying to evade his mouth. 'Don't let it be so soon. Give me a little time, for decency's sake.'

'The decision doesn't rest with me, lady, but with the king. You'll have noticed that he's not a man who cares overmuch for decent intervals between thought and deed. He acts on impulse and expects everyone else to keep up. We are to go to him and the archbishop. He wants it settled before anything else goes wrong. 'Tis not so unusual with him.'

'And afterwards?' she said, dreading his reply.

He smiled in the darkness. 'Why, afterwards, my lady, you'll be able to make a few comparisons, won't you? I'll do my best not to disappoint you, but you must not raise your hopes too high.'

'This is barbarous,' she whispered. 'Let me go home, sir.'

He took her damp hair in his fist to stop her struggles. 'Is it indeed barbarous, lady?' he scoffed. 'Was that word on your mind a moment ago? Was it? I think not. You cannot have it both ways, you see. You cannot lock your heart in its iron-bound chest and then claim that it's been affected by a little harmless barbarism. You'll have to make your mind up whether to let it mend naturally or throw away the key and remain unaffected by anything, painful or pleasant. Which I've just proved to you that you cannot do, otherwise you'd not have melted into my kiss, would you?'

'Please…don't say any more.'

'I don't intend to, except that this little episode has told me what I needed to know about your antagonism towards men. You're making the usual mistake of believing that they're all the same, which is as blind as believing that all women are too. I happen to know the opposite, as you do, at heart. I shall find a way in, my lady, believe me.'

'If it's my heart you're speaking of, sir, then this is at odds with your assertion that you have no interest in it. What's changed since then?'

'You have,' he whispered, fondling her brow with his lips. 'Then, you were more sure of yourself, needing nobody and nothing except your own property and peace. Now, you've lost both, and you need me. That's what's changed.'

'And you have started to care about the state of my heart?' She felt his smile against her skin and knew she'd got it wrong. He didn't care.

'Only as much as it goes with the property,' he said, predictably, unable to prevent a tactless rumble of laughter. 'And to keep it beating until you've born me a litter. As I said, it's up to you what state you keep it in.'

But while her skin crawled at the pitilessness of his reply, she realised she should have expected it after watching his merciless treatment of Warin. She should have known better. Now, she had brought more pain upon herself with her needlessly provocative question. 'Of course,' she said, coldly. 'You know nothing much about hearts, do you?'

'No,' he said. 'I wouldn't know where to start looking for one. But never fear, I'm surer about other parts of the anatomy.'

This man was an enigma, she decided, a puzzle far more obscure than those they had fun with in the evenings after supper. So cold and disciplined, yet burning with a passionate energy in his lovemaking, he had already awakened her curiosity in spite of her protestations that it was all too soon. And now, when she was losing control of everything, including her integrity, her self-imposed chastity would be the next thing to go.

The driving rain had found its way through the rotting thatch, and they were forced out at last to make their way back to Toft Green on foot, the squire and horses having disappeared. Holding her wrist, Jude clamped her arm under his, and together they squelched their way in tense silence with only the sacking to cover her head, though this time she was able to see where she was going.

Jude's first mission was to visit the stable. 'You go inside,' he called through the roar of the rain. 'I'll come in a moment.' When he returned, both his squire and Els were with him, guiltily eager to take up their duties again. Els's conscience suffered, however, when she saw that, while she had been 'helping' Jude's young squire, the refugees had returned home, assured by one of Jude's men of Rhoese's safety. They had now stripped off before the fire while their clothes steamed above them on a line. Rarely had Rhoese's household accommodated so many near-naked men, especially when Jude and Pierre, his squire, joined them to sit like members of the family with cups of ale and honey cakes, their torsos reflecting the glow of the flames like so many ripe apricots.

After changing her clothes in her bower, Rhoese rejoined the company, but would have much preferred to see the intruding Norman being treated with less warmth, though English courtesy demanded that anyone who asked should be admitted to one's hearth and board. Even so, the degree of amity that had instantly sprung up between him and her brother came close to treachery, she thought, though she dared not show her disquiet. 'Neal,' she said, as he came to her at the far side of the hall, 'is my brother all right? He appears to approve of his future brother-in-law. I didn't think he'd take my news quite so well.'

'Never better, m'lady,' Neal replied, sliding his fingers through spikes of thick blonde hair. 'The Norman put a guard on Father Leofric's house. We were all safe enough, thanks to him.'

Her eyes strayed to the Norman's magnificent body and the great muscular legs splayed out to the warmth. His arms rested on his knees as he listened to what Eric was saying, their heads close. 'Really?' she said, taking a leather flask of liquid from the table. 'That's very gratifying. Would you bring me the Norman's cup to replenish?'

Obligingly, Neal brought both men's cups, wood-turned vessels made on Coppergate, and placed them at the side of hers on the table.

'Oh, and Brother Alaric's and Pierre's too, if you please.' As soon as his back was turned, she gave the flask a quick shake and poured the love-potion into the Norman's cup, topping it up with ale from the earthenware jug just as Neal returned with two more. He placed them down as a half-drenched figure was shown into the hall to stand dripping on the threshold, his tonsure shining as black as his habit, his dour expression reddened by the stinging rain.

'I have come from the Abbey of St Mary,' he announced, pompously, 'with a message from Abbot Stephen for Master Eric. Which of you is Master Eric?'

Eric stood up, unselfconsciously naked. 'I am, Brother,' he said. 'But I've already received Abbot Stephen's message, I thank you. Is this to make sure I understand it?'

The monk quickly lowered his eyes. 'Er…no, I think not. The abbot wish…er…instructs me to say that he is willing to accept you as a novice after all. There was some mistake. He bids me say you'll be welcome.'

Eric faced the monk, smiling. 'A mistake. Yes, I believe Abbot Stephen came to certain conclusions about my character while I was away from home well before he had any evidence, let alone proof. Not what I would have expected from a truly unbiased Christian in charge of others' souls, Brother. Pray tell the good abbot that I must decline his kind offer and say that, whatever my future holds, it will not be in the Abbey of St Mary. Now, would you care to remove your wet habit and join us here a while? There's good ale and honey cakes. Or is it a fast-day?'

'Decline? You mean—?'

'Yes, I do mean it, Brother. I have discovered that I have pride instead of sight, and pride has no place

in a monastery, does it? I would rather have no place
to go than accept the rule of a bigot.'

Jude stood up by Eric's side. 'You will never need
to look for a place to live, Master Eric, as long as I
have a house. You and Neal are as welcome to live
in my home as your sister is, in London.'

Eric turned towards him. 'I thank you, Jude. I must
admit that the problem has been preying on our minds
for a while.' He sat down, and the monk was shown
to the door, strenuously declining the repeated invitation to wait until the rain had stopped.

Jude strolled over to where Rhoese stood by the
table with one hand over her cheek, completely taken
aback by this newest development, not to mention the
generosity of this Norman whose chivalric gestures
seemed to contradict his bouts of indifference. 'Is that
not what you wanted, lady?' he said. 'Had you set
your heart on him going to the monastery?'

Automatically, she poured ale into the cups to
avoid looking at him. 'No, on the contrary, I never
wanted him to leave me. I am relieved. Thank you.'
The warmth radiating from his skin reached her, and
she could not help a sidelong glance at the powerful
swell of his chest, the thick cords of his neck and the
wide sinewy shoulders that bulged with strength.

'Then I have managed to please you. That's a good
start on your feast-day, lady.' His platitude meant far
more than that, and the blush that rose into her cheeks
made her turn away as Eric, Neal and Brother Alaric
came to join them.

Passing the cups of ale to each of them, Brother
Alaric proposed a toast. 'To Eric's secure future.

You'll drink too, my lady?' he said, handing her the last cup.

'To my brother's secure future,' she said. Hiding her blushes in the bowl, she drank the contents in two long draughts, and only on the last swallow did she bother to look at the few dregs clinging greenish to the sides. Horror-struck, she coughed, suddenly paralysed with fear, her throat constricting.

Eric took her by the shoulder and slapped her back. 'What is it, love?' he said. 'Was there a spider in it?'

'No,' she choked. 'It went down…the wrong… hole. It's…all right.' But it was not, and nothing now could make it so, for the love-potion she had taken so heedlessly would do its work upon her instead of the Norman, and she would be even more disadvantaged than she was now with her heart in turmoil. It was a disaster she could not have foreseen, even in her worst nightmares.

She would have gone to her bower for a private attempt to bring up the contents of her stomach, but Brother Alaric wished to speak with her. Having understood that the household was to be disbanded, that Eric and Neal would go with her and her future husband, he naturally had concerns about where he and the rest of them were to go. Did she have any comfort to offer them? Rhoese could hardly refuse to discuss the matter.

'I'm afraid I don't know, Brother,' she said. 'Not yet. We've not had much of a chance to come to any agreement.' That much, at least, was true. 'I cannot believe Jude de Brionne will be unreasonable. A lady always wants to retain her own chaplain. Don't worry.

I'll speak to him about it as soon as the opportunity occurs. The others will want to know where they're to go too, though I think they may be absorbed into my stepmother's household along with everything else.'

'They're not happy about it, my lady,' he said.

'Nor am I, Brother. But ultimately it depends on the Norman.'

'You wish me to come to the palace with you this evening?'

'Of course I do, you and the others. You of all people understand how I feel about all this.'

He looked across the hall, smiling at the scene. 'Then we'd better start getting this crowd clothed again. And *you* try not to worry, too. You'd surely rather be wed to *this* Norman than the previous one, I take it? Sad that he met a violent end, but he'd not have made you happy.'

'And you think this one will?'

Brother Alaric withdrew his eyes slowly from the Norman's superb physique. 'I think it's time,' he said, significantly, 'for you to make an effort. To resist change doesn't always help, and you're going to have to adapt your whole way of life. You'll need all your courage.'

'And tonight?' she whispered, turning her back on the scene. 'He's determined to stay here, Brother, despite knowing my disinclination.' She hugged her arms across her body, a gesture not lost upon her chaplain.

'We'll all make it as easy for you as we can, my lady. No coarse revelries. That would be inappropriate. He will, after all, be your husband, so there's no sin in bedding together.' He placed a hand on her arm. 'He doesn't strike me as being insensitive,' he said, softly.

'He's a soldier,' she said. 'And a Norman one at that. And I don't want him.' A slow chill rippled over her arms and neck, and panic rose again to the surface, underscoring the wavering and devious route of her emotions that told her she was lying, that the potion was starting to take effect, that she *did* want him. 'This is an ill day,' she continued. 'And now Warin may even lose his life, and whatever bitterness I feel in my heart, Brother, I cannot be glad that this has happened. The Norman believes it was partly my doing.'

'Do you want me to tell him what happened last year?'

'No.' She looked at him in alarm. 'No, Brother. He has no pity. It would do no good, I fear.'

'You're sure of that? He doesn't appear to lack understanding, and a marriage founded on secrets and ill will isn't going to prosper, is it?'

She supposed he was right, but the man was still a complete stranger to her, walking into her life just as it was beginning to mend, splitting it apart once more in the name of avarice and greed. How could she lay her heart open and trust him with its painful contents? 'No, Brother,' she said. 'Probably not.'

Claimed by Eric once more, she was mercifully allowed to bring the abortive conversation to a close, which meant that she did not see the kindly chaplain pour ale into her empty cup, swill it round, and tip

the contents on to the boards by his feet, replacing it
before Hilda came to clear up. Inside one wide black
sleeve, he hid the flask that had contained the potion,
to be returned later.

The archbishop's palace at night was heavy with
the dank odour of wet clothes and male sweat, of
tallow and the acrid fumes from charcoal braziers.
Lung complaints were one of the commonest ail-
ments, the chaplain mused as he led the small party
from Toft Green through ranks of guards into the
main hall. He had managed to persuade the Lady
Rhoese to dress richly so as not to snub the Norman
by her unwillingness. It was too late, he had told her,
for that kind of statement, and now she must summon
all her dignity and show them the unlimited courage
for which Englishwomen were famed.

She had to admit that the clothes helped to draw
her mind towards what must be done rather than what
could never be, for she was still mistress of a household that looked to her for direction. So she wore
plenteous gold about her brow and round her neck
and wrists, on the hems of each flowing garment of
fine wool and linen. Cream and palest yellow were
her colours, and her shoes of soft kid that had not
been worn for a year tinkled with tiny gold bells as
she walked, turning heads and drawing low whistles
as they went to meet the archbishop. Her long plaits
were braided again with gold and silk ribbons, and
her head-rail was of sheer silk that her father had
bought at great cost from a Byzantine merchant. It

had been his last gift to her. The archbishop was waiting for them.

'My dear lady,' he said from inside his stiff cocoon of sparkling jewels and silk. 'You are well come.' One by one, they knelt and kissed his large topaz ring, Brother Alaric, Eric, Neal, Hilda and Els then stood aside as he offered Rhoese a few last-minute words of advice, which came far too late to be of much use to her confused mind. She found it impossible to concentrate, but knew only a feeling of sickness as the essence of his meaning flowed past, that she must be dutiful and obedient as her father would have wished, remain dignified for her husband's sake, and turn a blind eye to his infidelities, for she ought to know that he had a reputation with women. She must have looked particularly blank at that, for the archbishop waited for some response, then said, 'You understand what I'm saying, my lady?'

'I know nothing of his reputation, my lord. I know less about him than he knows about me,' she said, suddenly breathless.

'Ah, then I would not want this to be a shock to you. Such failings are not condoned by the church, of course, but I'm afraid we have to accept that full-blooded males in their prime, soldiers into the bargain, have lusty appetites. As soon as you begin to breed, my lady, he's sure to need another outlet for his energies, and you will have to bear whatever comes your way.'

'Yes, my lord,' she whispered. *Accept it? Accept his infidelities? God's truth! After what I've had to sacrifice? That, too? Is there not a single man on this earth who can stay faithful?* 'What of Warin, my lord? Have you heard when his trial is to be?'

The archbishop touched his nose with a knuckle and coughed discreetly. 'Ahem! Er…yes. Your late father's foolish assistant. Yes.'

'He'll not be executed, surely? Will he?' she said.

His voice dropped to a whisper. 'No, my dear. The king has already had the punishment carried out. It was for murder, you see. One of his own men. He was *very* angry indeed, and quite rightly so.'

'My lord, please tell me. Has the king outlawed him?' To place a man outside the law's protection was, apart from death, the thing most to be feared.

'No, not that. Blinding and castration. He's back home with his…er…with your stepmother. That's why she's not here.'

How Rhoese managed to walk the rest of the way to where the king stood with Judhael de Brionne and his supporters she would never be able to remember, for the marriage ceremony was like a dream in which her responses came from the far end of a tunnel, distant and resonating. *Warin, blind and mutilated. Warin, the one she had once loved. She knew he would rather have been killed.*

To his credit, Jude must have guessed by the terrible shock on her face that the archbishop's disastrous timing was responsible. The king was not in the best of moods, impatient to get this business over, totally unsympathetic to any reason for Rhoese's stuttering replies. Jude supported her, prompting her answers, placing the quill in her hand to make a cross by her name that the scribe had printed, and almost

having his finger marked by the signature that
emerged, neater by far than the scribe's. Astonished,
he caught Brother Alaric's eye, and the signal that
told him quite clearly that there was more to this
woman than met the eye.

Still numbed and horrified, and far from jubilant at
Warin's terrible fate, Rhoese allowed her hand to be
taken again into Jude's, this time feeling the pressure
of the gold ring between her fingers while her eyes
skimmed over his courtly tunic of blue and red and
gold, his short cloak lined with marten fur. His black
hair shone with highlights of silken blue, and her
heart suddenly ached for the future infidelities she
would have to turn a blind eye to, to the women
whose looks of pity she would have to suffer, and for
the coldness she would know while she was breeding.
The love-potion had not been a good idea, for not
until the spring would she be able to find those same
ingredients again.

A chorus of male cries went up as Jude kissed her
lips. 'I've won!' one yelled. 'I've won my wager!
Well done, de Brionne. We knew you could do it!'
Others howled similar absurdities until they were
hushed by a bark from the king's chaplain, Ranulf
Flambard. 'Hold your noise!' he told them. 'Show
some respect, will you? Or leave.'

'Amen to that,' said Archbishop Thomas. 'Come,
lady. Shall you kneel to your new husband now?'

Jude's grip on her hand was firm. 'No, my lord,
she will not.' He faced the king. 'By your leave, sire,
I beg you will release us.'

'To your bed?' the king said, standing up. 'Aye,

get off to your wife's bed and see if you can stir up some heat. She's as cold as midwinter. You're released from duty tomorrow, de Brionne, since I doubt you'll be up before midday and you have some new property to attend to. Your wife's stepmother is your responsibility now, and I hope she realises how much she owes to your intervention. She'd have lost the wretch altogether if I'd had my way, but he'll not be a lot of good to her now, will he? It's up to you whether to let her have Toft Green or put her somewhere else, man. In any case, we leave York the day after tomorrow, so you'd better get this one packed up and ready to go. Eh?'

'Yes, sire. I thank you.'

The king nodded, casting his eyes several times over Rhoese. 'Let me know how you get on,' he said. 'That woman's wardship of you has ended,' he said to Rhoese. 'You belong to de Brionne from now on. You'll attend my court with him whenever I wish it. The place could do with a bit of class, and even English class is better than none.'

Rhoese bowed, acknowledging a quick squeeze of Jude's fingers at the king's only attempt at a compliment, so far. They left, before he changed his volatile mind. The short journey through York's dark streets, however, was cold, cheerless, and anything but relaxed after the wine and warmth, the congratulations and smiles. Echoing in Rhoese's ears were the humiliating cries of joy from those who had won heavy bets on Jude's success, intermingled with Ketti's ghostly howls of anguish at Warin's dreadful injuries. She had been prepared to suffer her stepmother's impotent jealousy, even Warin's treachery and stupidity, but never in the bitterest days of her heartbreak had she wanted the woman's inevitable hatred on this scale. And the night was yet to come.

The heavy rain had passed over, but now the gales buffeted the sturdy walls of her bower and whined over the thatch as she lay snugly under the fur coverlet, the wool and the fine linen. She was still not sure how she would deal with Jude's invasion of her privacy, or with his teasing hopes not to disappoint her. If anything, it would be the other way round; she had no intention of making any kind of response to whatever satisfaction he might seek.

Someone, probably Hilda and Els, had bedecked the bower with fronds of golden bracken and magical mistletoe, and had left a bowl of lavender and dried rose petals on her chest to scent the air. The white curtains round the bed stirred in the draught, and she snuggled further down on to the feather mattress, remembering Eric's brotherly embrace that had lasted far longer than usual in the corner of the hall. They had all behaved lovingly, understanding the harrowing events of the last few days. 'I'll keep him talking a while,' Eric had whispered to her. 'I think we shall get on well together. He likes me.'

She had smiled at that. 'Everybody likes you,' she replied. 'And I'm so glad you're to come with us to London. Did you find out what's happened to Father Leofric?'

'Yes, I did. Archbishop Thomas has released him.

They didn't believe a word of his confession. What's happened to Warin?'

'I'll tell you tomorrow, love.'

Jude had hardly spoken to her except when he placed his fur-lined cloak around her shoulders and to ask if she was all right. On dismounting, he had held her against him and kissed her in the darkness before someone brought a torch, but there had been no cheers at their arrival, and her departure to bed had hardly been noticed, only Brother Alaric and her two women taking her across to the door of her bower. It was exactly as she had wanted it to be. Without comment.

She knew that she had been asleep for some time before the bed moved, covers were lifted, and a cool draught of air caressed her back, holding her rigid and dreading the hours to come that no amount of preparation could resolve. His warmth enclosed her back and bent itself into her shape, laying an arm around her waist and gently pulling her in, like a comfortable garment on a raw day. Her skin, alive and vibrant, registered every muscle, every soft scratch of hair from his legs, the softness of his folds and surfaces, each breath as he snuffled and yawned like a sated pup into her hair. One hand rested tenderly upon her ribcage and then, as if asleep already, moved up to cup one breast, relaxed, and fell off again.

She had never slept in a man's arms until now; not even with Warin had she passed the night, only a stolen hour or two in the afternoon. Tentatively, her fingers explored the soft-haired skin of his forearms and wrists while her mind recalled his many acts of protection over the last few days. Not since her father died had she experienced a man's direct authority, and now she wondered how easy it would be for her to submit to him in every way, or whether he would leave her alone to do as she pleased. Norman men were known for being allowed to beat their wives; the Anglo-Saxons had no such tradition of chastisement. But this Norman had refused to allow her to kneel to him.

Several times during the night she wakened with a fearful start, only to be caught in his arms as if he'd been waiting for that to happen. Thoughts of Warin's fate and Ketti's distress plagued her, haunting her dreams not with sweet revenge but with guilt and acts of penance. Each time she woke, he pulled her back to him, face to face or however she happened to fall, and not once did she resent it or fight him. Once, his hand wandered over her buttocks and stroked like a rider with a restless mare, his voice hushing her thoughts and unspoken words before they came, holding her like a child until sleep returned. Once, he lay over her, kissing her sleep-laden mouth to stir a slow-burning fire in her thighs, but no more than that before sleep came again, leaving her edgily unsatisfied and vaguely wanting more.

And when the cockerel crowed in the croft and the sound of church bells drifted on the wind, he had gone and there was only a patch of warmth between the linen sheets to remind her of his compensation for her catastrophic feast-day.

Chapter Five

In an effort to avoid reaching any conclusions about her chaste night in her new husband's arms, Rhoese spent her last day in York attending to matters that kept her mind thankfully engrossed in preparations, though the funeral of Ralph de Lessay was an engagement she would have preferred to miss, if she'd been allowed to. Standing by Jude's side in the little church of St Martin's, she recalled yet again the bizarre events that had clouded the last four days, leading her thoughts inevitably towards her father and the funeral that had never taken place. His companionship and advice were what she needed now more than anything, his dependability and constancy in all things. Brother Alaric was steadfast, but he was no real substitute for Lord Gamal who would heartily have insisted on having her marriage bed blessed, whether she wished it or not.

The Norman, on the other hand, was bent on surprising her, for no sooner had they returned to Toft Green for their morning meal than he announced to the household what their various fates were to be without any consultation with Rhoese. She was offended by this, even after Eric pointed out that Jude was the new master and that he had had time to decide what was best for them all. She did not want to be reminded in quite those terms. 'Oh, for heaven's sake, Eric, go and get dressed. You can't walk round like that all day. Neal!' she called. 'What's happened to my brother's clothes?'

Neal instantly appeared with an armful, grinning and showing his white even teeth against a skin as tanned as Eric's by summer days spent out of doors. Totally loyal to his blind master, Neal could have taken his pick of the local women at any time but, for Eric's sake, stayed within his call day and night. Not even for an hour with a lover would he have done otherwise. Strong, quick-thinking and slow to take offence, he was grey-eyed and golden like the native Icelandic ponies, his stamina as durable as theirs.

Big-boned Hilda, plain, reliable and happily middle-aged, had almost wept with relief at being allowed to go to her mistress's new home with Els and Brother Alaric. She hugged Rhoese with sturdy arms and felt it not out of place, as her nurse, to ask if all had gone well last night. 'You know what I mean,' she whispered, knowingly.

Rhoese had no qualms about the ambiguity of her reply, which Hilda would be sure to misunderstand. 'Yes, thank you, love. It was everything I hoped for.' It was the reply Hilda had hoped for, too.

'Oh, my dear, I'm so glad.' Hilda beamed, tearfully, and Rhoese knew exactly what was in her heart after the miscarriage that had distressed her greatly. 'He was not unkind, was he?' And then, before Rhoese could demur, she had moved on to the new arrangements. 'Fancy him putting Bran and his wife and Master Steward and his woman in here instead of Ketti and Warin. They're to have your bower, and serve them both right. Though he's a hard man is your husband, m'lady.'

A dry chill October morning it was after the storm, with the sharp fresh smell of autumn in the air that sent a sudden shiver along Rhoese's arms. She had felt the same tingling of ice in the church earlier, when they had lowered the shroud-wrapped body of de Lessay into the crypt as if he had fallen in defence of his country instead of a brawl to avenge his thwarted ambition. She had felt Jude's cool appraisal, but had shown no sign of gratification, only sadness at the waste of a life and bewilderment that it should have happened in her name.

The rest of the day had not improved with her visit to Ketti, which, for sheer unpleasantness, was on a par with the funeral. This time, it was Brother Alaric and Els who accompanied her, standing like buttresses on either side as they waited in the dim hall with the odour of sickness assaulting their noses. It had been a most distressing interview, with Ketti, at her most malevolent and the unfortunate Warin groaning on his sweat-soaked pallet, sedated and heavily bandaged, shaking with pain and the onset of a fever. Understandably, Ketti was not receptive to the conditions under which she and her immediate family were to receive accommodation at Toft Green;

at first surprised to be given anything at all, then indignant that, as Rhoese's kin, they were not to be given more, then accusing. Finally, when Rhoese told her of the minster clergy's need for a good seamstress to repair the church vestments, Ketti's world apparently collapsed as the notion of working for her living registered in her mind, and her outrage overflowed into a stream of self-pitying abuse that Brother Alaric dealt with by reminding her that she was fortunate not to have lost Warin altogether. She did not appear to be convinced of that.

But for Rhoese there had been no pleasure in the mission, and she left with wretchedness lying heavily over the heart that should, according to her former intentions, have been impervious to such distress. 'What a pity,' she said to Brother Alaric, 'that the Norman could not have delivered this news himself and allowed *me* to give my household the comforting news concerning their futures.'

'Ah,' said Brother Alaric unhelpfully. 'Perhaps the Norman has his good reasons.'

'Then I wish he'd tell *me* what they are,' she said, tight-lipped.

Toft Green had been in turmoil since dawn, for although most of the household were to stay there with Bran as the new fee-paying tenant, there were still Rhoese's belongings to be sorted and packed ready to load onto the ox-wagon before dawn the next day. Having heard the news, friends called to say congratulations and farewell and to bring gifts for good fortune and fertility: chunks of amber and rock crystal, a precious cowrie shell, and a less-controversial roll of fine linen for some new chemises. The shoe-maker sent her a pair of fur-lined bootees, the comb-maker an ivory comb, and the weaver several bobbins of linen thread far finer than she could have spun herself. Several of her father's merchant friends had also heard the scandal of the previous days and, to show their regard, had sent her boxes of spices, a set of walrus-ivory chess pieces, a rug of lynx fur for the coming winter and a carved whalebone box to keep her trinkets in. With her thanks, she had sent each of them a curl of her hair, which they had often teasingly asked for but never thought to receive. To Father Leofric she sent a note, thanking him for his kindness and affection to both herself and Eric.

As far as she was able, she avoided any contact with Jude, telling Els, who had remarked on it, that they'd be together enough on the long journey to Lon-don. But despite her attempted uninterest in his whereabouts, Rhoese would still have liked him to know that she was intentionally avoiding him. With-out telling her, he had gone up to the castle to arrange the journey for the morrow, to see his men and Count Alan, his lord, and by suppertime he had not returned. It was clear to everyone then that autumn would soon turn into winter.

As darkness fell, her hours after supper were spent with Bran the bailiff and the steward, for provisions had to be taken on the journey south and she was adamant that Ketti and Warin should have enough food to last them at least until All Saints' Day, if not longer, in spite of what Jude had decreed. The lad

Thorn would have to work for his bread like everyone else, and so would Ketti.

She told herself repeatedly that her conscience was clear, that it was entirely Warin's doing, not hers, brought on by her father's disappearance. She must look to her own future now. Nevertheless, in the time between business and sleep, it was not to the future she looked but to the past, to a small corner of the croft behind her bower where crab apples still clung to the gnarled branches, where browning meadow-sweet shed dust over a patch of carefully tended grass. A heavy square-cut stone from the nearby Roman wall marked the spot before which Rhoese knelt in the night air, her fingers resting on the stone as if to draw something from it. So engrossed was she in the painful memories, the farewells, the silent plea for this place not to be disturbed, that she was quite un-aware of the tall figure who watched from the end of the croft against the wall of her bower.

Eventually she rose and turned to find her way back through the darkness that swam with tears and, not surprisingly, she stumbled and was caught by strong arms that she fought against in fright, and then in furious indignation. His deep calming voice did noth-ing to ease her resentment at his intrusion upon this most private of all moments, and she fought him in the blind rage of a bereaved mother who fears for the violation of a sacred memory. Emotionally exhausted and quite unable to explain her anger, she used her body like a weapon against him, unthinking, reckless, and hopelessly outmatched by his strength and ex-perience. Soon, she was held, panting and howling with anguish at the loss of everything in her world, a dark world that was suddenly tipped sideways as she was lifted and carried into the warmth of her bower, her sobbing buried in the soft linen of his tunic.

A cresset lamp with four wicks burned in a corner, casting a glow over the untidy interior where baskets and chests were piled against the walls and her bed was now a stack of planks and posts roped into bundles. Her mattress and bedding was all that was left in a heap on the floor, and it was on this that Jude laid her, wrapping her tightly in his arms until her weeping subsided.

She made no resistance, having been starved of such tenderness over the past year, telling herself that she could live without it for ever. Drained and weakened, she slept like a child without a word being exchanged, still in her clothes and, when she woke, his arms were still around her and the lamp still burning.

'Is it dawn?' she whispered, through her hair.

His hand came up to sweep the auburn veil from her face. 'No. Go back to sleep. I'll wake you when it's time to go.'

'To London?'

'No, we're not going to London.'

Her eyes opened again. 'Not...not to London? Where, then?'

'To Durham. Northwards. Not so very far.'

Sitting up was not easy to do without co-operation, but she managed to lean on one elbow and look down into the lamp-lit face beside her that watched through narrowed eyes with neither amusement nor obvious desire. 'Are you serious?' she said. 'We're to go up to Durham?'

'Quite serious. Flambard told me only this eve.' His fingers touched the curtain of hair that spread across his chest like a red-wine stain while his eyes wandered over her face, still swollen with weeping. 'I'll tell you why tomorrow. It's not your concern. Go back to sleep.'

She did not understand him. They were together, in private, and he had shown no signs of wanting to consummate their marriage which, by law, should have been consummated immediately. Did he truly have no desire for her? Unable to resist a probe, she said, 'Hilda thinks we've…'

He blinked, slowly. 'I'm sure she does. And do you care what she thinks?'

His mouth, she thought, was beautiful in repose. Wide, firm, mobile, manly. 'No,' she said, aware that the pause had been too long to mean what it said.

'Good,' he said, gently pushing her head down on to his shoulder. 'Then what Hilda thinks doesn't concern either of us. Go to sleep now.'

If only I had not mixed the drinks up. If only he had taken the one meant for him. She yawned and closed her eyes, breathing in the male scent of him and using her thumb to twist the strange gold band on her finger. *He's a Norman. A greedy self-seeking Norman with a reputation for seducing women, a man on whom bets are laid to see how quickly he can take them. And leave them. Well, this would have provided him with almost no challenge to speak of. And obviously no interest, either.*

Her brother had offered only scant commiserations, which she knew to be an indication of his excitement at the thought of the future. St Mary's would have been an interesting change for him, a challenge, but a life in London was a more attractive lure than a monastery for which he had no real vocation. He had not seen how men looked at him as much as at her, and she did not know whether he understood the dangers of being both attractive and sightless. Her father may have told him. Or Neal.

So her thoughts swam round aimlessly like fish in a bowl seeking an escape. 'Are we to stay in Durham?' she asked.

His hand covered hers on his chest, and she felt the turn of his head. 'We have to make an arrest,' he said, 'and then escort the prisoner back to London. We shall be on the road for some little while, and this is not the best time of year to be travelling.'

'Who is it?' she said.

'One who was not at the ceremony the other day. William of St Calais, Bishop of Durham.'

Rhoese tried to lift her head but it was too heavy. 'You're going to arrest him? A bishop? Why, what has he done?'

'He took sides against the king. You remember that the king's elder brother, Duke Robert, was given Normandy to rule while William Rufus was given England. Well, Robert wants England too, and he's got the backing of his uncle, Bishop Odo of Bayeux, and other powerful men like the Bishop of Durham. But the king has dealt severely with them, which is why he needed your father's men to help restore order.

He's exiled his uncle and he's about to do the same to William of St Calais. He'll be sent back to Normandy.'

'Does he know?'

'Oh, he'll have a fair idea by now. He'll be packing his bags.'

'So Durham will be without a bishop?'

'For a while, until he's allowed to return.'

'Years?'

'Oh, certainly years. Go to sleep.'

'You could leave me here,' she said. 'You could collect me…us…on the way back down to London. It would save you some time.'

For a heart-stopping moment she thought he was about to agree, and in the silence she could hear his quiet sigh and feel the gentle lift of his chest. But the sigh continued into a soft laugh as he eased himself up to tower over her, blotting out the light with his shoulders and bending his head down to hers. Mechanically, her palms pushed against him, feeling his resistance.

'Would it indeed?' he whispered. 'And what would it save *you*, my lady? Your conjugal duties? Eh? Your dues to your husband? Is that what you have in mind to avoid? And would you still be here when I returned? I very much doubt it. No, lass. It was a good try, but you cannot buy time so cheaply. You're coming with me.'

Vexed at being read so easily, she pushed harder. 'You don't need me with you,' she said. 'If your conjugal rights are all you're bothered about, there are plenty of camp followers who'd be glad to service you meantime. There were wives of courtiers who couldn't see enough of you when we married. They'd oblige, I'm sure. You need not bother about what I get up to, now that you've got what you wanted.'

'I haven't got what I wanted, Rhoese of York. Not yet.'

'Ah, no, of course. There was some talk of a litter, I recall.'

'Which I'm not going to get simply by talking about it, am I?'

'Another time, then,' she said, coldly. 'I need to sleep.'

She tried to turn, but her body was held by his and he was not about to release her, and she knew that the ruse to test the inclination of his mind had led her into deep water from which there would be no escape. Nor had it helped that now it was her own mind that she didn't understand while her body ached to know more about his, in intimate detail.

It was too late to pretend that it was sleep she needed. Since her visit to the stone in the croft, her womb had been sending messages of emptiness and longing that not even sleep had calmed. Now, it was her rekindled body that responded to his virile maleness, and her confused mind that reminded her that Rhoese of York was not to be bought and sold without some show of pride, especially to a Norman.

Her initial attempts to resist had no effect as he held her chin in one large hand for his first kiss, pressing her into the fur rug and holding her there easily until she weakened. Already she could sense the hunger in his lips as they searched and dared her to follow

him, to reveal the same unpredictable flame of keenness she had shown once before, but this time to make
it to the end. Part-committed, and half-drowning in
the heavenly weight of him, she tried one last attempt
at rebellion, aware of its feeble implications. 'I
warned you,' she panted between kisses.

'Of what?'

'That I shall make you a poor wife. You may have
won what I owned, sir, but you'll never take my pride.
Or my honour.'

'Then I'll do my best to manage without them,
lady. Meanwhile you'll have to suffer in silence while
I enjoy my wager, won't you?' He made it clear that
he understood the terrible conflict that raged within
her, for even as he spoke the uncaring words, he knew
how to draw sighs of capitulation from his willing
victim. As she had said, he also knew his way round
a woman's anatomy and her garments without the
slightest help from her, showing how dexterously his
warm experienced hands could send immediate shiv-
ers of delight along the surface of her thighs.

Preparing herself for a hasty and somewhat bois-
terous use of her body similar to Warin's crude fum-
blings, with an embarrassing commentary on his find-
ings, her fists wound themselves into the stuff of his
tunic like two anchors. But there was no such boyish
assault, no resemblance to anything in her limited experience and, under his practised hands and lips, she
could not remain impassive, as she had intended. Nor
did she know how to keep her body rigid and her
mind distant when the first knowing touch of his fingertips in her groin made her gasp and soften, betray-

ing her interest with a parting of her legs that she had
no power to prevent.

Delaying and prolonging the surrender with consummate skill, he kept her engrossed in the play of
his lips upon hers, his hands tenderly exploring the
soft folds between her legs as no other had done before, melting her body and the tension in her fists and
drawing them gradually upwards to delve into the
thick silky hair of his head. Unconsciously, blissfully,
she stretched herself under him, wrapping her arms
around his neck.

Quick to recognise her change of allegiance, he
took advantage as any soldier would. 'That's it, my
beauty,' he whispered. 'Lay down your weapons.
Submit to me. I won you fairly. Easy now…' Nudg-
ing her legs further apart, he came between them and
directed himself into her with the hand already there.
Smooth, practised, assertive, he felt the shudder of her
body in the first of his slow thrusts that brought a cry
of surprise before a deep sigh. He watched her eyelids
droop and close, her head lift to reach him with her
lips, and his heart sang with admiration of her fierce
beauty.

For Rhoese, there could be no turning back, no
more mindless resistance during this time of truce
while the same joyful spark of rapture, glimpsed at
his first embrace, danced before her and led her on
with each stroke and caress into a place where pride
had no meaning. He was unhurried and in complete
control, and she waited like a slow fuse for every
move that would carry her further towards his com-
pletion. Warin's hurried performances had been com-

pletely selfish and had left her knowing only about giving, never about receiving.

But though the Norman's cold words about taking what he wanted without her permission had sent a chill through her heart, she found no evidence of that same callousness in the hands that gentled her in the dim untidiness of her bower.

There was no haste in his first possession of her, no trace of that earlier, almost violent passion that had had every hallmark of lust. In the carefully controlled consummation he now displayed, Rhoese began to sense that either he was making it last as an exercise in self-discipline, or that he intended by his leisurely approach to give her the pleasure that he had previously denied caring about. He could not, she thought hazily, have been in any doubt about that, for she was not so good at pretence, and her sighs, her writhing, her disobediently wandering hands told him what she would never have admitted in words.

Slowly, languorously, stretching time and rapture into light years, he used his body to close her mind to guilt and resentment and to lead her further than she had ever been before towards her own finale. And just when she was about to protest that she could bear the incredible suspense no longer, his rhythm changed in response to her cries and she felt a surge of power fill her lungs and halt her breath, centring every sense into her womb, bringing it madly to life. Seizing her in its hold, it thrust her hips upwards to meet him, quivering with tension just before the release, then hurling her away into a void where she heard her own echoing cry for help. Her body and mind floated, borne by wave after wave of tingling bliss.

In response, she heard the distant answering groan and felt the hard beat of his loins before he slowed and reached far into her, pulsing, throbbing. Above them, a star burst and shattered, then reformed into the cresset lamp in which only one wick burned. And at last she remembered to breathe out in a sobbing gasp, feeling the damp skin of his neck against her lips.

Dawn filtered through the wooden shutters before she remembered to try to make light of it all, to make some derogatory remark regarding his performance that might conceivably spoil his enjoyment or, at best, deflate his ego. But by then it was too late; she was alone and already awash with contradictions, her mind and body once again at opposite ends of the argument over whether she should be holding on to the rapture of last night or discarding it as meaningless.

The memory of his hands and lips, the weight of his body and the bliss of his invasion held her weightless for a moment or two before she pulled her mind back to the tousled state of her dress and hair. It was ironic, she told herself angrily, that this pile of furs and tangled blankets should have been no more fitting for her lovemaking as a married woman than it had been for Warin's lover, for then there had been no bed either. No sheets, no proper pillows, no rose petals, and no erotic undressing to aid the romantic preparation. Of that, there had been not a trace.

She stared at the pile of bedding resentfully while her hands stole up to hold her face, as he had done. *How can I hurt him? How do I pay him back for taking everything that was mine, even my body? How can I make him suffer jealousy when I cannot reach his heart? How shall I bear his indifference when I become pregnant? How can I hide my feelings when I've never learnt the art? And those two men, one dead and one maimed, helpless, useless and undergoing all the torments of hell for wanting what I cannot give. Why me?* 'Why me?' she said out loud.

'Why you, love?' said a soothing voice.

'Eric! You startled me.'

'Sorry. Are you with someone?'

'No, I'm on my own. Talking to myself. Come inside.'

He closed the door behind him and stood for a moment with one hand reaching out. 'Sounds strange,' he said. 'You packing?'

Rhoese took his fingers in hers and led him forward. 'Yes. Be careful. Nothing is where it should be. Chest behind you. Sit a while.'

'That's what I came to find out. Where's the book? You've packed it safe, have you?'

'Yes, you're sitting on it. It's in with my gowns, quite safe. But you and Neal will not be going with us up to—'

'To Durham. Yes, I know. Jude just told me.'

'Oh. Did he?' Her voice was flat and suddenly distant, and she was glad her brother could not see the state of her, or of the makeshift bed. 'He tells you more than he tells me, I think.' Instantly, she regretted the admission.

'It's all right, love,' he said, smoothing her ruffled feathers. 'I know you're finding it hard after all that's happened, but he's not a bad fellow. He and I will get on well enough, I think, as long as he's kind to my sister. And if he's not, then you must tell me and I'll thrash him without mercy.'

She couldn't help smiling at that. 'Thank you, love. There's been no unkindness.' *It's his indifference that will hurt me more.*

'He's not as indifferent as you think, you know.'

She was used to him reading her mind. Second sight, some called it, but Rhoese knew better. 'He's not indifferent to my property certainly,' she said, taking a comb to her hair. 'We shall see about the rest in due course. I had thought,' she said, quickly changing the subject, 'that I might leave the book here with you, but it's a responsibility, and I may as well leave it in its usual place. Eventually, when we can take it down to London, we stand a good chance of returning it to Barking, at last.'

'Did Archbishop Thomas ever ask about it?'

'Only indirectly.' She replaced the comb in her girdle-pouch and gathered the thick hair behind her head, dividing it into three. 'When Father didn't return, he sent for me to commiserate, though he was also quite keen to know what Father had been bringing back from his voyage.'

'Why didn't he ask Warin?'

'He probably did, but he'd want to know if our accounts tallied, I suppose. But more than that, he also asked me if there was anything that Father had left that we'd like him to keep safe for us. Temporarily, of course.' She smiled, and Eric sensed it.

'Of course. Temporarily. Cunning old fox. He meant the book, naturally. But you didn't tell him we'd got it, did you?'

Rhoese's hands were busily plaiting, pulling the hair over one shoulder. 'No, silly. Father had only brought it back with him on the previous voyage while the archbishop was away in London, otherwise he'd have handed it over.'

'And would not have been paid for it.'

'Certainly not,' she agreed. 'Archbishops take their time over that kind of thing.'

'Did you ever discover its history?'

'Oh, yes. It began before you were born. When the first Norman king stayed at Barking Abbey just after the battle at Hastings in 1066, he and his army were quite ill with stomach upsets. When they left after about three weeks, they took with them things his light-fingered greedy nobles thought they had a right to, things that had been donated to the abbey, and things the nuns themselves had made. The gospel-book was amongst the treasures they took, but the fool who stole it sold it for cash to a Norse merchant. The abbess protested to Archbishop Thomas.'

'Why not to the Archbishop of Canterbury?'

'Stigand? His position was too precarious, love. As an Anglo-Saxon, he'd not have been inclined to stir up trouble with the Normans. He lost his job soon after, anyway.'

'So Archbishop Thomas asked Father to look out for it.'

'Yes, on his travels to Norway. And, as it happened, he found the same merchant and bought it back, then brought it home with him.'

'While the archbishop was in London.'

'Right,' she said, binding a ribbon into her plait. 'It was to wait here until he returned to York, but then Father disappeared, and I didn't feel inclined to tell the archbishop that it was already here because both Brother Alaric and I believe it should be returned to the nuns at Barking, not to some greedy Norman's library already overflowing with our treasures.'

'It's more likely it would be sent over to Normandy, like so much other valuable stuff.'

'Very probably. It's time something was returned to its rightful owners, for a change.' They both recognised that there was more to her words than concern for a book.

'Give it time, love,' was all he said.

'Time,' she replied, throwing the plait over her shoulder. 'Ah yes, that's the stuff I was trying to hold on to. And now look what's happened to it.'

'Shall I call for Els and Hilda?'

'Yes, love. If you please. I need some hot water, for a start.'

Missing Rhoese's presence in the great hall at the beginning of their last day at Toft Green, Brother Alaric found her instead sitting on the only piece of luggage left in her bower, the clothes-chest. She folded the book she was reading, enclosing one finger inside it, but made no attempt to prevent her chaplain from removing it to see what she had been quietly reciting to Eric's wolfhound.

'Oh, dear,' said Brother Alaric, softly. 'No wonder your audience doesn't look too impressed.' He sat on a large stone that was part of the central hearth, oblivious to the dusting of fine white wood-ash. 'You've never needed to practise this kind of thing, have you?'

Rhoese looked down at her hands and twisted the gold ring until it sat more comfortably into a fold. 'No,' she said. 'Even less than you, Brother.'

He smiled. 'That's debatable. But incantations are not going to help, you know. For one thing, they're rubbish. And for another—'

'They're against Christian teaching. Yes, I know that. But I don't suppose there's a prayer you know of which will make a man fall in love with a woman, is there? Around Michaelmas, preferably.'

He was not affronted. 'No,' he said. 'But what you've just been reciting in Old Norse is a charm to make a woman fall in love with a man. Isn't that what you had in mind?' He saw by her shocked expression that it was not. 'Oh, dear,' he said again. 'That's the trouble with this old script. One letter can make all the difference.' For several moments he did not encroach upon her despair, for he was not unsympathetic, despite the pagan solution to her problem. There was still so much of the old religion in every aspect of their lives that would take centuries more to forget. 'Tell me,' he said, gently. 'Is there a need for you to force-feed love with incantations? His love for you will grow, if you nurture it, my lady.'

'Yes, Brother. There is,' she said, on the verge of tears. 'I took…'

He waited, then finished the sentence for her. 'You took the potion meant for him. I thought you were perhaps trying to give him a sleeping-draught.'

'You…?' She sat bolt upright, her brown eyes like polished topaz in water. '*You* handed the beakers round. You took the flask? Why? Whose side are you on?'

'Yours first and foremost,' he said. 'Why need you ask?'

'Because…'

'Because I have little liking for this kind of stuff?' he said, handing the old tattered book back to her. 'It may have a tooled leather binding, but that's all one can say in its favour. Listen, my lady. Potions and charms are not the answer to your problems. You're full of resentment. And anger. And grief. And you feel that every bit of precious life is being taken away from you.'

'And there's Warin, too,' she whispered.

'You still care for him?'

'No, Brother. But I never wanted *that* kind of revenge. How am I to live with it? A man blinded, terribly mutilated, made useless. That was never what I wanted. How can I even *think* about my own happiness after that?'

The chaplain took her wrists and held her hands between his. 'The Norman interceded for him,' he said, 'with the king. Warin would have been hanged, had it not been for Judhael de Brionne.'

'Then he should not have!' she cried. 'He should

not have, Brother. I know Warin would rather not have lived at all than be granted this terrible half-life.'

'You think so now,' he said, 'and so may he, for a while. But think straight, if you will. He will be blind. Yes, well so is your brother, and does *he* have half a life? I think not. I am celibate, but nor do I live a half-life, I can assure you. Give it time.'

'That's what Eric said.'

'Then we can't both be wrong, can we?' Watching her, he noted the slow shake of her head. 'Why, what is it? Is there something else?'

She spread her hands, and the book slid onto the wooden floor with a bump. 'Everything,' she whispered. 'Ketti and Warin and their kin will be living in here, and you know what lies yonder, outside the walls?' She pointed to the place where the stone marked the tiny grave. 'What if *she* finds it? Or that dreadful child of hers? What if they—'

'Shh!' said Brother Alaric. 'Leave it to me. I'll get some of the lads to pile a load of the old Roman stones on top of it.'

'Oh, *would* you?'

'Yes, and I'll get them to move that old Celtic cross-shaft there too, so they'll believe it's a holy place. They wouldn't dare shift that. Now, go out there and look as if you haven't a care in the world. Eh?' He stood up, placing a kindly hand beneath her elbow. 'There's rather an interesting-looking gelding in the yard, and I think it might be intended for a lady. Best go and see.'

Jude was one of a group of men who stood beside a handsome dark liver chestnut, but he saw Rhoese as soon as she arrived, watching her every stride as she approached. 'Come, lady,' he said, taking her hand.

She was glad even of that small gesture, not being sure how to look at him after last night's experience. Her glance was rewarded, for he showed none of the signs of their tempestuous encounter as she had done earlier. He was clean and newly shaved, neatly dressed in deep blue and red, with clean cross-gartered hose and polished leather ankle-boots. A light woollen cloak hung casually over one shoulder with a large golden brooch to pin it together, a huge amethyst in its centre, and his sword-belt gleamed with more gems, the hilt of his sword catching the rays of fitful sunshine. His grasp was warm and firm, gently pulling her into the discussion.

Eric was running his hands over the creature's shoulder and neck while Neal and Pierre moved round to the tail-end, admiring every angle.

'Like him?' said Jude. 'He's almost your colour.'

'For me?' she said.

'For you. Can you ride him?'

'I can ride, sir. But I already have a mare of my own.'

'Yes, I've seen it. Your maid or your nurse can ride that one. I prefer to see you on something more handsome. His name is Ar.'

'That means copper, in English.'

'Really? Aptly named, then.'

'New harness, too?'

'New harness for a new ride. New master and new mistress.' He was smiling wickedly, and she knew he was not talking about the horse. 'Well, lady? Will he do?'

Metaphorically, he had backed her into a corner, and now there was no chance for her to chasten him as she had intended. She looked down at his hand holding hers and was bound to give him the reply he wanted. 'Yes, sir. I thank you. He will do very well, I believe.'

'He'll look after you,' he said for her ears alone. 'Trust him.'

'I have no choice, do I?' she said. 'From owner to owned in less than a week. That must be some kind of record for the daughter of a thegn.'

'Strange,' he said. 'I could have sworn that there was a period only recently when you seemed to have put all that to the back of your mind. Perhaps I was dreaming.' He loosened her hand and lifted a rein as Eric ducked under the horse's chin. 'Your sister likes him,' he said.

'So do I,' said Eric, patting the glossy neck. 'He's as sound as a bell. He'll stay for ever.'

'I wonder,' murmured Rhoese.

Chapter Six

'Won't be long, love,' Rhoese whispered into Eric's ear as they hugged their farewells. She felt him clinging, childlike, though he was as manly as any to look at. 'I expect we'll get as far as the borough bridge before we stop for the night, then Catterick by the next night. We'll be at Durham by the fourth day. Soon be back.'

They had never been parted before, and both felt it keenly now that the moment had come. But the yard was full of men; only Rhoese knew how they watched from a respectful distance, and only she sensed the change in their former manner, from a thinly veiled incivility to deference. As the wife of their commanding officer, she was due every courtesy, but was there more to their almost unnatural reserve than mere respect for a superior's wife? Was there perhaps a hint of awe in their demeanour, now that some had profited by their wagers?

'Did Els not say her farewell to you?' said Rhoese. The young lass sat behind Pierre, Jude's handsome young squire, snuggling into his back with a look of utter contentment and pride on her vivacious face and the sun catching the bright sheen of her fair curls.

'Nah!' said Eric, grinning. 'It's Neal she should have said her farewells to, not me. He's the one.'

'Neal? Are you sure?'

Laughing, he hugged her to him with one arm as Jude approached. 'You're a bit behind with your pairing, love. Where is he?'

Neal was only a few yards away, his expression verifying what Eric had said. He caught Rhoese's enquiring glance and came to them, sheepishly flicking an eyebrow in brief display of defeat. 'Women,' he muttered, trying to smile.

'Oh, dear,' said Rhoese. 'I didn't realise. It'll not last, Neal. You'll see. You know what she's like. She's still very young.'

His mouth stretched into a simulated grin that quickly faded. 'Yeah,' he said, his bright eyes reflecting his doubts. 'God go with you, m'lady. We'll keep the place running smoothly until your return.'

At any other time she would have made an appropriate reply to that, but now Jude was by her side to remind her by his presence that the place was now his, and that he had put some of his men there to keep an eye on things.

He was light-hearted. 'And don't lay wagers with the Normans,' he said. 'Not unless you have money to lose. They'll bet on anything.'

Rhoese turned away as a sudden heat burned along her neck.

The cavalcade of ox-wagons and packhorses, men and supplies had already begun their slow rumbling

procession out towards the great wall across Micklegate. The same kind of traffic squeezed through the
gate in the opposite direction, for it was a market day
and traders had waited since dawn to be first into the
city. Mounted on her new showy gelding, Rhoese
could not help but be aware of the stares of her countrymen as they parted to make way for the company
of Normans, none of them calling out their usual
greetings this time, nor could she catch their eyes to
send them a smile. It was as if they had written her
off as Norman property.

For some time, her thoughts were occupied with
the ancient Roman road known as Ermine Street, a
straight cobbled track wide enough for traffic to pass
without detours on to the verges, still soft after the
heavy rain. Swathed in blue with a woollen mantle of
violet and a fair white head-rail, she drew Jude's eyes
constantly to her, though he refused to comment on
her appearance. Indeed, he said very little to her on
any subject.

Hilda had been given Rhoese's mare to ride. It was
a mistake, for the mare's reaction to the stallion's
interest caused quite an upset until they were both
relegated to a position behind the ox-wagon where
Rhoese could not reach Hilda. The clouds thickened
across the sky and the wind whipped at the women's
veils and sneaked into their wide sleeves, bringing the
first fine mist of rain to dampen their faces. Rhoese
waited for Jude to ask after her welfare, but he did
not, and the slanderous names she called him under
her breath went thankfully unheard in the clatter of
hooves and the rattle of cargo.

But while Rhoese's new husband was uncommunicative, there was one who was happy to step into the breach as Jude's continued absences left her with Brother Alaric's silence on one side of her and Els's continual chatter to Pierre on the other. It was easy for Ranulf Flambard to wedge himself between them just as Rhoese delivered a rebuke to her maid. *'Genog, Els,'* she said in English. Enough. The maid's chatter stopped immediately, but Rhoese's expression remained.

'My lady, can I assist you?' said Ranulf. 'You wish to stop?'

She wound her flying veil once more around her neck and forced a smile at the royal chaplain's gallantry, observing the pale fur edging to his cloak, the embroidered borders, the fine linen at his neck, and the jewels. Everywhere was gold. And gems. His hair was sleek, like a dark basin over his head, the fringe touching the level brows as precisely as every other detail. He caught her examining glance and held her eyes without embarrassment or the usual quick withdrawal of men in holy orders. His look held nothing but approval.

'No, I thank you Master Flambard. I was telling my maid to cease her chatter, that's all. This is her first trip out of York.'

'And you, my lady? Did you travel as far as your father?'

'My father didn't take women with him.'

'Too dangerous?'

'It would not have been proper. Merchant ships don't cater for women passengers.'

'No, of course not. Yet you ride a horse well. You are practised.'

'It would have been inconvenient otherwise. With my father away from home so much and my brother unable to travel far, someone had to assume the role of master. Some of my property is—' She stopped, suddenly aware of her mistake.

'Your property is?' the chaplain reminded her.

'I was going to say, is some distance away from York. Now I shall have to get used to being property-less. Do you think I shall be able to find someone to teach me how to fill my days with idleness? Women's gossip? The latest fashions? Court scandal? Do Norman women hunt, sir? Do they read poetry as well as embroider? I really will have to learn some kind of nonsense, otherwise I shall go mad with boredom.'

When Master Flambard made no immediate reply to this, Rhoese feared that it must have sounded to him like a foolish woman bewailing her new status before she had had time to get used to the idea which, in a sense, it was. But as yet, she had no household, nor had Jude given her the slightest indication of what to expect when they eventually reached London. Would there be many servants? Was it a large estate? Would they be in lodgings, or housed in one of the new castles that the Normans were erecting like a rash of ugly pimples everywhere? She had been told to attend at the royal court with her husband, but what was she expected to do there except be decorative? Could she stand the interminable boredom of it, and would she be able to hide her contempt of the king's lewd behaviour, the hostility of his mincing courtiers?

'I think, my lady,' said Master Flambard eventually, 'that you may well be glad of a few ready-made friends for at least a while. I shall be happy to consider myself one of them, if you agree to it. I know better than most the kind of life you are moving into, and I can give you any advice you require. Jude is one of the best, but as an officer he'll often be occupied with his duties, whereas mine are more flexible.'

On her other side, Brother Alaric cleared his throat with more gusto than usual, but since Rhoese believed herself to be fully aware of the implications of the offer, she ignored him. Here was Jude's close friend, a worldly and unquestionably ambitious man, volunteering his companionship at a time when she needed it most. Jude's interest in her would ebb and flow with the hours of darkness, it seemed, whereas this personable man would be consistently available to her. And she would need all the good advice she could get. What was more, if anything could be guaranteed to cause her husband even the slightest pang of jealousy, a close and daily friendship with Master Flambard could. They would, in fact, make a rather handsome pair. What else the friendship would yield would remain to be seen but, whatever it was, she would be able to handle it.

'As you say, Master Flambard, I'm going to need advice on so many matters, and I should not like to cause any embarrassment by my ignorance. You could perhaps tell me who people are and brief me on protocol. I know how important that is.' Demurely, she directed her gaze between her horse's ears and waited for some affirmation of the contract. When there was no reply, she glanced sidelong at her new friend's profile and saw, to her astonishment, that he was smiling broadly. 'Excellent,' was all he said, but so softly that she might almost have missed it.

Brother Alaric, whose response she could well guess at, was as impassive as usual. But that was because he was well disciplined and because he of all people would be able to speak to her privately before she placed herself more deeply in this man's influence.

Fortunately, Rhoese didn't have to pretend to like Ranulf Flambard, for she found him both easy to talk to and to listen to, and within the first two hours of that damp journey, he had explained to her about the seemingly vast network of officers, marshals, constables and keepers whose involvement with the king was jealously prized. At the same time, she saw that Master Flambard's own position in the king's court was an important one, which he took very seriously.

'So how will the king manage without his chaplain?' she asked.

'Oh, he has several chaplains. We take it in turns to serve his Grace. He has, however, only one Keeper of the King's Seal.' He patted the leather saddle-bag behind his thigh, smiling at her with white, even teeth. 'He won't miss it until we meet again.'

'Really? Why ever not?'

'Hunting, dear lady. The king's passion is for hunting rather than affairs of state.'

'And you, Master Flambard? You don't share that passion?'

'My passion is for politics. And the church, of course,' he added.

Overhearing the exchange, Brother Alaric would have expressed it differently. *Power, my friend,* he thought. *Your passion is for power.*

At the pace of the plodding oxen, the cavalcade could make no more than the twenty or so miles to the borough bridge, by which time the clouds had descended again, extinguishing what little light was left of the restless day. Jude had been preoccupied with his duties, so his contact with Rhoese had been brief, confined to enquiring looks and the occasional curt command to keep up. With Flambard, he was more inclined to discuss the route and the resting places, agreeing that messengers should be sent on ahead to warn the occupants of the manor house at the old Roman village of Aldborough that they would require hospitality, on the king's business.

It was not so much the idea of resting and eating that filled Rhoese with a guilty anticipation, but the possibility that at last she might have Jude to herself. And although she tried to push the flutter of excitement to the back of her mind, telling herself how she disliked the man, it would not stay there. Jude's interest, however, did not extend to Rhoese on that occasion but to his friend Ranulf, to his Norman host and his pregnant young wife, to Brother Alaric, to anyone and everyone except her. If he was waiting until the very last minute, she thought, she would deny him the opportunity by retiring early to the room she was to share with Hilda and Els, the only other women in the party. Not for the world would she indicate that she courted his company.

'Wait!' In the dark passageway, his command caused a moment of panic.

The three women stopped. 'You two go on,' Rhoese said.

'No,' said Jude. 'You two can wait here.' He took Rhoese by the arm and steered her forward, opening the heavy oak door into a roomy solar where a log fire burned in the large stone fireplace. The house was new, and a fire in the wall was a novelty. He closed the door and released her, producing the leather-bound recipe book from beneath his cloak and holding it out to her. 'Yours, I believe,' he said.

She took it from him. 'Yes. How did you come by it?'

A blazing torch in a wall-bracket lit the planes of his face and cast his eyes into deep shadow. 'It was on the floor of your bower. Pierre went in there to check that all had gone. He passed it on to me. Careless, lady. Have you need of such charms, then, after all?'

'Only to give me courage to face whatever is in store for me,' she replied, quick to defend herself. 'What would you suggest, were you in the same position? You have studiously ignored me all day, so why the sudden interest in what I read?'

'Ah, so it's needled you, has it, that I had duties to attend to? Well, you'll have to get used to it, my lady. This is a man's world you're in, so you'll just have to take each day as it comes, won't you?'

'Certainly, I can do that, sir. As long as you take

no interest in what I do, I shall do as I please. You can hardly grumble at that.' She turned away towards the large bed where new green curtains were drawn back to reveal white sheets, pillows, and a red woollen cover. It was obviously the host's chamber, relinquished to their guests.

Jude followed her and caught her arm, pulling her towards him until she was enclosed, rigidly aloof, though her heart was racing. 'Wrong, wife,' he said. 'I shall certainly do more than grumble unless what pleases you also pleases me. I brought you along with me so that I can keep an eye on you, not so that I can spend all day in your company and neglect my duties. If you've missed my attentions so much, then we can easily make up for it now while your women tarry.' Not waiting to hear her views on the suggestion, he picked her up like a puppet and dumped her on the soft bed, quickly holding her down with his body and hands to prevent her rolling away.

For Rhoese, the moment had passed when she would have made only a token protest and then capitulated. Now, she was stung and hurt by his manner, convinced that he was about to use her with contempt and with none of the tenderness she craved. 'Get *off* me!' she yelled. 'I want none of your so-called attentions, and least of all *this* kind. Get off!'

'Then tell me what charm you studied, wench,' he said, almost touching her lips with his. 'Was it to harm me? To make me impotent? To make you miscarry? What?' He could not have known the unfortunate and crushing impact of his words at that moment when her mind was already bruised and in chaos, nor could he have been prepared for the sudden contortion of her face and a rush of tears that flooded her eyes before she could say a coherent word.

Utterly bewildered, and shocked by her unexpected reaction after the anger he could have dealt with more easily, he pulled her into his arms, rocking. 'I shouldn't have asked,' he said. 'But whatever it was, don't rely on that nonsense. If you want to do me harm, you can achieve that in a fair fight, not by charms and such. And once you're in the family way, I'll leave you alone, if that's what you want. Now, stop weeping, lass. I'll send your women in. Sleep well. We have a long ride tomorrow.' He touched her forehead with his lips, a tender kiss that she felt through to the soles of her feet.

And when her dismayed nurse and maid rejoined her, they were obliged to make up their own story about what might have happened, for their mistress was unable and then unwilling to tell them. They were even more dismayed to see the blackened curling leaves of parchment like the underside of a mushroom on top of the flaming logs, the beautiful leather binding shrinking to nothing. It was a husband's right, of course, but what a waste, they said.

'And don't you go blabbing about this to that squire of his,' said Hilda to Els, handing her Rhoese's shoes.

On this occasion, Els had the good sense not to answer back.

Having so far believed that he had the measure of her, Jude de Brionne was now beginning to think otherwise. He had, in fact, been suspecting otherwise since the lad handed him the book, found in a dark corner of the lady's bower, which he had carried with him all day. There had been no convenient time to confront her about it until late and, even then, he had not expected tears, but a fierce contest that could have ended to their mutual satisfaction. Were the tears a sign of guilt? he wondered, holding out one foot for Pierre to remove his boot. Had he got it wrong about her showing signs of a thaw after all her angry protestations of dislike?

He sluiced his face and neck, dunking his head again into the water and holding out a hand sideways for the towel. Water ran in rivulets over his massive chest and back as he stood, half-naked. No, he thought. She had responded to him eventually, and her admission this morning showed that she had not found their night together distasteful. So why the need for charms? Was that what she had been doing when he had seen her kneeling in the garden last night? Reciting a charm? Was that why she'd been so angry?

It was pagan nonsense, when all said and done, but what disturbed him most was not that a charm might be effective, but that she obviously needed more than the help of her chaplain to carry her through this new phase in her life. And it was well-known that the charms the English used against the Normans were never for their good health or good fortune. The thought disturbed him. How was he going to be able to leave her alone, after last night? And what of Flambard? True to course, he'd wasted not a second there,

had he? That situation would have to be watched.
Closely.

Damp-haired, he rolled himself on to the bed and
pulled the blankets and furs over him. The nights
were already cold up here in the north, and not for
some time had he chosen to sleep alone when he
could have a lovely woman to keep him warm. Now
he wanted no other woman but Rhoese of York, and
for once in his love life, he was not sure that his best
well-tried plans would be good enough to win her
heart as well as her body. It was a long time before
he slept, aching with longing and the want of her,
asking himself questions to which there were too
many answers, none of them satisfactory.

The destruction of her mother's old recipe book
was a violation that Rhoese was quite unable to accept, let alone forgive. There was nothing that Hilda
could say in Jude's defence that made any difference
to her mistress's sense of outrage.

'Don't tell me again that it's a husband's right,'
she bawled at the placid and motherly nurse. 'I don't
want to know that. It was *my* book, handed down
through generations, and it was the last remaining
thing I had of my mother's. And if I could remember
the worst charms in it I'd recite the whole damn lot
at the waning of the next moon and feed him adder's
teeth in his porridge. And I shall never sleep with him
again, so he need not think it.'

The glances of Els and Hilda met in mid-air, round
like marbles. They had been up since before dawn,
repacking their belongings and finding more protec-

tive clothing against the inevitable rain, breaking their fast whilst preparing for the day's discomforts.

Hilda held out a hand to Rhoese. 'What about this?' she said. 'This came from your mother too, remember. You always kept it with her things.'

Rhoese picked up the small sharp object from Hilda's palm, a flint arrowhead no more than an inch long, still as sharp as a razor even through several centuries. 'Ah,' she whispered. 'I remember this. It has hostile powers, hasn't it?' Being sure she was right, she didn't wait to see Hilda's expression that would have warned her how she'd got it wrong again. But Hilda was not inclined to labour the point. After all, what did it matter to her whether the Norman had pains in his knees or not?

'What does it do?' said Els, ignoring Hilda's frown.

'It'll cause sharp pains in his joints,' said Rhoese. 'Elf-shot, it's called. That'll give him something to think about while he's so busy doing his duties. Let his men be on the receiving end of his foul temper.'

'But he's not foul—' Els looked pained, holding her arm where Hilda had knuckled her. 'What's that for?'

'It's for the door,' Hilda snapped, placing a heavy wicker basket into the maid's arms. 'Over there. Then come back for this one.'

Rhoese's morning prayers with Brother Alaric were understandably brief and, in spite of his scepticism yesterday, held no mention of the sins of clinging to pagan beliefs when there were better ones on offer. Nor did Rhoese tell him of the painful destruction of the book he had condemned only yesterday, knowing that he would find no sympathy for her.

Nevertheless, he did have a word of advice for her concerning the motives of the king's pushy young chaplain. 'Be careful,' he told her. 'When a zealous Norman like him offers you mead and sympathy, it's not usually for your sake but for his own.'

'Yes, Brother.'

'Your duty is to your husband, remember.'

'Yes, Brother.'

He looked at her steadily with deep brown eyes from beneath straight brows. His hair was silvered with fine strands of white, as if he'd been whitewashing a wall, and he was of an age not to be taken in by Rhoese's unusual docility. More advice along those lines was useless. 'He's over there,' he said. 'Shall you bid him good morrow?'

'Yes, Brother.'

It was not difficult for her to insert a tiny linen-wrapped arrowhead into her husband's saddle-bag under the pretext of packing an apple and some nuts for the journey. At her approach, men backed away and left her alone with him, their eyes averted, their manner even more obviously uncomfortable than yesterday. After last night's confrontation, Rhoese could only assume that perhaps Pierre had told them about the recipe book. If that were so, then he and Els were a dangerous combination.

'I wonder…?' she said to Jude, pushing the package well down.

'Yes?'

'I wonder if Els ought to ride behind me today, to keep my back warm.'

'That would solve two problems at once,' he replied, coolly. 'Pierre will be obliged to you.'

'Oh? I thought he liked her.'

'In small doses, my lady. She talks too much.'

'I see. Er…I've put an apple and some nuts in there for you.'

'I thank you.'

He lifted her on to the gelding and adjusted her skirts over her knees, and that would have been all except that he then went to his saddle-bag, removed the apple and fed half of it to her mount and the other half to his, while she watched, growing ever more indignant at his suspicions. 'The nuts,' she snapped at him. 'Who will you feed them to, the birds?'

'Depends whose horse dies first,' he said over his shoulder as he mounted. He was away across the courtyard before she could reply. The day had not started auspiciously, but worse was to come.

The relocation of Els caused a fit of the sulks that was entirely wasted on both Rhoese and Master Flambard, whose conversation was not in the least gossipy and so not to Els's liking. And since neither of them paid much attention, the journey for her quickly lost its appeal, the countryside became tiresomely dull, the temperature cooler, the rain sharper, more penetrating, her mistress's back not nearly as enticing as Pierre's. Her new position, she was sure, was due to Rhoese's intervention; she and the young groom had been getting on so well together.

The drenching rain eventually silenced even Master

Flambard and, as the ditches filled with brown gushing water, so did the narrow streams through which the cavalcade had to wade every so often, sometimes up to the horses' hocks. Inevitably, if a wheel was going to come off, it had to be at the most inopportune moment whilst crossing a ford, a catastrophe that tipped the ox-wagon sideways and threw many of its contents into the swirling water with sickening efficiency.

Master Flambard was quick to catch at Rhoese's reins, hauling her horse away from the disabled wagon as some of the contents hit the water in front of them. Els yelped as the mount swerved, and made a grab at Rhoese's shoulders to avoid falling off. But Rhoese had seen her own linen-chest fall with a clatter, bursting its lid open and washing its contents into the current out towards the shallow-growing banks of water-cress, wrapping them with colour.

'Oh, no!' she cried. 'Let go of me, Els. There's the book! Please, catch it, someone!' She was about to leap into the water, but Master Flambard caught her arm and held her back firmly.

'No!' he called. 'You stay on board, m'lady. I'll get it. Stay there!'

She had not thought he would do such a thing, for although he was already drenched, acts of heroism that ruined his clothes were surely not his strong point. Her horse plunged again over the slippery stones, sending plumes of water high into the air and Els hurtling backwards off the pillion-cushion, still clinging to Rhoese with one hand. It was enough to unseat her, and both riders fell as the horse bounded away towards the muddy bank.

Concerned more for the precious gospel-book in its linen wrap than for the screeching maid, Rhoese clambered heavily to her feet with the weight of wet skirts hanging like anchor chains around her, falling upon the sinking package just before Master Flambard's hands could reach it. 'See to my maid, if you please,' she gasped. 'She's tangled.'

For a moment, it looked as if the king's chaplain might argue the point since there were at least two other men now wading towards the tangle with grins already in place, eager to reach her first.

But another pair of arms caught Rhoese from behind, hoisted her high above the water and spilled her into the bend of his body with an undignified thud and a growl of annoyance. 'You and your damned books,' he said. 'What is it this time? More Latin charms for beginners?' Grim-faced, Jude strode across to the bank, hurting her with his vice-like grip.

She clung to the wet package, unable to speak and fighting a foolish urge to laugh, but whether from relief or from his welcome scolding she did not know. Even this, she thought, was preferable to being ignored.

Never having expected that the book would be seen by anyone, she had nothing prepared now that an explanation was imminent. Gospels were rarely owned by individuals except royalty: even high ecclesiastics borrowed them from the scriptoria of wealthy abbeys, and a book being in a woman's possession could only indicate one thing. Theft.

Jude's was not the only curiosity to be whetted, though he had no intention of giving his friend the advantage in the matter. He countered Ranulf's inevitable question with a quick pressure of his fingertips upon Rhoese's thigh, warning her to stay silent. 'Never mind the damn book,' he said dismissively to Master Flambard. 'It's mine. I thought it would be safe enough in there.' He kept Rhoese in his arms, though by now they were well up on the other side of the ford and she knew he was trying to evade more questions for her sake.

'What are *you* doing with it, then?' called Ranulf. He stood there, dripping and dark with wet, still irrepressible in his thirst for information, trivial or not. His eyes were lively and, some might have said, bright with cunning.

'Taking it to my cousin, if you must know,' Jude called back. 'To Durham. He's the *amarius* at the cathedral there.'

'Eh?' Ranulf started to run. 'He's…what? The librarian? He's one of the clergy then, is he? Your cousin?'

'Well, he'd have to be, wouldn't he? Thought you knew everyone.'

Ranulf stopped, unable to keep up. 'No,' he said, quietly. 'I don't.'

The travellers were near enough to the old Roman garrison at Catterick for Jude to have carried Rhoese across the field in his arms. But his squire brought the stallion, and she was hauled wetly up to sit behind him, still holding her precious bundle, which now appeared to have transferred its ownership to Jude's clerical cousin. All because of a broken wheel-shaft.

The situation had now become critical. 'Do you really have a cousin at the cathedral in Durham?' said Rhoese, clinging on with one hand.

'Of course,' said Jude. 'He came over with Bishop William eight years ago. You'll meet him.'

'Well, he can't have my book, if that's what you're thinking.'

'If it's like the other one he won't want it. One sent to the flames, one almost lost to water. Do you have a third one we could bury?'

'No.'

'Thank heaven for that. Perhaps the rest of the journey will be without incident.'

'I'm sure you'll do your best to make it as uninteresting for me over the next half as the first has been. I say thank heaven for Master Flambard's company.'

'Oh, he's a good companion all right. None more so.'

'You don't mind his attention to me?'

'Why should I? As long as he confines his attentions to the hours of daylight, I shan't mind at all.'

'And how will you know, I wonder?'

The question was too absurd to warrant a reply, and Rhoese was therefore not surprised when none was forthcoming, though she suspected that he was quietly laughing to himself as they rode through the gatehouse and across the moat-bridge into the courtyard.

The large stone manor house was another new

dwelling in the Norman style, fortified by a high wall with a moat beyond, and set around a courtyard in a series of adjoining parts whose rooftops were tiled with slices of local stone. Like the previous one, it was a far cry from her own thatched hall and bower, her humble stables and worksheds.

Rhoese was now shivering with cold, though courtesy required her to greet her hosts with some pretence of gladness whilst dreading the explaining she would have to do to satisfy Jude. Should she tell him the true story of the book and risk losing it, or should she ask Brother Alaric to say that it was his, on loan from the York scriptorium? And what of the librarian cousin? Naturally he would want to lay his acquisitive Norman hands on it. Permanently.

Unlike the previous hosts, the new Norman lord of Catterick and his wife were a middle-aged couple with a family of teenage sons and daughters, five noisy hounds, an exaggeration of servants by anybody's standards, a flock of elderly relatives and their companions, swarms of retainers who relied on the lord for hospitality and patronage, and several small children who seemed to belong to everyone by turns.

Their concern about the watery accident sent most of the menfolk down to the ford to help and the women to their chambers to find clothes for Rhoese and Els until their own could be retrieved and dried. 'Get you gone now,' scolded Alicia de Traille, wife of Catterick's new lord, 'and stop staring at the Lady Rhoese.' She aimed a blow at her eldest son's ears, which missed.

Neither Els nor Rhoese had been able to ignore the

stares, which they knew were for the wet fabric that clung from shoulder to ankle, about which they could do little except turn away and hold their arms close to their bodies. Els glared back at the lads, unamused by their boldness.

Jude had also noticed their teenage fascination, placing an arm around her shoulders with the beginning of a smile. 'Lead on,' he said to their hostess. 'My lady wife needs warmth, and so do I. Pierre! Come, lad! Attend me!'

While they struggled with wet cloth and ties that would not respond to numb fingers, the book lay in the shadows, still shrouded in its wet linen cloth as the last of the daylight slipped away unnoticed, and Rhoese began to hope that, after all, it would escape Jude's memory. They found clothes to fit them from an assorted pile of the family's best that Hilda doled out on the principle that if it would cover them decently and keep them warm, they should wear it. And though Rhoese emerged looking ravishing in a flowing gown of mulberry and soft madder-pink wool, Jude was given neutral tones of oatmeal and soft grey-greens, the only tunic and hose big enough to cover him.

He fastened the gold buckle on the belt around his hips and caught the wide uncertain gaze of his new wife upon him. 'Well?' he said, hooking his thumbs into it.

She hesitated, reluctant to concede even a hint of warmth with still so much bitterness at her disposal, yet unable to remain unmoved by his transformation from grimy traveller into this handsome creature. His dominant stance had once intimidated and annoyed her; now she was able to put a different interpretation on it. The memory of that single night of loving caught at her breath as she spoke. 'Are we to go in to supper?' The words sounded as if she'd been running.

He did not reply directly, but turned to the three servants, dismissing them with a wave of the hand and glaring pointedly at Hilda, who thought she might have been allowed to stay.

'I am usually able to dismiss my own women, given the chance,' Rhoese said. 'What's so important that Hilda may not know?'

'She probably does,' said Jude, delving a hand into the pouch at his belt. He brought out the small sharp arrowhead on his palm and offered it to her. 'Knowing your feeling towards me,' he said, 'I find it hard to believe you intended to protect me from elf-shot when I've never suffered any kind of pain in my joints. So I take it that you had something more malignant in mind, my lady. Am I right?'

Carefully, she took it from him and studied it. 'A man would be able to deal with matters more directly,' she said. 'Women must resort to more subtle methods. Yes, I did have something else in mind.'

'It doesn't seem very subtle to me,' he said, caustically. 'It's a charm usually meant to *protect* the wearer from pain, but it looks as if you should leave such matters to wiser women if you can't do better than that.' He removed it from her fingers and replaced it in his pouch. 'Still, I'm relieved to see that our mounts are still on their feet.'

'There was nothing wrong with the apple. Or the nuts.'

'I know. I ate the nuts, so I know.'

Sounds from the hall reached them through the heavy oak door as someone opened and quickly closed it again, yet neither of them showed any sign of noticing. 'You *ate* them?' she said. 'Then your mistrust was a *sham*, sir. Put on to make me feel guilt. Wasn't it?'

His stillness had fooled her, and now the quick step he took in her direction caught her completely off guard and, before she could evade him, his arms were around her and she was held close against his body with the soft texture of his woollen cloak against her cheek. 'You accuse me of sham, lady?' he said, harshly. 'Of trying to make you feel a guilt you ought to have felt already, with your charms and such? First an incantation, then an arrowhead, and you can talk to me about sham? What's in your head, then? Granite?'

As if to disprove the possibility, his kiss was persuasive and enticing, luring her hostile emotions to soften under the tender pressure of his mouth, searching every angle for some sweetness. Given more time, she would have responded, but now his kiss ended as abruptly as it had begun and she knew that, with her foolish and abortive attempts to claim his heart, then to punish him for staying beyond her reach, she had only managed to distance him further. Her body he made no secret of wanting, but his mistrust of her was impossible to disguise.

Matters had moved beyond her control, and now

she had few means to make him love her except to offer him hers in exchange, and that she was determined not to do. Besides, he had said that her heart did not interest him. 'Yes,' she gasped as his mouth left hers silently pleading for more, 'yes, it is. And so is my heart. You knew that. I warned you. It can come as no surprise. I was forced into this contract against my will. What did you expect of an English noblewoman, sir? Obedience *and* affection? After you've taken everything I possess?'

His arms dropped, and she swayed unsteadily with the sudden loss of his support. 'Oh, don't let's go through all that again,' he said sharply, turning away. 'The poor noblewoman in thrall to the conquering Normans. Yes…well, these things happen to us all eventually. It's a fact of life, lass. Most women make the best of it and see the advantages, then they get on with life. You seem determined to hark back to your losses instead of your gains. It's not every Englishwoman who's given hospitality with a noble Norman family, so bear that in mind when you go in to supper, will you? And if I find one more attempt to disable me with superstitious nonsense, I shall beat you. Do you understand?' He swung round to face her, and she knew he looked for signs of fear.

'I understand that Norman husbands beat their wives just as they do their dogs and horses, sir, because they lack the skill to communicate by any other method. All Englishmen know that. It causes them some amusement.'

'And have you seen me beat my hounds and horses, lady?'

'Not yet.'

'Then you'd better reserve your judgement about the reasons, hadn't you? When I beat you, you'll deserve it. Come.' He held out his hand to her, closing his fingers warmly over hers, reminding her far more of the intimate caresses they had dispensed than of any threatened beating.

Rhoese did nothing to delay their entry into supper, being far too relieved that he had made no mention of the book and, with any luck, would put it out of mind for the rest of the journey. She had not prepared herself, however, for the enthusiastic and, at times, embarrassing admiration of the two elder brothers who vied constantly with each other to gain her attention. Though they carried out their duties as servers at the meal, as did all the younger men, their rivalry was noticed even by Ranulf Flambard, who sat nearby and gently teased her about it.

Equally affected by the guests from York were three of the daughters, aged from around twelve to fifteen, who found in Judhael de Brionne the man who had inhabited their girlish dreams, both individually and collectively, becoming quite speechless each time he spoke to them. Henrietta, the eldest, was very aware of her fair loveliness and willowy form, and though Rhoese accepted Master Flambard's more-than-occasional glances in the girl's direction from under half-lowered lids, she found herself watching Jude to see if he was doing the same. Soon, she was wondering if he would dismiss her two women so that he could share some time in her bed, but that thought was soon dispelled.

'Well, my lady.' said Master Flambard. 'Isn't *any-one* going to tell me about this precious book? Is it badly damaged?'

'It's my husband's,' said Rhoese. 'You must ask him.'

'But you were the one to risk a wetting for it.'

'Yes,' she whispered. 'Shh! The harpist is getting ready to sing.'

'Tell me later, then?'

'Yes, of course.'

But the chance to explain was purposely not allowed to arise as Rhoese stayed quietly in Jude's company, a strategy not wholly to do with questions about the book. She knew that, if Master Flambard had asked then, he would be told to mind his own business. And if pretty Henrietta ventured too close, she would be sent about hers.

Chapter Seven

R anulf Flambard, the king's inquisitive and high-flying chaplain, was nothing if not tenacious, and several times during that evening he made attempts to draw Rhoese away from Jude's side for a private tête-à-tête. For different reasons, neither husband nor wife succumbed to his tactics, and finally she was handed over to Brother Alaric with a firmness that brought Master Flambard's endeavours to a close. The lady would say her prayers and go to bed, Jude told him.

Though privately relieved, Rhoese couldn't resist a word to Brother Alaric that was meant to emphasise a certain indignation. 'I haven't been told when to go to bed since I was a child,' she remarked in English. 'Shall I be told when to think, next?'

'Ahem!' Brother Alaric warned her, glancing at Jude. 'You must respect your husband's wishes in all things, my lady. Best for you to bid him a goodnight. In his language.'

'To go back to the hall and ogle that silly child, you mean.'

'Henrietta left with her sisters a moment ago. Why do you care?'

'I don't.'

Jude appeared to lose patience. 'Speak in French,' he said.

'No, *you* speak in English,' she said, walking away. 'You're in England.'

After that, her session with the chaplain lasted rather longer than usual, though Brother Alaric's homily about wifely respect received no convincing assurances of an improvement, and she lay in bed unrepentant, sleepless, and dreading the rest of the journey. If the Norman had wanted a meek and mild wife, she thought, he had chosen the wrong woman, but the threatened beating was not to be dismissed as mere talk and, although she was no coward, neither was she witless.

Following Rhoese's scolding from her chaplain, Hilda and Els had been expecting some show of irritation. Her marriage to the charismatic Norman had evidently not done much for her nerves these last few days, so they had not been too surprised when she delayed the order to go to bed and instead lavished her attentions upon the gospel-book.

They had seen it before, but now its leather and gem-studded covers with the scrolling border of long-tailed creatures were blackened with damp and the edges of many pages had warped, making it impossible to close the book properly. Mercifully, the inks had not run, so Rhoese's makeshift renovation was to interleave each page with linen torn from an old chemise to prevent the pages from sticking together. It was all she could do.

It now seemed inevitable that Jude's librarian cousin at Durham would have to see it, if only to prevent permanent damage. But it seemed equally certain that Jude had little curiosity about it, otherwise he would surely have shown more concern. She decided, therefore, before she climbed into bed, to pack it into her saddlebag for the next stage of their journey.

As it turned out, the dread of the journey was suspended for a whole day when it was seen that the wagon needed a new shaft that could be made in Hubert de Traille's workshops, and since Count Alan of Richmond was Hubert's lord as well as Jude's, he was duty-bound to extend his hospitality and aid. An extra day, Jude said, would give them all time to dry out, to rest, and fix the horses' loose shoes.

Rhoese found nothing to grumble about in that as she made her way to Alicia de Traille's south-facing garden where fruit bushes were laden with berries, their stems bent with droplets of sparkling rain. The early sun caught her shoulders and promised more warmth to come, steaming the mossy tiles on the rooftops and sending clouds up from the dung-heap in the stable yard.

She took the straw-covered path, followed at a distance by Els and the two younger daughters whose chatter added to a cacophony of men's shouts, dogs barking, oxen roaring, loud scolding from the kitchen, geese protesting and hammers clanging in the forge. Two squirrels bounded across her path and disappeared into the orchard beyond, ignoring the lanky figure that emerged, his hands juggling three rotten apples with limited success. Rhoese wished she had stayed indoors with Hilda to mend clothes.

Gilbert de Traille, Hubert's eldest son, was, at sixteen, on the verge of manhood yet still lacking in perception, so the absence of either greeting or smile from the woman he hoped to meet held no warning for him. He was fair, blotchy and garrulous, full of himself and mistakenly confident that Rhoese would want his company once he had commended himself to her. Diving in at the deep end, so to speak, he waded through the long wet grass to follow her more closely while throwing his apples at a feasting hedgehog and telling her with some pride and amusement that he was out to win a wager laid only an hour ago with her husband's men.

He was rewarded with a sharp enquiry. '*What* wager?'

Delighted by his two words at last, he laughed. 'Ah, that I'd get close enough to speak to you without…er…' His face squirmed as he sensed a blunder taking shape. That was the trouble with words.

'Without what?' Rhoese stopped beside a wooden bench and perched on one end. If she asked the right questions, this gauche lad might unravel the mystery that had plagued her since leaving York. She patted the seat and spoke more gently. 'Without what, blushing?'

'No.' He laughed and sat tentatively by her side. 'Well, without you putting a spell on me.' He peeped at her, watching for signs of a smile. 'They weren't serious, of course,' he assured her.

There was no smile. 'No, of course not. But why would I do that, d'ye think?'

'Because they say that's what you do. Only in fun.' He picked up another apple from between his feet and looked it over, poking at the rotten brown patch with his thumbnail. 'They say their master must have been bewitched to marry an Englishwoman when he could have had his pick of Norman heiresses. They say you're dangerous. But only in *fun*.'

'Do they?' she said. 'Well, well. And what else do they say? That I'm a witch? In fun?'

'Kind of.' Encouraged, he went on, heedless of the cynicism. 'Is it true that a man was murdered for love of you and that another lost his…er…sight?' He turned on her a look of such awe such as she'd seen on the men's faces for two days now, except that this lad's look was also innocently fearless. 'I bet them it wasn't.'

'It's only part true,' she said. 'You've probably lost that one.'

Sorrowfully, he stared at her. 'You're teasing me,' he said.

'No, Gilbert. Was that the only wager?'

Despairingly, he dropped the squashed apple. 'They say there were more.'

'More what?'

'Men. A merchant. He was found dead, too, wasn't he?'

'What? What are you saying?'

'They say you bring disaster. Of course, I don't believe them.'

'Gilbert! What *are* you talking about? What merchant's been found dead? When? Where?'

He picked up another apple, but Rhoese took it from him and tossed it aside, making him look at her. 'A merchant in York, they said. Murdac, is it? Found dead. And a priest confessed for your sake to something he hadn't done, and you have books of charms that Pierre found, and when one fell in the river you dived in after it, and—'

'Stop!' Rhoese insisted, dropping her tone as the young women drew nearer. 'Look, this is nonsense. When such disasters happen one after the other like that, that doesn't mean one person is actually *causing* them. And as for charms, forget it. I'm no witch, Gilbert. About the merchant being found dead…they were teasing you, surely.'

'No,' he said, 'I don't think so. He was found in his upper room, foaming at the mouth, all on his own on the day you left York.'

'Then they *were* teasing you,' she said, standing up. 'Now, here's a young lady who'll be happy to hear about your knight's training and more. Make the most of her company; she'll be gone tomorrow.'

Openly eyeing young Els up and down as he had seen the men do, his mind and attention veered like a weathervane, giving Rhoese a chance to continue her walk to the far end of the orchard where the flooded stream gushed its way towards the thundering paddles of the flour-mill.

Murdac…dead? Foaming at the mouth and alone?

He had been in a vile temper when he'd left her, days before their departure. She had encountered a side of him never seen before, angry, rejected and flaying her with his tongue, but he was not a man to take his own life. Never that. A seizure, perhaps? But why had they not told her? And what would happen when they called at York on their return journey from Durham? Would she be accused and arrested? Would she have to suffer the ordeal to establish the truth? Most of all, why had Jude said nothing of this? Because he believed her to be responsible, or because he did not?

The brown water slid past, tearing at fronds of weed along the bank, combing them straight and swirling crisp leaves into the eddies like boats in whirlpools. Patches of blue sky were mirrored like silken streamers, distorting the face and shoulders of the one who peered into its depths. 'What's happening to me?' she whispered. 'This is not me. I'm no witch. Why has my life turned so sour since Father went?'

Sour, perhaps, but tinged with a bitter sweetness that flooded over her and washed away all thoughts of revenge, holding her mind in a void of ecstasy as she felt again the vigorous pulse of his loins against her body, the thrill of his hands and the slow searching bliss of his lips on hers. There were places he had not yet investigated that cried out for his attention. How would he do it? Would it mean anything more to him than the others? He had offered more for her than de Lessay, but why *her*, if there were Norman heiresses to be had? Her property would be nothing to theirs. Would she be obliged to meet them at the king's court, and would this new and harmful reputation go before her?

'You're thoughtful, my lady,' said a familiar voice.

The vision swirled away downstream as another reflection appeared above hers, taller, and with dark basin-cut hair. 'Yes,' she said. 'And your fine chausses are sure to be spoiled by this long grass. Your mission must be important to risk such a wetting.' She had no need to ask why he had followed her here, sure that it was but a continuation of last night's foiled attempts.

Master Flambard looked down at himself, then held out a hand to help her up. 'And you,' he said, 'seem to be drawn to some watery places of late. Shall we move to a drier spot where the noise is a little less constant?'

For all his tidy splendour, the resistance in his arm as he pulled her to her feet was like tempered steel, and she knew that his vocation as a chaplain did not prevent him from taking part in the usual manly pursuits, including women. Jude's warning had made that clear.

He led her through a door in the high wall that sheltered a secluded place where a few white roses still bloomed on a trellis, and honeysuckle was loaded with red berries. There was a grassy patch, gravel pathways and a row of benches along one sunny wall and, as he swept away a scattering of brown leaves, Rhoese accepted that she would once again be pressed for information about the book unless she got her questions in first.

She arranged her soft woollen kirtle over her knees

and watched him do the same to his deep blue tunic, noting his immediate stillness as he leaned back and lifted his chin to the sun, half-closing his eyes in pleasure. There was a blue shadow over his cheeks where he'd been shaved, and his Adam's apple moved as he swallowed.

He caught her scrutiny and smiled, puckishly. 'Well, my lady?' he said.

'I have just discovered…' she said, pausing for effect.

'Yes?'

'That I have a reputation.'

His head turned fully. 'Yes,' he said.

She had expected more than that. 'You know, do you?'

'Yes, I know that.'

'That they think I have powers…charms?'

He hid his facetiousness well. 'All women have powers and charms, but I'd say you have more than your fair share. Is that what you meant? And who are ''they''?'

'Master Flambard, you *know* that's not what I meant. I'm talking about what the men are saying, about what happened in York. And now I discover, quite by accident, that the merchant Murdac was found dead and that I am being implicated. Did you know of that, too?'

'My lady, of course I knew of Murdac's death. Didn't Jude tell you?'

'No, he didn't. And I cannot understand why.'

Master Flambard leaned back again, his head half-turned in her direction. 'Well, he no doubt has his good reasons. Perhaps he's waiting for the best time to reveal such disturbing news. For a new husband to tell his wife of the sudden death of one of her former suitors within days of their marriage might seem rather insensitive, you must agree. And if you were indeed implicated, as you've heard, you'd certainly know about it by now, I can assure you. Put yourself in your husband's shoes, my lady.'

'Yes, but what about the other things? They're saying I use witchcraft…magic…and that's a punishable offence, sir. They think de Lessay's death and Warin's punishment are the result of…oh, heaven knows what nonsense.'

He put a hand out to cover hers briefly before withdrawing it. 'Soldiers,' he said. 'They're a rough bunch. Easily bored and avid for anything that makes their lives more colourful. They gamble and drink and fight and go whoring. They make up whatever they lack in hard facts. They're loyal to their master, but they're not best known for their reasonableness. They can put up with all kinds of hardship and they don't care a damn what they impose on others, and when they find a gullible young male like Gilbert, they'll happily relieve him of his money even before he knows he's wagered it. He'll learn, though he's not the quickest-witted young cock I've ever met.'

Rhoese watched him as he spoke, as she had done during their ride, and was impressed by his grasp of human nature. 'How did you know it was Gilbert who told me this?'

His grin made a small sound as it appeared. 'He crows a fair bit, doesn't he? He's just been allowed to sit beside the Lady Rhoese of York and speak with her in private. He's going to make sure we all get to hear about that. What else did he say?'

'Nothing,' she said. 'I'm beginning to understand, I think. All the same, I wish that kind of thing was not being said.'

'Leave it to me. I'll squash it, if that's what you want.'

'Thank you, I'd appreciate it.'

'There is an alternative, though.' A lazy honey bee swung off course and landed heavily on Flambard's embroidered cuff to clean its legs, but he made no move to disturb it. 'When you find you've been attributed with some kind of power, whether you believe in it or not, it can sometimes be quite useful to allow it as long as it's working *for* you, not against. In your case, they may like to believe you're able to wield some kind of magic over others because, to soldiers especially, women fall into very few categories: they're either goddesses, mother-figures, wives, sisters or whores. You're obviously up amongst the goddesses, my lady, which gives you a healthy advantage. Not to be thrown away lightly.'

Intrigued, and not a little excited, she stared at him. 'Good heavens,' she said. 'Now that's what I call an alternative. Tell me more, if you please.'

The bee lumbered away as one forefinger pointed. 'Not now. See, we're about to observe your husband being pursued by a would-be goddess. Relish the sight. Come to my chamber after supper, my lady, and I'll tell you more about how to enjoy your reputation. And bring the book with you.'

Whether the king's chaplain would have worded his invitation differently had they not been about to be interrupted, Rhoese had no way of knowing, but the sight at the other end of the garden was indeed entertaining and not to be missed.

Striding with fierce determination along the gravel path, Jude was about to break into a trot to escape the clinging attentions of the young woman in red whose matching complexion reflected an equal insistence. Her skirts were bunched up in one hand to free her cantering legs, her other hand was outstretched to catch at Jude's sleeve that flapped behind him like a loose sail. The effect was so much the reverse of what Rhoese had feared that she was hard pressed to obey Flambard's signal to silence.

When Jude stopped with unexpected suddenness, the young Henrietta cannoned into him, her face lighting with victory until she caught sight of her seated audience. Then, stopping a yelp with her hand, she turned tail and fled, her fair hair swinging from side to side. Jude stared, then swivelled to face them, doubling up with laughter, hands on knees, thankful for his deliverance but speechless to explain the matter.

'Judhael de Brionne in flight from a woman?' called Master Flambard. 'I never thought to witness such a thing. Is this what marriage has done for you then, man?'

'God's truth!' gasped Jude, striding towards them. Still laughing, he threw himself down beside Rhoese and ran both hands through his dark hair that flopped straight back again like a silken landslide. 'Nay, Ranulf. She's yet a child, for all her keenness. But you'd think they'd never seen a man before, the way these lasses behave. You'd better have a care. I swear she nearly had me on my back.'

'And you wouldn't like that?' asked Rhoese, sweetly.

'I wouldn't like anything that chit has to offer, my lady.'

Master Flambard leaned a little towards her, conspiratorially. 'He prefers a challenge, does our Jude. Now, I've heard there's to be some fun and games out on the green in a while: archery, wrestling. I wonder if our hero will be taking part, or has marriage softened him, all of a sudden?'

Jude leaned back against the wall and closed his eyes. 'I'll take my part,' he said, 'then I shall claim my prize.'

Master Flambard's eyebrows lifted as he winked at Rhoese. 'Over-confidence, my friend, has its dangers,' he said.

'Not this time it doesn't,' said Jude, softly.

'I must confess,' Rhoese later remarked to Hilda, 'that I was a bit surprised to hear a king's chaplain talking about goddesses and whores.'

Hilda dumped an armful of folded clothes into the dried-out chest with a grunt and stood up straight, wincing at the pain in her back. 'He's a man, love. No need to be surprised at anything a man says. Or thinks. Or does, for that matter,' she added in a whisper. 'And anyway, that young man intends to go places by the shortest route. He won't be one to mince words. Takes too long.'

'Think so?'

'Oh, I certainly do, love,' Hilda said. 'And if you'll take my advice, you'll not get too involved with him.' She gave Rhoese a light woollen mantle to wear, holding the hole open for her head to pass through. 'Come on. If you're going out again, you'd better put this on.'

'It doesn't match.'

Hilda insisted. 'That need be the least of your worries with this colour-blind family to see. I never saw such an assortment in my life.'

Emerging through the hole, Rhoese hauled her long plaits up like an anchor chain. 'That Gilbert is becoming a pest,' she said, 'but what am I to do about the lass? I feel irritated and sorry for her at the same time.'

'Don't you go feeling sorry for the little minx, love, or she'll think you're holding the door open for her. Firmness is what she'll understand, not sympathy. Lasses like her will take a yard if you give 'em an inch. Heaven knows where she'll end up.' Her tone implied that, if heaven knew, then Hilda could also make a very good guess.

Prepared to take her nurse's advice about Henrietta's capers, if only because it seemed the easiest course, Rhoese was less sure of the warning not to become too involved with Master Flambard. For one thing, she had already toyed with the notion of a flirtation there, since she had begun to like the man and, as Jude's friend, it seemed a reasonably sure way of provoking her husband to jealousy, if anything could. That, at least, would indicate whether she was to him merely a piece of property or something more, though the process would no doubt be a joyless one with a bitter outcome. It would even be worth a beating to discover that he had a heart, and even more to find that she could warm it—then, she would know real power, the only kind that mattered to her, and then, she would break it, slowly, painfully, and with sweet revenge for the pain she had suffered.

The words in her head sounded savage and melodic, yet when she listened to that same fierce harmony in her heart, and to savour it, she was aware instead of a fearful uncertainty that made her sit down rather heavily on the bed and clutch the mantle closer to her breast. For some moments, while Hilda bustled about, Rhoese was cocooned in a recent memory that promised yet more to come, reminding her of the potion she had swallowed that held her daily in its power. Helpless, without an antidote.

Then there was the pity of Warin, whose terrible injuries had brought her anything but the satisfaction she had hoped for. Was that the kind of power she wanted, the kind to ruin a man's life? Had she not recently found a brief bright flame of rapture in yielding to a man more skilled at loving than she?

'Well,' said Hilda. 'Are ye going?'

'Eh? Oh, yes. Shall you come too?'

'Aye, when I've done in here. Keep an eye on young Els. She's taken a shine to that lad Gilbert. She'll need watching.'

Rhoese groaned. 'Oh, Hilda! I can't keep up with all this.'

* * *

Even so, she did keep up with that side of things remarkably well, as she had been trained to do as mistress of a large household and, in the horseplay between Els and Gilbert she saw little harm. She took part in the skittles competition and almost won, then stood aside as the younger lads played a rough game of pick-a-back wrestling that ended in tears as well as laughter.

The fourteen families on the lord of Catterick's estate were joined by ten more smallholders and their priest, whose young concubine carried a toddler so like the priest himself that her claims to be no more than the housekeeper were sadly out of date. Celebrations after harvest came later to these northern counties, with ripening oats and fruit reaching well into September and even October. This year had seen floods and ruined crops, and the games were small compensation for the extra work before the first frosts and the inevitable hunger next year.

Despite the Norman and English rivalries that stopped only just short of real damage, there was plenty of good-natured fun that placed everyone on the same level as long as the games lasted. Yet Rhoese's enjoyment was moderated by Gilbert's mooning presence, hanging around her like a shadow and waiting for courage to build on his earlier success, if only she would look at him. She encouraged Els to speak to him instead and moved away to stand near Jude, hoping that Gilbert would be distracted. But he followed her, standing on her other side and plying her with doleful stares.

Her unease must have transferred itself to Jude

who, without pausing in his loud encouragement of
the young sword-fighters, took her arm and drew her
firmly across to stand in front of him so that she felt
his warmth on her back. Sliding his arms beneath her
mantle with no attempt at concealment, he spread his
hands across her ribs where they were muffled by the
fabric, holding her close enough to feel her trembling.

Before she could settle into this new tenderness,
she felt his hands move upwards to hold her breasts,
cupping them, his thumbs brushing idly across their
soft peaks and hardening them in an instant. Her
knees weakened, and with unfocussed eyes she arched
against him, her breathing suddenly losing its rhythm.
Over one shoulder she pleaded with him to stop, holding his hands with her own. 'Please,' she whispered,
'not here.'

Obediently, the caressing ceased and his arms
crossed her, preventing her escape. 'It worked,' he
whispered in her ear. 'Look at his face.'

If she had been able to anticipate the expression of
lovesick anguish on young Gilbert's face, she would
not have made matters worse by letting him see that
he was observed. But she was in no fit state to think
of that, and by the time both she and Jude had caught
the pain in his eyes, followed by his embarrassed departure, bumping blindly into people as he went,
Rhoese realised that it had been a crude ploy to get
rid of him. And in seeking her husband's protection,
she had been used like a toy, her emotions mangled
and then left to untangle themselves the moment it
had worked. Of course the lad had seen what was

happening but would Jude, she wondered, have used the same low trick to get rid of the girl?

'Let me go!' she whispered, angrily. 'That was ill done. He doesn't understand.'

'Stand still!' he growled into her linen veil. 'If he doesn't understand by now, he soon will. Bravo!' he yelled at the swordplay before them. 'Go on, lad! Come at him again. Now!'

'You *are* heartless,' she snapped. 'Like all the rest. Harsh. Pitiless.'

'Yes, my beauty. You'll be able to watch it in action soon enough,' he replied. 'Come on now, you lads. Keep at it!'

But she did not strive to free herself after that. Seeing the girl glowering at them from the other side of the circle, it suited Rhoese to adopt an expression of contentment. Just for the girl, she told herself.

The men's wrestling was always a highlight of such games, for it was a serious affair where men could settle scores of long standing and where reputations were made and demolished in public. Having guests willing to participate heightened the excitement, Count Alan's men being expected to cut some of the village men down to size. Tough, mean-looking individuals on both sides.

Rhoese sensed that this was what Jude had been waiting for when his arms moved upwards underneath her chin, pushing her head up to meet his mouth and kissing her before she could prevent it. Urgently, he held her close to him in a strong embrace while he whispered, 'Just this once you can lie to me. Tell me

you want me to win…that you'll cheer me on. Can
you do it?'

'I can do it, just this once,' she said. 'I'll cheer for
you, and you'll win.' She sounded convincing and
Jude was not to know that she spoke the truth, for her
eyes were closed as he kissed her again before them
all, the envious, the curious and the furious.

'I shall win,' he said. He released her quickly and
walked away to his calling men, laughing at their applause as if he'd won her out of all those who'd tried,
and failed. And she, after the pretence of pulling her
garments straight, caught sight of what he had missed;
Gilbert's angry sidelong glance before he turned away
to join the competitors.

The ground was cleared, stones removed, teams
chosen and insults exchanged with no anatomical detail exempt from descriptions of the most outra-
geously defective to the super-human. The women
were as inventive as the men, but there was not one
whose eyes did not linger over the magnificent Norman who had just kissed his new wife, the one whose
half-naked torso rippled in the sun as he tossed his
tunic to Pierre.

'My, but he's a big 'un, is that,' muttered Hilda in
characteristic to-the-point northern style. 'There's not
a woman here who'd refuse him, I reckon. Aye, and
look ye where *I*'m looking.' She nudged Rhoese's
arm. 'Look.'

Henrietta and her sisters stood on the far side of
the crowd, their eyes caressing, their mouths for once
slack and still, their thoughts as transparent as water
as they examined the mighty back turned towards

them. One of them leaned to the other to whisper some comment, but the lass continued to gawp, making no response.

Rhoese turned away, suddenly protective of the man who, in theory, belonged to her. 'Let them look,' she said. 'That's as near as she'll get.' *Lie to him? Why should it matter to him that she should cheer him on?*

'Wait!' Hilda whispered. 'Look over there.'

'What? Where?'

'You missed it. Young Gilbert's up to no good. He's just signalled something to his sister and she nodded. I saw them.'

'It's nothing, love,' said Rhoese.

'All the same, he's up to something.'

Two by two, men entered the arena, fought and departed limping, staggering, swaggering or thrown out of it bodily. Jude fought two cruel rounds, one English, one Norman, winning them both by his superb agility, cunning and strength. Clearly, he was the favourite to win the contest. As she had agreed, Rhoese cheered as loud as any and made sure that he knew she had kept their bargain, even though she prayed he would not suffer any real physical injury.

Then there was a noise behind the crowd, a shouting and waving of arms, and finally the pink lanky frame of Gilbert de Traille stalked backwards into the circle, beckoning derisively to a reluctant Jude, who was pushed forward to yells of encouragement. If that's what the lad insisted on, they hooted, let him have it.

Both Gilbert's mother and Jude protested that it

was absurd, but Hubert de Traille saw nothing amiss that his eldest son should learn how to lose to a better man. 'Get on with it!' he bellowed. 'Get it over with!'

Disturbed at this escalation of Gilbert's grudge and puzzled by his foolhardiness, Rhoese tried to will Jude to look at her, but he kept his eyes firmly on his opponent even before the signal to begin, as if he already knew that the lad would cheat, just to hurt him. Had Jude presented his back at any time, Gilbert would surely have leapt on him like a leopard, rules or no rules, for they were as unevenly matched as it was possible to be.

At first, Jude toyed with him, fending off every attempt to throw him, circling in a wrestler's crouch, dodging every kick and armlock, avoiding each twist of the body with a counter-twist that did no harm except to infuriate Gilbert more. Quick, and superbly fit, Jude brought the first phase to a conclusion when Gilbert rushed clumsily at him and was caught easily in his arms, swung over his back and hurled away to land in an undignified sprawl at Hubert de Traille's feet.

The crowd yelled with approval while Jude waited for him to recover, hands resting on narrow hips and legs apart, just as Rhoese had seen him stand to face her in her own compound, tall, imposing and commanding the scene.

Over behind the crowd, screams pierced the hooting and yelling, and the loud roars that followed were at first absorbed into the general clamour until the arena began to fragment, sway and fall about. Heads swung round to look with expressions that turned to horror as two terrified black bullocks leapt through crouching bodies and knocked others aside, their eyes wild, their shoulders and flanks bloodied. Another two followed close behind, tossing and churning the solid wall of people, trampling them like corn. Then, seeing a lone figure in a space, they headed for him as if he were the one responsible for their terror.

Swinging, leaping and bellowing in a maddened rush of hooves, they charged as he faced them with outstretched arms in a vain attempt to head them off before they reached the children behind him. Catching him between them, they knocked him over like a skittle, kicking and trampling him as they galloped past.

Yelling even before she was halfway to him, Rhoese came closer to a bullock's pale slimy nose and rolling eyes than she'd ever been before, hitting out at it wildly, making it duck and try to reverse. 'Get *off* him…get off…get…get off, you great brute!' she screamed, punching at its blood-streaked hide. Putting her shoulder to its hind quarters, she heaved with all her strength to prevent the creature from straddling Jude's curled-up body with its four legs. But it had to put its hooves somewhere, and Jude's back was in the way as it swerved aside to join its mates.

In a screaming fury, she pounded its back with her fists, catching her wrist painfully on its sharp hip-bone, then making a grab at its huge hock before it could trample him again. With its hind leg restrained, the steer kicked out at her and she was thrown backwards on top of Jude as yet another black shape backed into them to escape the waving arms. Instinctively, she swivelled and threw herself over his head, pushing his damp hair down into the two large hands from which it was about to emerge.

'Stay down!' she yelled into the back of his neck. 'Stay!'

Legs, hooves and roaring muzzles came at them from all sides, stamping within inches of Rhoese's feet and legs, but her face was in Jude's hair and she saw very little of the bullocks' departure, and soon there were hands plucking at her shoulders, lifting her away to the distant sound of crying children and wailing mothers, the angry shouts of men and the yapping of excited hounds.

Curiously then, it was not her injuries that concerned her most, nor even anyone else's, but why she was here, protecting this man, a Norman to whom she had virtually been sold, to whom she meant so little that he could disregard her feelings as if she had none, and who she had sworn to hurt, one way or another?

Jude turned his head, and she saw blood pouring into one eye from a cut on his forehead. There was a bruise already forming on his cheek and his braies were hanging off in tatters. 'Speak to me,' she urged, suddenly sick with fear.

He opened the other eye. 'I can do better than that,' he whispered. 'Are you hurt?'

She heaved herself off him. 'Not where it shows,' she said, quietly.

Supper in the large Norman hall was served later than normal that day in an atmosphere of unusual restraint, in view of the size of the de Traille family and their household. Alicia de Traille had done her best not to comment on the absence of Gilbert and Henrietta, but she found it impossible to enjoy her food, knowing how they were being deprived of theirs. She saw that their chaplain was having no such problem with his appetite after his whipping of Henrietta, but poor Gilbert had been banished to the cold tower room after his beating, and the nights were chill. Poor dears, she thought. What could have possessed them to do such a thing? Her eyes slid involuntarily across to the Lady Rhoese of York who looked as if she might be having similar difficulties herself.

As soon as she was able, Rhoese summoned Els and Hilda from their places lower down the table and together they retired to the north-south solar below the chapel on the excuse that she needed rest. Jude had asked after her bruises, knowing from his earlier enquiries that they were not serious but that, even if they had been, she would have avoided telling him.

Jude himself had not been badly injured, and had helped Rhoese to carry several of the trampled children away before being tended for cuts to his forehead and back. But he could see how the incident had shaken her, and far from being satisfied by his performance that afternoon, his lack of chivalry towards her sat like a black cloud over his successes. His treatment of her while he had held her before the wrestling had been selfish and insensitive; a bungled ploy that he had privately tried to condone with the absurd excuse of irritation for a lad almost old enough to be his own son. Rhoese had turned to him for protection and he had used the situation, already delicate, in a way that took no heed either of her antipathy or of her finely balanced responses. She had every right to be angry, and now his slow progress would be even harder to maintain.

Unhappily, he watched her leave in a swirl of green, gold and white and suspected that her wish for rest was only half-genuine, her frosty politeness revealing far more than he would like to have seen of her disgust. Yet now he relived once more the soft shelter of her body as she lay over him, pressing her face into his hair and even confronting a bullock to protect him, when he should have been protecting her. What a rare and complex woman.

Ranulf Flambard leaned across to him, hiding his mouth from onlookers with a half-eaten apricot. 'I suggest that you go to her, my friend,' he said, following Jude's gaze. 'You both have prizes to claim, I believe, and who knows where we shall be laying our heads tomorrow.'

Making no reply, Jude tried to read more from Ranulf's eyes. There *was* more, of that he was certain.

Smiling at his apricot, Ranulf continued, 'Go and ask her where she's taking the book. She'll be getting it out now.' He glanced at Jude, still smiling. 'How do I know? Because she and I have an assignation...no...don't look like *that*, man. I asked to be allowed to see it, and she agreed.'

'Alone? Tonight?'

Ranulf nibbled at his dessert. 'Probably. Yes, alone.' He turned to face Jude, dropping the smile. 'We've talked for two days, Jude, she and I. You allowed it. You were glad of it. You're surely not expecting that I haven't learnt a thing or two about her feelings for you in those two days, are you? Eh?'

Jude's silence failed to discourage him.

'Well, I'm glad to hear it or I'd have thought I was going senile already. She was angry before she met you, you know. I told you as much when you first saw her. She's going to try every trick in the book to make you pay over the odds for winning her, so it's no good expecting her to fall into your hands like a ripe cherry, Jude my friend. You're going to have to work harder than that.'

'I don't recall your earlier advice being particularly inventive, either.'

'No…well, I'm not the one with the reputation or the wife, am I? I've got other things to strive for. But let me tell you this: trying everything in the book means just that. Everything.'

Jude leaned back and swung one long leg over the cushioned bench, tapping Ranulf on the arm. 'Put that thing down,' he said, 'and come with me. I think we'd better have this conversation in private. Come.' Without leaving the hall, he led his friend to a small room in the thickness of the wall from which a narrow flight of stairs spiralled upwards to the gallery. A wooden bench ran along one side, and there they sat together, each leaning into the corner with one foot on the cushion, their faces half-lit by distant torches. 'Now,' said Jude. 'Tell me exactly what you're talking about.'

'She likes me,' said Ranulf, candidly. 'She's ready to do some serious flirting. Don't worry, it's not going

to come to anything, but if you know about it beforehand you can behave accordingly, can't you? Instead of inappropriately, I mean.' He waited. 'Oh,
come, Jude. You're not usually as pole-axed as this.
Did the steers kick your head in as well as your
back?'

Touching his forehead tenderly, Jude frowned.
'What d'ye mean by accordingly?' he said. 'Or inappropriately, for that matter. What am I supposed to
do?'

'I never thought to hear you ask that of *me*. You
really do want to win her, don't you? Completely, I
mean. All of her.'

'What else do you know without me telling you?'

'I *am* a chaplain, Jude.'

'Sorry. I know. I don't mean you to…you know…
confidence and all that. Did you think I'd beat her?
Is that the inappropriate bit?'

'No, I know you're not disposed to behave like
that. Mind you, I don't think a threat does much harm
now and then, but what I'm trying to say, my friend,
is that she needs to know where she stands with you.
Security has not figured large in her life over the past
couple of years, apparently, and as long as you let her
believe you have no feelings for her, she's hardly going to trust you with hers, is she? Is that what you
want?'

Leaning forward, Jude clasped his hands around his
knees and took a deep breath that ended in a sigh
long before the words came. He shook his head, ruefully. 'Listen. I know you've studied humans and
their foibles, but this is not nearly as straightforward

as you seem to think. Something has set her against men. All men. Any man. It can't simply be that oaf she hoped to marry; there's more to it than that. Much more.

'Me being a Norman doesn't help either,' he continued, 'because to Yorkists, there aren't many good Normans. We're barely tolerated, you know that. It isn't just because she's lost all her property to me, either; she knew she'd have to lose it some time, I expect.'

Ranulf went even further in her defence. 'It was not a very dignified process, though, you must admit.'

'Far from it. It was a disgraceful business. But, Ranulf, if I show softness now, she'll despise me. If I show her that she can reach my heart, she'll try to break it. I know it. Something's hurt her, and she can think of nothing except how to hurt back. She's already tried it, so I know what I'm talking about.'

'Yes, and all it's done is to get her a reputation she can't handle. You heard what that young cockerel called her to his father, didn't you? She knows it, too.'

'Argh! That's all nonsense. She cannot believe it.'

'She doesn't believe it, no. But she is affected by it. Not many women want that kind of reputation. But, Jude, you can be firm and masterly without being quite so cold, can you not? A little more husbandly, perhaps? A public kiss is one thing, but appearing to enjoy her company too is quite another.'

'While she's flirting with the king's chaplain, you mean?'

'Try it,' said Ranulf, ignoring the sarcasm. 'You've not seen how her eyes follow you. She'd not have gone to your aid this afternoon if she really wanted you hurt, would she? I don't know many Norman wives who'd do that much for their husbands. And anyway, I don't think she's the kind of woman who appreciates softness in a man in the way that you mean. Any woman who can wrestle with a bullock would be quite capable of holding her own in a marital argument. You don't have to let her win, but nor do you need to beat her for opposing you. That's not what she needs.'

What Rhoese of York *did* need was not voiced by either of the men who both thought they had a fair idea of the answer to that delicate question. The unusual circumstance of Ranulf Flambard offering advice to Judhael de Brionne on his wife's state of mind, however, was to be the turning point in a relationship that was nearing stalemate within days of marriage.

'What is it I'm supposed to be asking her about? Ah…yes…'

'The book,' they said, in unison.

'That,' Ranulf said, 'could be quite a useful tool.'

'What d'ye mean?'

The chaplain stood up and carefully removed a cat-hair from the skirt of his tunic. 'Oh, go and find out, lad. D'ye need me to tell you everything?'

'No, thank you. There are some things I can manage on my own.'

They moved away into the light of the hall. 'And, Jude…' Ranulf said.

'What?'

'It was not she who made the assignation, but me. You know nothing about it. The possibility of a flirtation is a manifestation of her desperation, not her depravity,' he said, slightly pompously.

'You mean a woman would have to be *depraved* to flirt with you? Nay, man, surely not. Patient, perhaps, but not depraved.' Jude grinned.

Ranulf placed a knuckle to his nose to hide the smile. 'Well, no. Perhaps not. Unconventional, though. Eh?'

Chapter Eight

Contrary to Jude's suspicions, Rhoese's tiredness was genuine, and her exit from the hall into the peace of the solar was a relief to which she'd looked forward throughout supper. Privacy for anyone, whether high or low, was a rare commodity at all times; almost every chamber in the house had several functions, and solitude had to be sought anywhere. With Hilda and Els, Rhoese was as close to it as she expected to get, Els being deeply sulky at Gilbert's punishment and Hilda letting loose a volley of remarks about their host's daughter at every opportunity that showed exactly where her sympathies lay.

'Little hussy,' she muttered. 'If she goes letting steers loose on all her father's guests, she's never going to find a husband. Thank heaven you never got as steamed up as that.'

Rhoese didn't think that Henrietta made a habit of it, but nor could she respond in the same colourful vein. It was not only because of the acrimonious wrestling match but because, once again, others had been injured for something she had neither wanted nor done anything to incite except to be herself. Nevertheless, somehow she was responsible, and the sooner they left this over-reactive family the better she would like it.

Then there was Jude, who had thanked her politely for trying to protect him, but had then told her *not* how brave and wonderful she was but how foolhardy. She must never do such a thing again, he told her severely. She had assured him that she would not, ever, picturing as she did so how she would rejoice to be able to tell her Yorkist friends how her Norman husband had been killed by a herd of bullocks let out by a sex-crazed fifteen-year-old in collusion with her pea-brained brother. The idea of an hour or so with Master Flambard at this time of the evening would not go down well with Brother Alaric, though she doubted that Jude would either know or care. But now the situation had worsened, if anything, and advice on the power thing was required more than sleep. She took the parcelled book into her arms. 'Pass me that woollen wrap,' she said to Els, 'and for pity's sake put your face straight, girl. Go and turn the covers down on the bed.'

Hilda pursed her lips. 'Is it wise, love?' she said.

'Probably not,' said Rhoese. 'I really don't care any more.'

The door-latch clicked upwards seconds before she could reach it, the door swinging open and hitting her knuckles, making the book slip from her grasp and slither down to her knees. Jude caught it and took it from her. 'Ah,' he said, patting the damp linen cladding, 'this is just what I've come to see.'

'Of course,' said Rhoese, sucking at her knuckles. 'Why else would a husband visit his wife's chamber at night but to see a book?'

Looking at Hilda and Els, he kept the door open. 'Ladies,' he said, 'I believe there's a particularly fine troupe of jugglers in the hall at the moment. It would be a pity for you to miss them.' Ignoring their reluctance, he closed the door behind them, replacing the book in Rhoese's arms. 'Now, my lady, tell me what you were about to do with this, if you please, so that I know what to expect in the next few days.'

'If you must know, sir, I was about to take it to Master Flambard. He asked if I would show it to him,' she said, thrusting the book back at him. She took off her wrap and threw it across to the bed.

Jude looked as if he was about to smile, but then thought the better of it. 'Did he, indeed? At *this* time of the night?' He took her elbow to steer her away from the door. 'Well, that's not a very original trick, is it? I must remember to suggest some new ones to him.'

Crossly, she removed her elbow from his hand. 'I'm sure you'll not find that difficult. But it was no trick, sir. I've told you, I find his company agreeable, and that's quite a rare thing of late. I seem to recall you saying only recently that you didn't mind him paying me attention.'

'Correction, lady. I said, as long as he confines it to the hours of daylight. After supper, and I *do* mind.'

'Why should you?'

He took the parcel to the cushioned bench by the fireside where light from the blaze cast a sheen upon his cheek. On his forehead, a blood-red cut glistened with recently applied salve. 'You wouldn't like it,' he said. 'He gets very wordy after supper. I know from experience.' His fingers had already begun to peel away the linen to expose the gospel-book upon his lap, its jewels catching the flames in their colours and flashing them over the gold settings. Jude held it up, tipping it this way and that. 'Good God!' he whispered. 'Where did this come from?'

'I think I could tolerate his wordiness,' Rhoese replied, keeping her distance. 'I find that idea more to my liking than simply being an appendage in a baggage-train.'

Smiling, Jude closed the book and held out a hand to her. 'Come over here,' he said. 'Come on. I'm not letting you go to Flambard, so that's that. He's had your company for two days and now it's my turn. Come to me.'

Rhoese looked away, tense with anger. 'I don't take turns,' she cried. 'I am the Lady Rhoese of York and I saved your life this day, sir. And I do not appreciate your magnanimous gift of a few memorable moments in your company when it happens to suit you. Take the cursed book. Everything is yours, but don't expect me to sit with you and be grateful that it's my turn at last. You're as clumsy with words as you are with your hands, sir, and it will not have occurred to you that what happened today was due to something that *you* did. I've had my turn with you for today and I didn't enjoy it nearly as much as I enjoy Master Flambard's respect. To him, I am a lady. To you, I'm just another woman. Now be pleased to leave me alone.'

Very slowly, he put the book aside and stood up, his smile replaced by an expression she might have called tenderness, had she not known him better. 'And you cheered for me, too,' he said. '*Was* it a lie, my lady? Did you really mean me to hear you?'

She swung away as his hand reached out for her, but he was too quick, and she was brought to a halt, bristling with anger at arm's length. 'Men's silly games,' she said, trying to free her arm. 'What does it matter? Yes, it *was* a lie to save face, nothing more. It would have reflected badly on me if I had not done. There. That's the truth.'

Holding her fast, he reeled her in like a fish on a line. 'That's all right, my beauty. I can accept that. As long as you keep on telling me the truth and lie only when I ask it, that will do for a start. Yes, I admit to a certain clumsiness this afternoon, but it'll not happen again in public. You have my word on it. Hold still, Rhoese.' He pulled her wrists to his chest, keeping her confined. 'But we'll come to that later,' he said.

'We will *not* come to that later.'

'First, I want to know about the book. Where did you get it? Will you show it to me? I'm willing to listen.'

'Hah! It takes a book to get you to listen, does it, when only a moment ago that was not a very original method. Well, it seems to have worked on you, except that I don't want to talk to you about anything.'

'Nevertheless, my lady, if you want to get to bed tonight, that is what you will do. Come on.' He released one wrist and drew her by the other to the bench where he pushed on her shoulder. 'Your tongue's been sharpened on my hide, so now let's see it in action.'

With the book once more on his knee, he lifted the gem-studded cover beneath which lay crinkled layers of vellum with strips of linen to keep them apart. The pages were masterpieces of calligraphy, each representing weeks of long and patient work and the very best skills that the artist had to offer. Overall, it was only the size of a jewel box and about three inches thick, but it contained all four gospels written in Latin in a beautiful round-hand inside decorated borders, with initial letters of huge proportions, headings and whole pages of interlaced pattern. Colour glowed from every page, the words unspoiled by the effect of water, the oak-gall black as firm as ever, the gold leaf as shining, the lively creatures as fresh as the day they were painted. Except for the warped edges and softened corners of leather, the damage was minimal. 'This is a gem,' said Jude. 'How did you come by it?'

When Rhoese remained silent, he turned to look at her, noting the rebellion in the set of her mouth, the high spots of colour on her cheeks. He took one of her hands in his. 'Rhoese,' he said. 'Flambard believes this belongs to me. I told him so, remember? He doesn't understand why I've not shown it to him, which is why he's asked you to, I expect. He believes I'm taking it to my cousin at Durham who will expect me to explain how I came by it. Flambard will no doubt make a point of being there too, and it's going to look a bit odd if I can't tell them anything about it, isn't it?'

'Not at all. You can tell them without a lie that you now own everything belonging to your Anglo-Saxon wife and that you haven't yet had time to count it all. Or to look at it, in this case.'

'Very true,' Jude sighed. 'There's something else that I own that I haven't yet got round to looking at. Thank you for reminding me.' He closed the book and put it on the chest, standing up and pulling at her hand. 'Shall we?'

'No!'

'No to everything, is it? Didn't you promise me obedience the other day?'

'Under duress.'

'Then that's the way it will have to be, I suppose.' He pulled again.

'No…no! I'll show you the book, then you can go.'

'Go where?'

'To hell!' she muttered. 'What is it you need to know?'

In all respects the same as the one she related to Eric, the tale didn't take long to tell while Jude sat motionless without interrupting, only looking at her directly once or twice when her voice wavered at mention of her father.

'Nuns?' said Jude, eventually, looking hard at a page of intricate scrolling patterns. 'Do *you* think the nuns at Barking could have done this?'

Rhoese tried not to let her enthusiasm show. 'Barking Abbey,' she said, 'has always had a reputation for learning. I don't know what the present community is like because Barking is nearer to London than York and I've had no contact with them, but the abbey was founded by a bishop of London for his sister, and it drew the noblest and wealthiest women to it. They've always had strong connections with continental abbeys and the royal court. Perhaps that's why William of Normandy—'

'King William,' Jude corrected her, softly.

'Yes, why he stayed there after the invasion. I don't know what else was stolen at the time, but the abbess was particularly anxious to get this back. It's a wonder it didn't find its way to Normandy instead of Norway. Which it will do, I suppose, if you let Archbishop Thomas know you have it.'

'You think he'd keep it rather than return it?'

'Wouldn't you?'

'If that's where it really belongs, I'd probably return it to the abbey. I do have *some* scruples, my lady, despite what you believe. But how do you know this is actually the one?'

'My father seemed quite certain of it.' She took the book from him and turned carefully to the back. 'There's something here, where you can see that a gloss has been added to the text.'

'A what?'

'A gloss…glossary…translation. It's written in a different smaller script between the lines, look, and it's in English so you won't be able to read it, nor will your cousin at Durham. If you look more carefully,' she pointed out, 'you can just make out the word *abbodisse*, which means abbess, followed by *Baercinge*, which suggests that the book may actually have been made by one of the previous abbesses. Some of them were scribes and artists, you know, just as men are.'

'Can you read the rest of the gloss?'

'Eventually, I suppose. It's quite small, so I never have done.'

'Who taught you to read?'

'Our chaplain before Brother Alaric. My father said one of us ought to, and since it couldn't be Eric it had to be me.'

'A wise man, your father,' said Jude, taking the book from her. 'Is there anything else I ought to know about it before I allow the others to see it?'

'No…only…'

'Only what?'

She watched the last lazy flames flicker over the charred logs. There was little she could say now that would affect the outcome. 'Only that if you truly believe my father to have been wise, then you might consider respecting his wishes for the book to stay in English hands.'

Jude was silent for a moment, and Rhoese was sure he was deliberating the issue, though she was unprepared for his question. 'Rhoese,' he said, 'it's now well over twenty years since this book left Barking Abbey and, in that time, many things have changed. Might they not have forgotten about it, after all this time?'

'It's possible, I suppose. It's quite some time since Archbishop Thomas asked my father to look out for it, and anything could have happened since then. But I still think it belongs there more than anywhere else.'

Jude let the subject drop. 'Was he a good husband, your father?'

This was another unexpected question to which, surprisingly, Rhoese did not have a ready answer, despite the love she had borne him. Ketti's loud complaints echoed in her head, but had that been more to do with Gamal's continual long absences from home, rather than her natural shrewishness? Had he not left his motherless children for months at a time while he went voyaging when he could just as easily have sent others? And had he warned her about Warin's unreliability with women when he could have done? Had he not left to her the business of Eric's future? Had there not been a strong element of irresponsibility in her father's eternal adventuring that had quickly killed Ketti's enthusiasm?

'I loved him,' she said at last. 'That's as much as I know.'

It may have been this talk of her father, or the emotional day, or the dark warmth and this man's nearness that eventually took its toll of her, or even the unwelcome premonitions of another argument with him, which on the one hand she didn't want to lose nor, on the other did she want to win. It might also have been her bruised foot that a steer had caught, or indeed several other pains including her recently grazed knuckles that caused her to sway as she rose to her aching legs, putting out a hand to steady herself.

Jude was on his feet immediately, supporting her with an arm about her waist. 'Come, lady, you've had enough questions to answer for one day, I think. Time you were in bed.' His arm tightened around her.

But to Rhoese's contrary mind, that could only mean one thing and, even in her exhaustion, the angry flame of rebellion still burned hot enough to make a show of protesting. She tried to turn away from his support, but his hand pressed on a forgotten bruise on her side and her first words of dismissal turned into a yelp of pain before she could catch it. Grasping at his arm, she threw it aside. 'Go!' she yelled. 'Just go…before…you do any more damage.' Tears of pain welled up, brushed quickly away with the heel of her hand. 'Please, leave me alone.'

Although it was past time for verbal arguments, Rhoese's hurt pride would not allow her to yield as Jude's authority began to overwhelm her by sheer strength and determination. 'You're hurt, brave lass. You didn't tell me all of it, did you?' He caught her again, pulling her into his arms and lifting her like a child, in spite of her struggles.

'No…no, leave me! Hilda and Els will—'

'Will find somewhere else for the night. You need me.'

'I don't! I don't need you. Put me down.'

'I'm going to. Then I shall find those bruises.' He placed her on the bed, keeping hold of her.

'No, no, please,' she whispered. 'They're nothing.'

He took her protesting hands and held them away on the coverlet while she pushed and squirmed against his restraint, her hair wisping loosely across her face in a halo of dark red spirals. Her eyes, huge and dark, sparkled with tears of vexation. Panting, she lay still at last, glaring at him with the soft pink light from the dying fire reflected on his face while he waited, feeling the fight drain out of her, drooping her heavy eyelids and thick lashes like deep pools in a river bed, watery and alluring.

'Are you going to fight me every time, Rhoese of York? Shall I have to master you to make you submit to me? Is that what you intend?'

Her voice was tired and deep with anger. 'I've told you, Norman, that I do not want you. I don't want *any* man...shiftless...untrustworthy...'

'After what you told me tonight, my lady, it would appear that there are exceptions to that. Are you not willing for me to prove it?'

'You?' she whispered, scornfully. 'With *your* reputation?'

He lowered himself on to his elbows, releasing her hands. His eyes were alight with amusement. 'Reputations are usually bestowed upon us by others, are they not? So if I agree to ignore yours, could you do the same for me? Eh? Then we can reach our own conclusions like two reasonably intelligent people. Is that a deal?'

'I can try. But that doesn't make me want you in my bed.'

He smiled again, almost melting her heart. 'And I told you earlier that there are some things you cannot lie about and *that*, my beauty, is one of them. I'm glad to say that pretence is not one of your strong points.'

'It's not a lie,' she whispered. 'You are arrogant

and thankless, and I shall never lift another finger to protect you. Never.'

'And if you ever throw yourself into a herd of steers like that again, for any reason, I shall personally beat the hell out of you. I want you for the mother of my bairns, and I haven't gone to all this trouble and expense just for you to get yourself crippled before we've made a start on it.'

The sudden blaze of fury in her dark eyes and the fractional lift of her lashes warned him to catch her hands before they could reach him, wrestling her into his arms and silencing her with his lips over hers that she had neither strength nor will to resist for long. It seemed to her like everything she had wanted from him for days, drawing her mind away on to another level and focussing it on sensations alone rather than her own injuries. And in those moments as his lips warmed and seduced hers, the world darkened and slid away, time stopped, and her body began a slow melting like the first days of spring after a hard winter.

Her eyes were still closed as he slowed and drew away, and she made no move either to help or hinder him as he began to remove each layer of her clothing, all of it loose and tied with a girdle. 'Where are these bruises? Show me, Rhoese,' he whispered, not expecting that she would. Piece by piece, he tossed them aside, turning her this way and that whilst examining each part of her revealed by his search, removing the reticent hands that covered her breasts and slowing his softly sweeping strokes into lingering caresses that were nothing like the sensation-seekers of earlier that day that had both aroused and angered her. Slowly, and with delicacy, Jude used his hands over every part of her, sparing no detail, missing no crevice or fold. When he found bruises and scratches, he kissed them tenderly while his hands gentled her, scattering her mind like shattered reflections over water.

He spoke to her at last. 'Well?' he said. 'Is it still no, or can I do more for you?'

Drowsily, she touched his shoulder. 'Are you going to keep your clothes on again?'

'Do you want me to?'

'Another no, then.'

Smiling at the wordplay, he lifted himself away and threw off his clothes so quickly that her body still tingled warmly as he rejoined her. He lay over her, taking her mouth with an urgency that swept her back into the darkened world where now her hands and arms could add another dimension to the body she had seen earlier, the rippling muscles and wide shoulders that tapered down into a deep curve beyond her reach.

She felt him flinch as her fingers made contact with his wounds and, inside herself, she felt the ache and yearning of her belly as his fingertips raked softly across her breast, then held its firm fullness to his mouth. Every sense melted at the tugging of his lips, senses that never before had been stirred, making her cry out and twist beneath him while she grasped at his silky hair, calling his name.

She thought that, like last time, he would delay the consummation when he parted her legs with his hand and ran the same intimate fondling, but now his entry was quick and sure, matching her own demands, and instead of the prolonged and exquisite stroking with all its variations of timing, he was forceful and fast, sparing her nothing after the languorous seduction.

Wave after wave of joy swept through her and tossed her into the deep currents that penetrated every part of her body. At first enclosing her face for his hungry lips to feed on, his hands moved further down to her tender parts to add to her pleasure and, as she cried out again at the surfeit of arousal, he braced himself above her to release a burst of energy that gave no hint that he had won two punishing wrestling matches that same day.

Thoughts tumbled headlong past her mind of how different this man was, and how much she had missed until now, of how much she herself could bring to this loving if only it would bring her his heart. Then she was swept along once more into his virile buffeting that was drawing her towards the same bliss she had experienced last time. 'Go on…go on,' she whispered, her voice ragged with approaching ecstasy.

Reaching up for him, she drew his head down to where her lips could reach his skin and, as he buried his forehead in her hair, she delved her fingers into his, revelling in the thickness of it, but not realising that her intended gentleness was in fact both rough and provocative, or that she had pressed upon a new injury, just as he had done earlier.

His roar was muffled in her hair, but now his arms came round her like a wrestler's, rolling her over and under him again, hardly pausing in his fierce possession of her while she clung, gasping with excitement. On the very edge of the bed, their journey to the floor was controlled by the step of the shallow platform on which the bed was raised, now scattered by their garments. But this was no impediment to Jude who swung her down, pushed a handful of clothes beneath her head, and continued with an arm under her thigh, his exploring hand wasting no opportunity to excite.

As if in answer to her cries, the moment of release burst upon them like a summer hurricane, unleashing in them a power that not even an intruder could have stopped, and Rhoese heard herself calling out words of rapture in her own language, words of love and surrender that joined his words of sweet conquest, over and over, again and again, safe in the knowledge that he would not understand. She held him into her as he slowed and stopped at last, but there was no need, for she was discovering that, unlike Warin, he was not one for hasty withdrawals once the deed was done, and for some time she was able to savour the delicious warmth of him both inside and over her, linked, joined and still gently pulsing.

'Are you asleep?' she whispered at last, sure that he was not.

He moved his face through the veil of her hair. 'In this position, my lady, that would be unforgivably churlish of me,' he said.

'You said you'd leave me alone once I was breeding. Did you mean it?'

'No. Not a word. Why?'

'Just wondered, that's all.'

'D'ye want me to?'

His reply pleased her beyond dreams, but could she believe him? The smile, however, was in her voice. 'Oh, I can take it or leave it,' she said, softly.

He began to move gently inside her again. 'And I,' he said, 'shall put a limit on your fibs to one a day from now on, and that was *well* over the limit.'

After the autumn gales and the daily soaking, the countryside had turned to a bedraggled mellow gold in the bright sun and the air was fresh with bracing westerlies, scattering the riders with leaves as they passed. To the English, October was known as Winterfylleth, and in defence against that prediction, village men and boys waded knee-deep into ditches to clear them before the next downpour. Others lopped branches and piled the wood on to ox-carts or stood to stare as the long slow cavalcade lurched and clattered past, touching their forelocks and responding to Rhoese's English farewells with shy smiles.

By her side, Jude and Ranulf Flambard made no comment on this breaking of her self-imposed silence; it was the first time she'd spoken more than two words together since they'd set out, and not even the chaplain's smiling enquiries had drawn her out of her reverie. He was not dismayed, and his discretion was far too seasoned for him to show outwardly the smugness he was feeling at his friends' acceptance of his advice. It seemed to have paid off for them both.

As for Jude, no one could quite put their finger on exactly what had happened between him and his English wife because, to all appearances, nothing much seemed to have changed except that he was not letting her out of his sight. And he was certainly not leaving her alone with the king's chaplain, either. Jude's men thought it might be to do with what had taken place yesterday. They'd been hauled over the coals this morning about their teasing of their host's son and had been promised a flogging if anyone spoke another word about the Lady Rhoese's charms, about her wrestling with steers single-handed and saving her lord's life while not having a mark to show for it. It didn't stop them believing in her amazing powers, of course, for not even de Brionne's threats could stop them looking at her, at the proud set of her beautiful head and the rich wine-red plait that swung down her back. She was a rare woman, they whispered; a goddess, even. Why, she'd even left money for the families of the injured men. No wonder they waved and smiled.

Rhoese was relieved to pull out of Catterick and to head northwards along Dere Street again with the sun on her back, but her thoughts were her own, very private, very womanly, and unsuitable to share with Brother Alaric at her morning prayers. He was several paces behind her now with Pierre, Els and Hilda, and even the casual observer might have noticed the absence of chatter there too, that seemed mercifully to have afflicted the maid since yesterday, Pierre's interest having waned faster than hers.

When no one else had been there to hear, Rhoese had, in fact, said more than two words to Jude by asking why he'd not thought fit to tell her of Murdac's strange and sudden demise. Why had she to hear of it from a sixteen-year-old stranger? To this Jude had replied with little sympathy. Murdac, he had told her, had suffered a seizure brought on by extreme anger, which apparently the man had been warned of more than once. The king's physician was certain that no other reason need be sought. There was no need for her to be told of it, Jude said, and if he'd been aware that Gilbert had passed on soldiers' gossip he'd happily have broken his neck before throwing him out of the ring.

He had left her so abruptly and with such a stern expression on his face that left Rhoese in no doubt that, whatever passion was contained in their night-time loving, he was not going to let it affect his day-time disposition. She was relieved, in a way. It was disconcerting enough to have him ride beside her without having to respond with false amity.

The miles passed in virtual silence, and Rhoese withdrew into her dreamery again. Jude had possessed her twice more last night, each time differently, masterly, even tender at times. Yet few words had passed between them, even afterwards when she lay in his arms, and though this was perhaps understandable she would like to have known whether his heart was as involved as his body. In the circumstances, she thought, it was safe to assume that it was not.

Nor had he made any attempt at conversation this morning while the chamber swarmed with their servants, although her initial fears that he was angry with her melted away when, in the middle of having her hair braided, he had taken her into his arms without warning and kissed her, none too gently. His voice had matched his mood. 'We set out before the sun touches yon tree line,' he growled. 'Get a move on. I'll be in the hall. Join me there to take our leave. Come, Pierre!'

This time she had done exactly as she was told whilst studiously ignoring Els's beetroot-red complexion and Hilda's round-eyed poker-face. Now, several miles north of Catterick, she glanced sideways once more at her husband's long cross-gartered limbs and spurred heels, his strong brown hand resting on the pommel of the high saddle, holding the reins. His wrist was cuffed with a band of green on deep gold sleeves that blended into the distant fields, and his glossy hair was like the sheen on a rook's wing. A gold brooch as big as an apple shone upon his shoulder, and though he had none of Master Flambard's ostentation, Rhoese found her breath catching in her throat at the sight of him. What were those words she had called out in English last night? *Beloved. Adored one. Brave heart.* Thank heaven he would not understand, for only yesterday Master Flambard had reminded her that Jude liked a challenge, and once he discovered her heart's betrayal, then he would lose interest and look elsewhere, despite what he'd indicated last night. Why else would Warin have left her for Ketti if not for the pursuit of a new conquest? That, and the money. Obviously they were not so very different, after all.

'We'll stop at the bridge,' Jude called to the leaders.

Ahead of them, the broad sweep of the River Tees cut a shining swathe through woodland and fields, past the crofts of meanly thatched dwellings where blue woodsmoke was snatched by the wind. She was sure he would not allow them to linger here.

He came to lift her down before Master Flambard could reach her. 'Over there,' he said, pointing to a thicket of elders and mossy boulders nearby, 'you'll find some privacy, if you look.' It was always the first thing women needed after hours in the saddle.

Being choosy, the three of them searched for some moments before finding suitable places to squat and, as soon as Hilda and Els had left her, Rhoese stayed to rest her back upon a large rock to watch the river glide past and to enjoy the sound of the water. A gust of wind swirled leaves across her feet, masking the sound of footsteps and, when Jude appeared round the side of the boulder, she assumed he had come for the same purpose as herself.

She heaved herself away to leave him in peace but he held her back, taking her so much by surprise that her first resistance gave way under the pressure of his hands on her arms. 'Now,' he whispered, 'why so silent in my company, my lady? Are your thoughts like mine, eh? Are you feeling it again… tasting…smelling it? Are you?' He could not have expected an answer, for his mouth was over hers before she could think of one, before she realised she was not meant to speak or to think at all.

Since that was exactly what she had been experiencing and what she craved more of, there seemed to be little point in trying to deny it, for her body was already melting in the cruel grip of his hands and the second ungentle kiss of that day, and it was too late

for her to lie about her needs as she would like to
have done. Caught up like a leaf in a squall, helpless,
directionless, her arms enclosed his head then slid
down to enclose his great shoulders while she drank
in his kisses and felt again the hard length of his body
pressing against hers, his legs on hers as they had
been on his stallion, controlling, restraining. Drunk
with the taste of him, with the soft-hard pressure of
his lips, she felt him move down over her throat, holding her head back as he lingered over the white skin
of her neck and shoulder. She made no protest when
he pushed her woollen kirtle down to free her taut
pointed breast, for by that time her need was as fierce
as his, and the sweet ache under his hands and mouth
was suddenly unbearable. Voraciously, he covered it
with lips and tongue as if this was the only kind of
hunger on his mind, not the other, while a craving
weakened her limbs and sent a surge of excitement
into her lungs, making her gasp and moan into his
hair.

'More,' she cried, in English, forgetting herself.
'More…love me again, beloved…quickly…now.
Take me here.'

As if he had understood every word, Jude pulled
up her skirts and, with his hands beneath her buttocks,
lifted her on to a ledge of the boulder, pulling his
braies undone beneath his tunic. 'Put your arms
around my neck,' he commanded, hoarsely. 'Spread
your thighs for me, my beauty. There…here…'

And there, as the river slid past and the wind sang
through the berry-laden elders above them, Rhoese
became oblivious to the harshness of her bed and felt

only the fierce and turbulent storm of Jude's passion, the crazy dappling of the sun through the leaves matching the disconnected thoughts in her mind, tossing them into oblivion. There was little in the way of finesse this time, no seduction to speak of, commands taking the place of loving words. Craving and urgency was upon them, and satisfaction was all either of them wanted, instant, immediate, rough-hewn and raw like the rocks, the water, the trees that sheltered them, primitive and beautiful.

In an instant, their animal fervour heightened and rushed upon them both with the uncontrolled wildness of a burst dam, dizzying them with its force and drawing from them cries of ecstasy as the torrent carried them with it. Time hung, breathless, then came crashing down softly, and they heard their panting, their soft groans, their last gasps of bliss, and Rhoese felt her shame as the reality of it came seeping back. *What am I doing with this man? In God's name what has come over me? I love him. I need him. I am a fool again.* With her head buried in his shoulders, an odd tear escaped with the disastrous confession.

But something in her breathing made him take her face into his hand. 'What's this?' he said. 'I hurt you? Too rough?'

'No,' she whispered. 'Nothing. Just something I've discovered.'

'Ah,' he said. 'A discovery, is it? Or an admission?'

'Yes,' she said. 'We must get back to the others.'

For a few precious moments he hesitated. 'Rhoese,' he said at last, 'we make a good bonding, you and I.

It's nothing to be ashamed of, as man and wife. Wanting each other, I mean.' He held her to him, brushing away the tear with his free hand. Never had he appeared so tenderly concerned, even after the steers' incident. 'Is that part of the problem?'

Still half-dazed and without thinking how it would seem to him, she nudged his fingers with her lips, nuzzling at his knuckles. 'It's not what I had in mind for you,' she whispered. 'Not at all what I had in mind.'

'Good,' he said, smiling. 'Then I shall not spoil it by asking what you *did* have in mind. All the same, my beauty, it's what I've had in mind for *you* for the last four hours.' With the faintest of complacent smiles playing around the corners of his eyes, he removed himself from her at last and allowed her to slip to the ground. 'Did you feed me a potion then, lady?'

'Yes, sir, I did,' she replied. But her head was down as she adjusted her dress, hiding from him the frown that passed like a fleeting shadow across her eyes, and he took her answer for caprice, which is what she had intended he should.

Nevertheless, he took this new willingness as a step forward in their relationship and, because he believed he was on the way to understanding something of the conflict she was fighting, he kept up the appearance of severity for her sake. And while this convinced many in their party that nothing had changed, there were at least two who had other opinions.

Chapter Nine

By the time they reached Durham it was clear to Rhoese that her carefully nurtured ambitions of cold-hearted revenge were disturbing *her* far more than the man they were intended to disturb. Having reluctantly admitted to herself that, like it or not, she was crazily in love, she found it well nigh impossible to persuade herself that she was not, though she tried hard enough. Heaven knows, there were plenty of reasons not to be, and very few excuses why she was, and none of these made much sense in the cold light of day. The man was a Norman, for pity's sake, a man who wanted what she had, that's all, a man who had told her she would never reach his heart and who now suspected that, with all this talk of potions, she had already tried. Well, that would afford him some amusement. Imagine how he'd laugh if he thought she actually loved him, after all her threats and predictions. Worse still, imagine how he'd gloat if he knew she was going through all the torments meant for him because she'd swallowed her own medicine.

The situation last night had not done much for her

peace of mind either, when his men had turned an English family out of their home at Bishop's Oakland so that they could occupy it. She had been upset by that, but was quite unable to do anything about it, and they had spent the night in a thatched hall resembling her own at Toft Green, divided into cubicles by curtains with the firelight filtering through them. On a pile of furs she had slept in Jude's arms, hearing every cough, snore and murmur from those nearby and fearing that any activity on their part would also be heard. Apart from some very intimate caresses, there was no activity, but Jude's whispered reminder that she needed him gave her no hope at all that his feelings were involved, as hers were. He was right. She did need him.

With the hostile scowls of the dispossessed families still clear in her mind, Rhoese had tried to look apologetic as well as helpless as they set out on the last leg of their journey, this time not daring to offer them money, which would certainly have been thrown back in her face. They had reached Durham by noon and had been quartered in the bishop's palace, now rebuilt after the notorious fire of 1069 which not only burnt the place to the ground but, in true Anglo-Saxon style, the men inside it too. Those who perished on that fateful night had been Norman to a man, including the brutal new governor sent to keep the rebellious northerners in their place. That act of revenge had brought the whole force of King William's army, led by the king himself, to eradicate every village, every human being, animal and crop between York and this spectacular town of Durham. Nineteen years later, the countryside was still struggling to recover, and although Rhoese was too young to remember, there were plenty of Yorkists who did and who vowed never to forgive. Except for a few renegades in the fens near Ely and their leader, a man named Hereward, that was the last uprising against the new Norman king, though who knows how many plans had gone adrift through lack of funds to raise an army.

The bishop's palace was a far more substantial building than the previous one: thick stone walls and rounded arches with heavily patterned columns to hold them up, massive timber ceilings and stone staircases on the outside to take them up to a first floor with halls, side-chambers, chapels and offices leading off. Rhoese couldn't help comparing this solid grandeur with the close earthy warmth of her own simple hall and bower, the muddy stockade, stores and workshops.

No one had expected the turncoat bishop to come rushing out to meet them, but he did, as if he'd known of their coming. Which, in a way, he had, through a complicated network of messengers who were paid handsomely to tell him what was happening as well as what was about to happen. As if nothing was, he smiled courteously at the invasion of mounted men, ox-carts and packhorses that poured into his courtyard at noon. He smiled with especial warmth at Rhoese, being an admirer of beautiful women, and no outsider would have guessed by his welcome that he was about to be arrested for treason.

They were in time for midday dinner, and here again there was no sign that their arrival had caused the slightest problem to the cooks, or that over one hundred extra posteriors to be seated in the hall had upset the chamberlain's calculations. And if Rhoese had thought she might be the only lady there, it just went to show what kind of a man the bishop was when he introduced her to Anneys d'Abbeville, to whose imperious manner and arresting good looks the servants deferred as if she were very important.

Anneys d'Abbeville and Bishop William made an incongruous pair, as lovers often do, she being an inch or two taller than he, more slender, and looking considerably younger than his middle age. Greying of hair and balding, he was nevertheless genial of face and with a certain shrewdness in his deep-set eyes. She was a black-haired Juno with an unsmiling wary expression that Rhoese saw instantly as hostility, but which Master Flambard put down to the insecurity of her position. Which amounted to much the same thing.

Like flickering candlelight, Anneys d'Abbeville's hooded eyes washed over the principle guests and settled at last upon Rhoese as if to weigh up the competition, travelling over her figure in what she intended to be a message of superiority, in case the lady from York was in any doubt.

Whether because of her natural defensiveness amongst Normans or because of a new confidence as Jude's wife after the last unusual twenty-four hours, Rhoese held the woman's stare with unwavering composure that had the startling effect of turning it aside in sudden uncertainty. Just over the cold shoulder, Rhoese caught the eye of Master Flambard whose ex-

ceedingly slow wink told her what he had so far failed
to impart in words about the use of power.

Emboldened, she pursued the success.
'D'Abbeville?' she said. 'Exactly where *is* Abbeville?'

'Not too far from Amiens.' The reply was unusually subdued.

'Ah, on the Somme river? Near St Valery, where I
believe Duke William held his troops before the wind
changed? Very flat there, I believe.'

'Warmer than it is here, too,' said the lady, bristling.

'Then you'll be happy to return, I'm sure.'

With that brief and conclusive skirmish to her
credit, Rhoese turned away to find Master Flambard's
eyes upon her, dancing with laughter, though he was
in better control of his mouth. 'His mistress,' he told
her in an undertone as they were escorted across the
busy hall. 'Sure to be.'

'You don't know her, then?' said Rhoese.

'No, but your husband does.' They turned together
through an arch, then had to walk in single file as far
as the next large chamber.

'How d'ye know that?' Rhoese said, catching him
up.

'I saw how they looked at each other. Recognition.'

She felt an insidious nausea ripple upwards from
her stomach, its fear-provoking effects out of all pro-
portion to the innocent sound of Flambard's words.
*Was that the deadly sickness known as jealousy?
Damn the observant chaplain. Why did he have to tell*

her this? Could he be wrong? 'Oh, really?' she said. 'As far afield as Durham. Well, well.'

'She's a good-looking woman,' Flambard said, as if to justify it. 'And Abbeville is not far from Brionne, either, though she was careful not to say so.'

Rhoese refused to be drawn along that line of enquiry. 'Mmm. I take it she'll not be going down to London with the bishop, will she?'

'Well, now,' he said, looking round the solar into which her baggage was being carried, 'that's an interesting question, my lady. She'll either want to accompany him into exile or she won't, if you see what I mean.'

'Not really,' she said, wishing he would go away. 'But no matter.'

He bowed and turned to go. 'No, of course not. No matter,' he said. The door closed, quietly.

Accusingly, Rhoese glared at it. 'Where's Brother Alaric when I need him?' she snapped.

'Over here,' said a quiet voice by the deep window recess. 'Just come and look at this view.'

Shamefaced, she joined him. 'I'm sorry,' she whispered. 'I think I'm letting it all get to me. I mustn't, must I?'

'I heard what Master Flambard said,' Brother Alaric admitted, still looking down at the astonishing view. 'You're doing very well.'

From a high window, they looked down a sheer rock-face to the silver blue curve of the river upon which tiny dots scudded with the current like midges on a pond. Beyond that, the sunwashed thatches of dwellings sat beside narrow crofts and tracks leading to distant hills and woodland where clusters of home-steads now belonged to men like Count Alan of Rich-mond and Bishop William of St Calais, instead of to the English Earl of Northumberland and his descen-dants.

Rhoese heaved a sigh at her chaplain's attempt at comfort. 'What are we doing here?' she said. 'It's only a short while since we were taking in our dues and minding our own business. And now…'

Brother Alaric remained very still. 'There are peo-ple out there,' he said, 'who've lost far more than you, m'lady.'

'You're asking me to be thankful?' she said, sharply.

'Shh. Sit down,' he said, turning to sit on the cush-ioned stone ledge. 'Come on…' he patted the cushion '…sit and tell me about it. What we're doing here need not concern us unduly. What *you* need to get straight is your heart. It's in a bit of a twist, isn't it?'

Though her lips compressed to stop her eyes filling, the picture he presented made her snort with amuse-ment. 'You could say that,' she croaked. 'Is it so ob-vious?' She lifted up a toeful of rushes and let them drop again.

'Only to me,' he lied for her sake, 'because I know you better than most. D'ye think it's time you told your husband how you feel about him now? That might help.'

'He knows how I feel,' she said.

'That you love him?'

'No, not as much as that. I cannot tell him that,

Brother.' She steeled herself for the inevitable 'why not?', but it did not come.

'You're not still thinking of revenge, are you? Haven't we passed that point now? Warin? Ketti? That fiasco at Catterick? Is it necessary?'

Her silence told him that it was.

'Listen,' he said, keeping his voice low. 'Things change. They always have, and we have to accept it. People change too. But to allow them to hold you back so that *you* can't change is…'

'I *have* changed, haven't I?'

'Emotionally, I mean. No, you've ground to a halt. And now when you can see the way forward, you're not taking it.'

'It's too soon,' she said, looking down at her twisting hands. 'I'm not ready.' *I'm not ready to trust him. I know nothing about him.*

There was one of their familiar silences, as if the chaplain was hearing all her reservations and was trying to resolve them. When he spoke at last, his change of subject took her by surprise. 'You've spent quite some time with Master Flambard,' he said, watching Hilda and Els unpack the pannier baskets and lay Rhoese's clothes upon the bed.

'You think I ought not to?' she said. 'Spend time with him?'

'I think,' he said, 'that you should be careful. No, I'm not suggesting that you suddenly shun his company. That would look very strange. But you must remember that he's a king's chaplain on the ladder to some high office, and such climbers don't usually mind too much how they get there as long as it's fast and safe. Do you see what I'm saying?'

'Well, no, Brother. I was aware of all that. Am I in some danger?'

'I heard what he said just now about the Lady Anneys and your husband recognising each other. Remember?'

'He's so perceptive,' Rhoese said. 'He studies human—'

'Perceptive my *foot*!' said Brother Alaric. 'He's no more perceptive than my…well, never mind. I'm not saying that he's actually out to make trouble, but there's absolutely no reason for him to suggest, as he was doing, that Anneys d'Abbeville and Sire Jude know each other. And even if they do, what's his motive in telling you except to upset you? As he suspects it will.' He looked at her sharply. '*Has* it upset you?'

'Well…' she whispered.

'Yes, of course it has. Don't let it. Whatever Master Flambard has in mind, you can be sure of one thing, that it's for his own ends. Not Jude's, not yours, but his.'

'You don't like him, do you?'

There was but a moment's hesitation before his reply. 'Oh, one cannot help liking him. He's clever, but I don't admire his kind. He'll get where he wants to go right enough and he'll not give a damn who likes or dislikes him. But if he gives you advice, m'lady, you can be sure it won't come cheap.'

'He's already offered me some, Brother.'

'About what?'

'About my so-called reputation. You know what was being said?'

'Yes, I do. What kind of advice?'

'Not to deny it, but to use the power it brings, in a nutshell.'

'The power. Ah…yes, of course. But as long as you use it for good, not for evil. I hope he said that, too?'

'Yes, he did.' Had he? She couldn't quite remember.

'Well, you have, haven't you? You used the ashes of that sloughed-off snakeskin you found to treat a wound yesterday, didn't you? They'd not come across that one before. And you picked blackberries to cure Ned's sore throat, and they did. And look how you had that thrush perch on your finger this morning. I've never seen anyone do that before, and nor had they. They were impressed all right, but don't let it go to your head.'

'So how am I to charm Anneys d'Abbeville? Be nice to her?'

'Of course, lady. You're Jude's wife, not her. You've nothing to fear. She's merely the mistress of a dissenting bishop, and if she's not tasting the bitterness of insecurity right now I'd be very much surprised. She'll have lost far more than you by the time this year is over, and her *curriculum vitae* won't look too healthy after this, will it? Besides, she's losing her looks.'

His throwaway line brought Rhoese's deep well of tension to the surface like a flash flood and, recognising the uncharitable remark for what it was, their chuckles were deliciously guilty. He touched her arm lightly with his fingertips. 'You need your husband,' he said as the chuckles faded. 'You can't afford to ignore or reject what he's offering you, my lady.'

'Aye, Brother. But I know so little about him. Purposely I've not asked, just to prove my uninterest.'

'Well, then, if you're balking at asking him, ask his cousin. We'll be taking the gospel-book to him while we're here. The topic is sure to arise.'

'You'll come too, won't you?'

'Of course I will. Now, I suggest that, instead of skulking up here, we go down to dinner. You act the perfect wife and I'll act the perfect chaplain. Eh?'

'Yes, Brother,' she smiled back at him. 'Give me but a moment. My acting skills need honing.'

If Prior Turgot had not been otherwise engaged in the cathedral when the party from York arrived, he would have been able to greet them along with the bishop. His apologies as they went in to dine were exactly the right tone, sincere but not grovelling, and Brother Alaric took to him instantly in a way he'd not been able to take to Master Flambard. His being a Lincolnshire man, the chaplain told himself, had nothing to do with it, nor had the fact that, after only thirteen years as a monk, he had been elected prior a year ago. A meteoric rise worthy even of Flambard's respect.

Rhoese was equally impressed by the Benedictine prior who had once been one of Lincoln's lawmen, dispossessed by the Normans as she was, and replaced by a Norman family. He had resisted the invaders and had been held hostage by them before settling into the monastic life in Northumberland, and though his ability shone through everything he did, his engaging modesty was in stark contrast to Flambard's brilliance.

Speaking in her native English, the prior was seated next to Rhoese at the high table with Jude on her other side. 'Yes, dispossessed, my lady,' Prior Turgot repeated, smiling at her astonishment. 'My family held lands in Oxfordshire and here in the north as well as in Lincolnshire. It happens,' he said, ruefully. 'One has to accept it and carry on.'

All this talk of carrying on. 'That's quite remarkable,' she said, watching his workmanlike hands take a sop of bread to his mouth, well able to imagine how he had fought to retain what was his by right. His face was strong, craggy, and lined like folds of linen, his skin pitted with signs of living, loving and hardship. Eyes of green surveyed her as he munched, then swallowed. 'No, lady,' he contradicted her gently. 'Hundreds…thousands have had to do it. Take Queen Margaret, for example. Now she *is* remarkable.'

Jude leaned forward to offer her a morsel of goosewing from their shared portion. 'What are you talking about?' he said.

Rhoese accepted the meat. 'The English Queen of Scotland,' she said in French. 'King Malcolm's wife.' She turned back to the prior. 'Shall we speak my husband's language?' she said.

'Certainly,' said the prior. 'Queen Margaret was obliged to marry a man she neither trusted nor liked. It was her brother, the Prince Edgar, who persuaded her that she must accept the king's proposal, though she protested that she didn't want to marry anyone. In fact, she'd have preferred to go into a nunnery.' His eyes seemed to miss little, though they did not see Jude take Rhoese's hand into his own beneath the white linen tablecloth and hold it still upon his lap. 'She's much younger than him, and a devout Christian. A wonderful woman. I have the honour of being her spiritual adviser.'

'That doesn't surprise me,' said Rhoese. 'Any woman in that dreadful position must need all the spiritual advice she can get.' The hand squeezed hers, and she understood that Jude was laughing to himself. 'Has she managed to overcome some of her repugnance, Father?' she said.

The prior sat back, wiping his mouth carefully with his napkin. 'Oh, she most certainly has,' he replied, smiling. 'They've been together since 1070 and she's borne him a large family and made a good Christian out of him too.'

'You mean, he was a *pagan*?'

'A borderline case. He certainly behaved like one.'

'How awful. And now?'

'Now she's tamed him, my lady. She has him eating out of her hand like a pet lamb. They adore one another. But…' his tone lifted from the tender to the brisk '…she's had to work hard at it and try to please him at the same time. It's not been easy for her. She saw what had to be done when many another woman would have given up. But not my Lady Margaret. Ah, no, she took the bull by the horns, as they say. I have

no doubt that she'll be canonised for her good works,
eventually.'

'Really?' Jude brought their joined hands up onto
the table and laid them down with a soft thud. 'Well,
I'm happy to say we shall never have to go through
all that, shall we, my love? Except for the taking of
bulls by the horns, that is. Shall you be writing the
queen's Life, my lord prior?'

'I shall be ready to do so whenever she asks me,
Sire Judhael,' said Prior Turgot, modestly. 'But now
I ask you to excuse me while I have a word with our
good bishop. It may be the last time we're allowed
any contact.' He stood up, brushing his habit down.
'Oh, dear. What a sad business this is.'

Rhoese kept her eyes upon the square of gravy-
soaked bread in front of her. 'If you think you've
deceived him,' she said, 'think again.'

'Be quiet, wife,' Jude said, shaking her hand
gently, 'or I may take you out into the dark passageway and make passionate love to you before the meal
is over and risk scandalising our hosts. In fact...' He
made as if to stand and pull her with him, and she
was obliged to clutch at his arm before she realised
how he was teasing her.

'Oh...*you*!' Her fist curled up to deliver a blow to
his ribs, but he caught it before it made contact. Then,
with both her hands caught, she was made to wait
upon his kiss before he would release her. It was not
the best table manners, of course, but no one seemed
to take offence at the newlyweds, and no one could
have known of the thrill she felt at the hardness of

his arms. Did he, she wondered, derive as much pleasure from her softness as she did from his strength?

Checking the faces as he released her, Rhoese saw
that the one whose eyes remained on them longest
without a hint of amusement belonged to Anneys
d'Abbeville. But the taste of Jude's kiss still clung to
her mouth and his light-hearted threat throbbed
through her veins, reminding her of the fierce beat of
his loins and the intimate pounding of his thighs
against hers. 'What?' she said, blankly, aware that he
had spoken to her.

His bellow of teasing laughter rang across the hall,
and Rhoese's ensuing blush persisted far longer than
the stares that followed.

Escaping at last from the noisy confines of the great
hall and the masculine odour of soldiers, monks, clerics and servants, Hilda and Rhoese passed out of a
side door and along a cool passageway into the
bishop's private garden, which, so he'd told her sadly,
he was going to miss.

The garden was brilliant with autumn sunshine,
better tended than the one at Catterick, larger and ti-
dier with raised beds of seeding herbs and benches
thick with camomile that made a permanently scented
cushion of greenness. Wickerwork screens made private outdoor chambers where the bishop and his staff
could sit in meditation, some of them canopied over
with convolvulus and climbing roses. In the distance,
monks strolled past narrow water channels while
other took shortcuts to the cathedral precincts now
that there was no one to stop them.

Hilda whispered like an intruder. 'We're going to have to leave young Els at York, you know,' she said. 'She's already homesick. She'll never make it down to London.'

'It's more likely to be a lack of male attention that's the problem,' said Rhoese, heading towards a trellis where pears had been fanned out sideways to show their ripened fruit to the sun. 'Not even Jude's men will bother with her. I think you may be right; we may have to do without her. We'll manage.'

'Well, if you ask me—'

'Shh!'

'What?' Hilda mouthed, silently.

'Shh, that's Jude's voice, surely.'

'No, he's in the hall still. Isn't he?'

'It *is* him. He's with that woman, Hild.'

Slowly and silently, placing their feet down like cats, they moved towards the screen until the voices percolated more clearly through the yellowing leaves. Here Rhoese stopped, quite unable to pass by or to prevent herself from eavesdropping.

'I can scarce believe it,' the woman called Anneys was saying. 'You…*married*? What on earth's come over you, Jude?' The voice came and went as if she was pacing about in agitation. 'Did you *have* to marry her?'

'Yes, I did,' said Jude. 'I'm past thirty, Anneys, and I need to take a wife. You know what my father was like.'

There was a gasp of quiet laughter. 'I know better than most what your father was like, don't I? Who better? A lot's happened since those days, Jude, but you know how I felt about you. Nothing's changed.'

'You're wrong, *chérie*. Everything's changed. In eight years, how could it not? You've moved up to higher ground till you reached the top and now it's all about to end for you. How can you say nothing's changed?'

'You know what I mean, Jude. Don't be cruel. I mean my feelings for you. We could keep it from your wife. She need never know.'

'Anneys, you're clutching at straws. I have nothing to offer you. I have a wife and I mean to keep her. A mistress would make for complications, and that's the last thing I need at this time, believe me.'

'You used to have two or three.'

'Those days have gone. If you're quite sure you can't go into exile with the bishop, then why not try Flambard? He might be interested.'

'Still so cruel, Jude. You make me feel like a parcel being passed on.'

'That's your choice. Try the one who's moving up in the world instead of down. Flambard and Bishop William have been friends for years, ever since Odo of Bayeux brought them over, but Ranulf has no trouble arresting friends as well as enemies. He knows what to do with a woman, too.'

'Really? But you did too. Do you still, Jude? Now you're married?'

'Ask my wife. She'll tell you.'

'Tch! I shall come with you down to London, then.'

'We have to take him to Sarum first, to stand trial.'

'Sarum?'

'It's in Wiltshire. I suggest you make yourself agreeable to the king's chaplain. There's a way out for you there, and the bishop needn't know anything about it.'

'I'd rather it was you, Jude. Shall I beg? Plead? Your new wife doesn't look as if she'd care one way or the other.'

'It would be dangerous, Anneys.'

'Then we keep it from her. I can be discreet, you know that.'

Caring for Rhoese as she did, Hilda could not allow her mistress to hear another word. With a firm hand over her wrist, Hilda hauled her bodily away from the pear tree, which had now grown eerily silent. Grim-faced, she sat Rhoese down near a pond where flashing trout twisted and curved in figures of eight, her matronly arms longing to hold her while her heart bled with pity. She looked at Rhoese's white face and was shocked by the tragic emptiness there, as before when she had lost all that she held dear in one, short, wicked span of time. And now, suspecting the workings of Rhoese's heart, she saw that it was about to happen again, so soon. The pain would kill her.

'Courage, love,' she whispered. 'Courage. It may not mean what it seems. We have to find out.'

The response was a long time coming. 'He *did* know her,' she said, hoarsely. 'They've known each other for years. In Normandy. She wants him back. Master Flambard was right and Brother Alaric was wrong. And he married me because his father wants him to take a wife, so he says. Isn't that flattering, love? Isn't it grand? Isn't it just about the best reason you've ever heard?' Her laughter was soft and brittle, made of gasps that sounded like sobbing, and when she looked up to watch a flight of white doves circle the palace rooftop, her eyes were awash with angry tears that she knuckled away before they could fall.

'Why?' she whispered. 'Why is this happening to me again? And why so soon? I expected it, eventually, but not so soon. Surely not now when it seemed to be getting better, when I thought I had his interest, if not his heart. What's the matter with me, Hild? What is *wrong* with me?'

'Nothing, love. Nothing,' said Hilda, taking her hand.

'I think I should just go back to York. I know the way, and we could make far better progress on our own than we did coming.'

'It's not like you to run away, love.'

'I know, but I can't wait around to watch this happening between them. It'll take weeks to get down to where we're going, and she'll be wheedling her way back into Jude's heart all the time. I know it. She almost said as much.'

'Then you must fight back. You didn't have the energy or the will to fight Ketti for Warin after your father died, did you? But now you're fit again, so fight for what you love if you want it badly enough. Do you?'

'Want him? I think of little else night and day, Hild.'

'I thought so. Your heart has softened, then.'

Rhoese placed a hand on her breast to feel the thudding beneath her fine mantle and kirtle. 'I dare not let him know it,' she said. 'It will never survive the damage.'

Hilda squeezed her hand. 'Aye, but you see, love, the way to soften *his* heart is to show him that you care, not that you *don't* care. Take this woman on. You can do it. It's no use standing back and looking helpless, is it? He's your husband, not hers. He's the one who'll father your bairns, and no matter how strong a man looks, you can't go leaving him wide open to a woman like that. She believes you'd neither know nor care, so show her…show them both…how wrong they can be. Men are so daft about women and their hearts.'

'He told me he'd not know where to start looking for one.'

'Nay, come on, lass. How many lies have *you* spun, just to hurt him?'

Rhoese was spared having to answer this tricky question as two shadows fell across the path and headed directly towards them, two Benedictine monks, one familiar and one not. It took no time at all to guess who the stranger was and, because of his distinguished appearance in contrast to Brother Alaric's brown ordinariness, she and Hilda stood up to greet them.

It had taken Jude's cousin the same short glance to recognise the private nature of the two women's conversation, one whose reputation for beauty had not been exaggerated but whose eyes were filled with pain and whose hand, held in her nurse's lap, was hastily snatched away. Jude, he reflected, had excelled himself this time, although the signs were disturbing.

His companion, the lady's chaplain, introduced them. 'My lady,' he said, 'will you allow me to present Brother Gerard, your husband's cousin.'

It was the custom to greet any man with a kiss to both cheeks, but there were some Norman ecclesiastics nowadays who took exception to that from a woman, so it was safer to bow one's head and smile. Brother Gerard was sensitive enough to see what it cost her to smile at such a time.

He would have been as tall as Jude, and as broadshouldered, had he not been shortened by a pronounced limp and stooped shoulders. His features were strong and well defined, his eyes dark and piercing beneath black brows pulled together as if by a drawstring above his nose. The hair around his tonsure was dark and too long for neatness, sitting into his cowl at the sides.

Hoping to see her lovely eyes lighten a little, Brother Gerard continued to speak in English as he had been doing to the chaplain. Her long spiked lashes widened to show him the soft-lit brownness of a river bed, and he was rewarded. 'I am honoured, my lady,' he said. 'And may I welcome you to Durham? Brother Alaric tells me that you are able to read and write. I wish one could say the same for all the monks here. It would make life simpler.'

'My father insisted,' she said. 'Brother Alaric and I were able to do our own accounts. May I present my nurse, Hilda? We've been together since I was born.'

They sat facing each other in the sunny secluded alcove where walls of plums and damsons spread their arms across the trellises, buzzing with winged foragers and festooned with gossamer webs. The formal arrest of the bishop had just begun, the two men told Rhoese, and now he would be confined to his quarters under heavy guard. It seemed bizarre to reward his courteous hospitality in this way, but that was how things were done, part-civilised and part-barbaric. Jude was arranging the administration of cathedral business with Prior Turgot, and they would see little of him for the rest of the day.

'You speak our language well,' said Rhoese. 'If you think it unusual for a woman to read and write, we think it far more unusual to hear a Norman speak in English. Why did you learn it, Brother?'

Brother Gerard spread his hands and looked at the inkstains in some surprise. 'Well, my lady, it would be hard for me to oversee scribes in an English scriptorium speaking only my own tongue. If I want the job done properly, I have to make the same kind of effort, initially.'

'So you've been in England some time, have you?'

'I came over with Jude eight years ago. I'm a few years older than he, but I lived with his family after my parents died. Bishop Odo was my patron, though he's now gone the same way as men like our good bishop who would have preferred William Rufus's elder brother to take the throne of England. They may even be in exile together, our bishops. Who knows?'

'I think *we* would have preferred an Englishman to take it,' said Rhoese.

'We live in a changing world my lady,' said Brother Gerard, quietly.

'Yes, Brother,' said Rhoese, unwilling to let it go at that and tiring of all the talk of change. 'But it often appears that we English have had more than our fair share of change, and not always in our favour, either. Have you seen the state of the villages and countryside between here and York lately? Try telling those poor souls out there that we live in a changing world and see if they find comfort in that. How much have *you* changed in your eight years in England, Brother?'

Halfway through this unexpected outburst, Brother Alaric had already given up trying to silence her with frowns and now sat looking at his knees with the occasional sidelong glance at the two disputants. 'Lady,' he said, 'Brother Gerard was only—'

The monk made a sign for him to cease. 'I will tell you,' he said, 'since you ask. 'Tis no secret. Ten years ago I had a hunting accident and was paralysed. I was totally unable to walk and hardly able to fend for myself. As his father's eldest son, Jude took on the duty of caring for me night and day. Nothing was too much trouble for him. He made me exercise, taught me to walk again, found books for me to read, made me take an interest in life and was my constant companion. I learnt the art of writing as a day pupil in a local monastery and came to the attention of Bishop Odo of Bayeux. He's a great patron of the arts, you know. He and Count Alan wanted Jude to come over here to England, but he wouldn't leave me, then eight years ago he brought me up here to Durham with

Bishop William of St Calais and I became a monk. In the last eight years, thanks to Jude, I've begun a new life, became the cathedral *amarius*, I can walk and praise God and do things for myself. So, from being close to death to this, my lady, is as much change as I can cope with, I think. Jude's father died, you see, and he's inherited everything, including all the responsibilities.'

'Died? I thought he was…'

'Oh, yes. Two years ago. Jude is now extremely wealthy, though he's never let it rule his life as others have. He's also been given land over here—'

'Yes, I know that.'

There was something in her voice that made Brother Gerard pause and look at her, sensing that here was perhaps the root of the problem. 'But he wouldn't marry simply to acquire more, my lady,' he said. 'Did you think he would? No, not Jude. If he'd been of that persuasion, he could have married half the heiresses in Normandy long before now. He's got his head on straight, has Jude. An idealist, perhaps, but when it comes to marriage he's taken his time, despite his father's nagging. And now I can see what he was searching for: a woman with more to her than wealth and health. A woman of character.'

'By all accounts, Brother, Jude's searches have become a highly enjoyable pastime. Men are used to laying bets on them.'

Brother Gerard did not smile at that, as she thought he might. 'With any good-looking wealthy individual, my lady, there's always speculation and laying of wagers. Jude is a man like any other who enjoys beautiful things, especially when they're offered at no extra expense. But there's no man more faithful to his relatives than Jude, no one more protective. I know him better than anyone, and I can vouch for it. I owe him my life, and I'm delighted that he brought you up here to meet me before you go south.'

Rhoese wiped something off her cheek with a dainty finger before she replied. 'I've brought a book to show you,' she said. 'It's in need of repair.'

Brother Alaric glanced at Hilda, then leaned back and heaved a silent sigh of relief.

'Constipation?' said Hilda. 'Who's got constipation?'

'Nobody has,' said Rhoese, unplaiting her hair.

'Well, what d'ye need—?'

'Just *tell* me, Hild. I've lost my recipe book, haven't I?'

'Well, thistle roots, for one thing.'

'I'm not going gathering thistles. What else?'

Hilda sat down on the linen chest with her chin resting on the pile of folded clothes, her jowls spreading sideways into her wimple like dough in a breadcloth. 'Well, let me see, there's houseleek juice. Elder bark. Brother Alaric will know.'

'I'm not asking him, either.'

'Why not?'

'He'll suspect.'

'Suspect what?'

'Oh, for pity's sake, Hild.' Rhoese took one unplaited rope of hair and threw it like a cloak over her shoulder. 'He'll suspect that I'm trying to dabble again, if you must know.'

'Dabble?'

'Hild, if you go on repeating everything like that I shall call you Echo. He'll want to know who it's for. Why. How. All that.'

'Well, who is it for?'

'For her. That woman.'

'She's constipated?'

The deep breath was let out slowly before Rhoese answered, 'No, she's not. But what happens if you give a strong laxative to someone who doesn't need one? Eh?' She stared at Hilda whose eyes had widened considerably.

'A *strong* laxative?'

'A *very* strong one. Yes.'

'Oh, dear.'

'Exactly. Oh, dear. Unfit to travel, wouldn't you say?'

Hilda chewed on her bottom lip, but this could not prevent her mouth from contorting into a grimace of pain, then into a grin as wide as a sickle. 'Oh, dear,' she said again. 'That's a bit wicked. Well, if we're into *very* strong purges, there's stinking gladwin.'

'Never heard of it.'

'Yes, you have. It's that little iris that grows in the King's Pond in York. We used to call it segg, after the leaves like little swords. There's nothing like it for a good purge.'

'The flowers will have finished long since.'

'It's not the flowers we want, it's the roots.'

'Ah, good. Have you seen any?'

'No, but we could go and take a look.'

So they did. And they found some, but before they could reach the bishop's kitchen with it, they ran into Brother Alaric who took one look at the flopping plants and their muddy roots and said, 'What's this for?', as if he knew.

'Constipation,' said Rhoese. 'I need a purge.'

He held out his arms to receive the bundle. 'I'll make it for you. You need some old ale, too. Come, trust me. They don't like women in the kitchens.'

With no proper show of gratitude, Rhoese handed the plants over. 'I need it soon,' she said. 'And strong. Very strong.'

'You shall have it soon. And strong. And by the way, I'm afraid you won't be able to take the book personally to the scriptorium because they don't allow women in there either.'

'Where *do* they allow women?'

He smiled. 'Well, wherever the Lady Anneys goes, I suppose. But don't mind about it. I'll be there and I'll tell you what's decided.'

'I think I can work that out for myself already. This is the last I shall see of it, isn't it?'

'I don't know, but I'll put your side of the case to them.'

'Thank you, Brother. We shall take our supper in private. Will you join us?'

'Certainly, my lady. I'd be glad to.'

And with that most unsatisfactory state of affairs she had to be content. Except that she was not. Not, that is, until Jude came quietly to her chamber that night without waking her, sliding between the cool sheets and pulling her into his arms, entering her dreams so that she had no need to wake to remember them.

She turned, welcoming him as if he were her other half reclaimed after a separation of years, pressing herself into his warmth, all resentments hidden by the intimate darkness, only joy surfacing into her lips, seeking him. If he had expected something less than this because of the lateness of the hour, his response gave no indication of it, for now he entered into her half-prepared dream as if he knew what had gone before down to the last confused detail, making them both whole again with artless simplicity and with no elaboration to wake her.

Her body and limbs opened to him, wrapping him as he entered her, clinging as she had done in the elder grove, with the same urgency but without the use of words. Totally fulfilling her need at that moment, naked and sweet, their union returned her to sleep in his arms with her lips against his throat, and it was not until her foot strayed into the warmth showing where he had lain that she recalled the grievances of the previous day and how she ought to have made him aware of them.

But by that time it was dawn, and his day had already begun.

Chapter Ten

$$\sim\!\!\sim\!\!\sim\!\!\sim$$

It was just after the office of Prime when Jude, carrying the book beneath his arm, walked across the deserted garden to the cathedral scriptorium in the company of Ranulf Flambard and Brother Alaric. A clinging October mist shrouded the towers and pale yellow trees, and the sharp air stung their nostrils, sending their words out in white clouds. If Brother Alaric had not been with them, Jude might have spoken to Flambard about what he'd seen late last night while on his way to share his sleep with Rhoese. Failing that, he recalled the scene to his memory.

In the dimly lit passageway leading from the hall, a figure had tripped ahead of him, believing herself to be unseen. Holding himself into the deepest shadows, Jude had watched her tap quietly on Flambard's door, had seen it open just wide enough for her to slip through, then close again. The lady had wasted no time in taking his advice. Nor was the king's chaplain a man to refuse a chance like that with so little effort on his part, though he must have tipped her out early so as not to miss seeing the book about which he'd been so curious. Well, Jude mused, once they'd got this over with, they could get on with the business of the day and prepare for an eventual departure.

The scriptorium was already occupied by scribes seated at their writing desks like so many magpies on tall stools, their heads bent over sheets of vellum. Quills scratched and dipped, candle flames flickered in the draught and shadows danced softly on the folds of curtains that partitioned each cubicle. Not a head lifted as the three men were shown inside by Brother Gerard, not a word was spoken to disturb the silence until they reached the library, where the door was closed behind them.

'Prior Turgot will be with us anon,' said Gerard. 'He's preparing for the Chapter. Ah, is this the book then, Jude? Come, lay it over on the table.' His face had the concern of a mother for a sick child.

'So this is where you work,' said Brother Alaric, looking around him at stacks of books on cupboard shelves, leather-bound and weighty. More volumes lay upon the table, their precious covers protected by linen cloths, one of them kept open by a narrow leather strip with a triangular weight at the end. The room was cool, far from cosy, and smelling strangely fusty, with benches where the four men arranged themselves with no expectations of the slightest comfort.

Flambard seated himself next to Gerard, pulling the single candlestick closer to the gospel-book as it was carefully unwrapped, and Jude saw how he shivered with excitement and craned forward eagerly. 'Where did it come from? Remind me, Jude,' he said.

Between them, Jude and Brother Alaric told all
they knew, but now there were questions to be resolved concerning the water damage and the book's
connection to Barking Abbey. They passed it round
the table from hand to hand like fathers with a new-
born babe. To Brother Alaric's prompting, Gerard
turned to the last pages where the tiny script in red
ink between the lines of text seemed to suggest a
connection of some kind.

'You've not read it, Brother?' said Gerard to the
chaplain.

'It's too small for my eyes. They're not what they
were, I fear.'

Gerard peered closely. 'Yes, it is indeed small.
Smaller than usual, even for a gloss. Perhaps the
scribe thought everyone had eyesight as good as his,
or hers. Now we just have to translate it. Give me
time. I'll manage it.'

The door opened, letting in a draught of cold air
along with Prior Turgot. 'Ah,' he said without pre-
amble. 'My word, what a little beauty.' His eyes lit
on the book at once like a bird of prey on a juicy
vole. 'Queen Margaret has one in her possession very
like it.' The men rose to their feet, but he waved them
down again, impatient to join in the conversation.

'We were discussing the provenance, Father,' said
Gerard. 'The abbey at Barking seems to be the most
likely place, as the Lady Rhoese said. Take a look at
this.' He passed the book to the prior, tapping the red
words.

The prior squinted at the page, nodding. 'You do
know, of course,' he said quietly, 'that the new abbess

is not English, don't you?' He lowered the book and
raised his head, looking directly at Jude. 'She's from
the nunnery at St Leger de Prieux, near Lisieux. A
Norman woman.'

It was exactly as Jude had feared. After twenty-two
years, it would have been unusual for the same abbess
to still be in office, hoping for the return of her book.
How would Rhoese feel about that? he wondered.

Whatever it was that had contributed so directly to
Rhoese's growing militancy, she took on the new day
as if she had drunk an energising potion rather than
the weak rosehip wine that Els had brought up from
the kitchen. The young maid was looking pale and
peaky, and Rhoese thought she looked as if she had
just been sick. But no, not Els. She was far too canny
to get caught like that.

At any other time, she would have pursued the matter, but on this day there was a brightly burning fire
inside her and a new spark of assertiveness to be directed, and Els's problems, whatever they were,
would have to wait. If that woman, Anneys
d'Abbeville, thought she could take Jude just for the
asking, then she'd better think again. Whether
Rhoese's heart was thawing or not, no one...*no
one*...was going to take her husband from beneath her
nose without a very hard fight indeed.

However, Brother Alaric's warning to her yesterday about using her so-called powers only for good,
never for evil, had found a niche in her conscience
overnight, and the nasty business of a purge and all
its possible dangers began to lose its appeal as a

means of keeping the woman at Durham. She went in search of her chaplain to tell him, but found Ranulf Flambard and her husband instead, about to part company after leaving the cathedral.

There was no question of a change to her usual cool greeting. Their physical need of each other, their undeniable alchemy, their day and night-time truces and the passion that followed were one thing, but any acknowledgement of a change in a heart so deep-rooted in revenge was quite another, and Rhoese had not yet found a way to show by day what she knew to be true. Having harped on that string at some length, backing down did not come easily. Besides, she had no assurance that her first opinions of him were in any way flawed, except that what his cousin had said about him and his faithfulness could not be totally discounted, even taking into account the ties of family. Yet that woman's years-old claim to him appeared to verify his vast reputation for heartlessness, and that would take some explaining.

As if he knew the kind of greeting to expect, Jude merely took her hand, kissed it, and made it clear that he did not intend to tarry. 'You are well, m'lady?' he said and then, as if he also knew the answer to that, said, 'Good. Then I'll leave you two alone. If you'll excuse me?' And he walked off with an enigmatic smile upon his face that Rhoese had not yet learned to interpret.

She could not help watching the swing of his arms and the long energetic stride of his legs, the black hair lifting in the mist-scattering breeze. A weak sun struggled through the cloud to catch a glint of gold somewhere and to swathe his wide shoulders in a wash of pale linen, and Rhoese's admiring gaze was too late in returning to Master Flambard's watchfulness to hide from him what was in her heart.

'Marriage is beginning to suit you, my lady,' he said.

She was not sure how to reply to that, so she remained silent as they walked slowly across the cobbled yard where two monks swept away crisp leaves and piled them on to a blue-smoking bonfire in the corner. Out of earshot, she found courage to say what was uppermost in her mind. 'That woman. You said she was sure to be the bishop's woman. Did you know that she's also one of Jude's previous mistresses? Is that what you were implying yesterday?'

Master Flambard's restraint came from many years' experience. He did not ask how she knew. 'Well, now, my lady,' he said, speaking softly, 'what I suspect and what I know for certain are not quite the same thing. Let's say there is evidence but no proof. I may be quite mistaken and I have far too much respect for you and Jude to lie about something as important as this, but I do know that they were together in the hall until quite late. At what time did he come to your chamber, may I ask?'

'I don't know. I was asleep.'

'Ah.'

Rhoese stopped, looking him full in the eyes. 'Why? Are you suggesting that…? What *are* you suggesting?'

He held out a hand, directing her towards a bench on the other side of the courtyard wall, holding the

ivy up as she passed through the arch and moving so
fluently into his next sentence that Rhoese lost track
of her question. 'My lady,' he said, 'do you recall our
last conversation in the garden at Catterick? Reputations?'

'Yes, I do. You said I should use mine to my advantage.'

'Exactly. And now I think the time has come for
you to assert yourself. Now, I'm not saying that the
lady in question *had* a liaison with Jude last night,
but I *am* saying that I distinctly overheard her this
morning describing her night's experiences with a
man of particular vigour and imagination. And since
our bishop is under lock and key, and since the lady
was in our company until I left the two of them together, I cannot for the life of me see who else—'

'Yes. Thank you. I think you've said enough, Master Flambard.' It was as much as she could say in one
breath when her lungs had suddenly squeezed all the
air out of them. Panting seemed to help, but it hurt,
and there was a ball of hardness pressing at the back
of her throat. When she could find her voice, she was
annoyed to find that it squeaked. 'She won't be going...ahem!...going down to York and London with
us,' she said. 'Well, at least, I don't think she will.
I've had doubts, and I'm still not sure.'

Flambard stared at her, genuinely intrigued. 'Really?' he said. 'May I ask what it is you have doubts
about?'

'About the ethics of...of exerting my...'

'Powers?'

'Yes. I had thought that a strong purge might do the trick.'

She was watching a flock of squabbling rooks on the tower as she spoke, so missed the expression of jubilant admiration that passed across her companion's face and disappeared as quickly as it had come. 'Er…' he said, unusually hesitant, 'well…yes, it probably would, but since killing your adversary is not always necessary, I would not advise it. Besides, it would not help your cause overmuch, or your reputation either, would it? Who's making this purge? Hilda?'

'Brother Alaric.'

'Good grief! Has he been informed of its purpose?'

'He thinks it's for me.'

He cleared his throat discreetly. 'Perhaps something a little more immediate would be better. You're not afraid of speaking your mind as a rule. To find her and have a quiet and reasonable word in her ear would probably be much better understood than the delayed action of a potion. After all, you don't want to give her time to be telling others what she gets up to at night, do you?' Purposely, he kept Jude's name out of the advice.

Rhoese stood, already fired up and ready to go while the seething hurt and fury were at their height. 'I shall go and tackle Jude first,' she said.

Flambard was on his feet before she'd finished. 'Er…no!' he said with some emphasis. 'No, it's *her* you need to target, my lady. Tackle her now, straight away before she has chance to speak of it again. You need not tell her how you know any of this. Remember, those in authority need not reveal their sources of information, they keep people guessing. That way, they're kept at a disadvantage.'

'Yes. Thank you, Master Flambard. I don't know what I'd do without your help. It's always so direct.'

'My lady, your happiness is my concern,' he said, bowing as she passed him on her way to the palace. He stood there for a moment or two, looking down at the kitchen cat that had come to examine the bench where they had been sitting. 'Manipulation,' he whispered to it. 'That's what it's all about, my friend, isn't it? Manipulation. Eh?' He pulled the smooth beaver-fur collar up around his neck and turned his thoughts back to the gospel-book, which he was sure was not quite what it appeared to be. But then, he thought, things seldom were.

The three remaining monks, one Norman and two English, sat back at last with faces that, whilst not exactly smiling, reflected intense satisfaction. The English text between the lines of Latin had kept them occupied for ten minutes, and now they understood at last.

'Let's see what we have,' said Brother Gerard, picking up the scrap of vellum on which he'd been hurriedly scribbling. He read, 'From Aaeldgyth'— which he pronounced Aeldith—'Abbess of Barking, greetings in Christ to our sister Christina: know that in these wicked and troubled times there is a brother fit to lead us to victory and who for lack of supplies was forced to flee once more from the invaders. I pray you let it be known to him therefore, that we have been the custodians of the treasure left here for safe-keeping in the days before the invasion, and though they searched elsewhere, we were spared. Since its many owners were slain, their wives and kin who fled to our doors are agreed on its use for the good of our countrymen. It is immense. Let it be for our freedom.'

'Well,' said Gerard, passing the message across to Brother Alaric, 'that's the most interesting gloss I've ever read. What do you make of it, Brother? Can you make head or tail of it?'

Brother Alaric pulled a downwards face. 'Only that it almost certainly refers to the treasure that our wealthiest thegns deposited in monasteries for safe-keeping before the invasion in 1066. Four years after that, I believe the new Norman king heard of it and ordered that every monastery in the country should be plundered. It looks as if his men may not have included nunneries in the search.'

'They more than made up for that omission,' said Prior Turgot, drily. 'As I heard it, the looters took far more than what belonged to the thegns and their families. Holy relics, gold plate, books, jewelled—'

'Ahem!' Brother Alaric interrupted softly, glancing at Gerard. 'Our Norman brother here probably knows about that, Father. But what of this "brother" who is to lead them to victory? Would that have been the aethling, d'ye think?'

'Yes,' said the prior. 'It sounds as if the former Abbess of Barking intended to send this message to Abbess Christina of Romsey, in Hampshire. She's the younger sister of Queen Margaret of Scotland, you know. You may recall that both Margaret and Christina and their brother Prince Edgar, the one we call the Aethling, had to flee from the English court in 1068 because there were still men who intended to put him on the throne instead of William. The three young people sought aid in Scotland because their ship to Flanders was blown off course by an ill wind, and Margaret was wooed by Malcolm, King of Scotland. No friend of the English, is Malcolm, but sensible enough to see the advantages of marrying into the royal house.'

'Ah, I see,' said Gerard. 'Being Norman, I'm not as familiar with these events as you.' He was too discreet to mention the other factor, his age.

Prior Turgot continued, 'The Aethling Edgar still had hopes of leading an English army against King William. He reached York and was acclaimed king by the northerners, but William marched up there and drove Edgar back to Scotland and made a mess of York once more. Edgar made another futile attempt, and now he's in Normandy to take sides with Robert, the brother of William Rufus, and no one has heard of him for years. At one time I expect he'd have been glad of extra funds to raise an army, but it's come a bit too late, I fear.'

'I see,' said Gerard. 'So this message was to have been sent by the Abbess of Barking to Edgar's sister Christina at Romsey Abbey, who would then—'

'Pass it on to Queen Margaret of Scotland, the other sister, who would then get the message to Edgar,' said Brother Alaric. 'And if he'd received it, King William could have faced some stiff opposition from both Scotland and England at the same time, since King Malcolm of the Scots would certainly have leapt at the chance to join in.'

'So didn't we ought to let our new king, William Rufus, know about this wealth?' said Gerard. 'Barking Abbey will still have it, I suppose?'

Brother Alaric shook his head. 'This,' he said, tapping the message with one finger, 'was written over twenty years ago. Edgar isn't a threat any more. He's no longer young, and William Rufus appears to be in complete control of the opposition. Look how he's dealing with Bishop William. Look how he's dealt with his uncle Bishop Odo of Bayeux and all those who were behind him. No, the message is outdated, Brother. And Queen Margaret's younger brother David is a hostage at William Rufus's court now. He'd be in mortal danger at any sign of trouble.'

'But the treasure is still there, presumably,' said Gerard, 'and it *could* still be used, once the present abbess understands what it's doing there. You said she's a Norman, Father, so what if her sympathies lie with Robert of Normandy instead of the king, his brother? She could pass the treasure over to the king's enemies, if she was so inclined. It's immense, apparently.'

'She *is* so inclined,' said Prior Turgot. The two brothers waited for him to continue. 'I met her while I was a hostage at court, so I know. And I would not want either of you to repeat what I'm telling you. Bishop William may be the only one of us to be arrested for his support of Robert of Normandy against his brother, but he's not alone in his views by any means, and if his schemes for the overthrow of William Rufus had been successful, there are few monks here, Norman or English, who'd be too put out by it. We're losing a good man. We want him back.'

'None of this could have been said,' Gerard told Brother Alaric, 'while Master Flambard was with us or he'd surely insist on taking the book straight to the king. The Abbess of Barking would immediately lose the wealth she's been keeping safe all these years since the previous abbess died.'

'That goes for Abbess Christina of Romsey too,' said Prior Turgot, significantly. 'She's certainly implicated here. The king can be very vindictive.'

'So we must keep this from the king's chaplain, and from Jude, too. He's loyal to the king and, if he were to find out, he'd insist on him being made aware of it. He would have no option,' said Gerard.

Brother Alaric sighed. The book had once belonged to Rhoese, and she had always been adamant that it must be returned to the woman who had requested its return after it had been stolen and sold. He could well imagine the worsening state of relations between Rhoese and the husband she was learning to love if, instead of acceding to her wishes on this, Jude insisted on telling the king of the subversive message it contained, resulting in raids on the nunneries of Barking and Romsey, one for hoarded treasure belonging by rights to the crown, the other to make sure that nothing illegal was being held there, too. And what *that* would do for Rhoese's increasing remorse over the havoc recently caused to men's lives on her account he did not dare to contemplate.

'In theory,' he said, 'there's nothing to stop either

Sire Jude or the king's chaplain from discovering that the book contains a message, especially as we shall have to carry it from one end of the country to the other. The answer is therefore…' he paused, aware of the intense interest '…to remove the gloss on that page and replace it with something else.'

'*Remove* it?' There was a creak of wood as Prior Turgot wriggled in alarm. 'You mean…remove… interfere with the text in a one-hundred-year-old book? That would be highly unethical, Brother Alaric.'

'The message is highly unethical too, Father,' said the chaplain. 'And if I may be allowed to remind you, the message is not one hundred years old. It's been added recently for unpeaceful purposes that have nothing whatever to do with the Latin text. I am amazed that the late Abbess of Barking could do such a thing.'

'She probably had her good reasons,' said Gerard. 'But I can see nothing wrong with any suggestion that the book should be restored to its former beauty. I can scrape the offending words away, as we do when we wish to re-use a page, and put new words in their place once a suitable base has been applied. It's perfectly feasible, Father.'

'Yes,' said the prior. 'You're right. It is.'

'But are we forgetting something?' said Brother Alaric, thinking of his promise to Rhoese. 'Should we not consult the present owner of the book before we interfere with it?'

The controlled sigh was threefold and, for a moment or two, the holy men struggled with the correct procedure for perverting the course of justice. Finally, it was Jude's cousin who broke the silence. 'Jude will have to be told,' he said.

'Not the Lady Rhoese?' said Brother Alaric, in alarm.

'No, the book lawfully belongs to the lady's husband.'

'But then we're back where we started, Brother. He wouldn't agree to any alteration. We've already established that, haven't we?'

'Stalemate,' said the prior. 'How do we get round that one?'

This time it was Brother Alaric who moved the discussion forward. 'Leave it to me,' he said, frowning. 'There's some unresolved business to do before we go down to York and beyond. Perhaps you could make a start on the water-damage restoration, Brother?' He had not, at that point, thought any further than the sudden and intense decision to put an end to the heart-rending, time-wasting, energy-sapping and unnecessary conflict between the young noblewoman he had grown to admire over the years and the man who had made her his unwilling wife. It could not go on, but how he would put a stop to it was another matter. However, stop it he would, even if he had to shake them both senseless to do it.

Ranulf Flambard's suggestion of a quiet and reasonable word in the ear of a woman who was well on the way to taking Rhoese's husband away from her was immediately discarded in favour of a full-scale, full-face, no-holds-barred confrontation. For

Rhoese to reveal anything other than her outright
fury—yes, and jealousy too, come to that—would not
have the intended effect of stopping the woman in her
tracks, and today there was no time for reasonableness. This was not a reasonable business.

It was true that Jude himself had much to answer
for, but since this kind of thing was what she had
been led to expect, one way or the other, it made
sense to show him indirectly that it was too soon to
begin the breaking of her heart. The notion of breaking *his* heart had had to be shelved. It was simply not
going to happen.

Still raging inside with indignation and the painful
fear of what she stood to lose, she strode into the
bishop's palace past guards, past clerics and chaplains, messengers and men-at-arms towards the place
from which the sound of an Irish harp floated through
an open door. She halted on the threshold to get her
bearings and to assess the competition, for Anneys
d'Abbeville was surrounded by a group of well-
dressed young men, whose laughter at some gossip
indicated the kind of gossip it was. Bellowing with
delight, they embellished it with quips of their own,
drowning out the harpist's strumming and not noticing when he stopped playing.

The woman at the centre of attention sat on the
edge of the bed with her hair unbound, black,
lustrous, and rippling in waves over her shoulders,
one of which was bare. Her maid held an armful of
silk, linen, soft wool and fur, a pair of green kid slip-
pers dangling from her fingers. She saw Rhoese, and
it was her stillness that conveyed itself to the group,

fading the noise altogether. Anneys looked over her shoulder, showing a moment of confusion before hiding it expertly beneath a mask of indifference. 'Yes?' she said.

Rhoese entered the chamber with an assurance that took the group by surprise, for at the steely glitter in her eyes they seemed to melt away round the edges. 'Yes,' she said, casting her gaze over them as if they were no more than serfs. 'You will leave. Now. Get out…go on…all of you.' Her tone was decisive and demanding, but still the men did not move fast enough. *'Move!'* she yelled at them.

Blinking, they scurried out as the bishop's mistress began her protest. 'You have no right to—'

As soon as the door closed behind the maid, Rhoese whirled round to face her adversary, mentally notching up the first point in her own favour for room clearance. 'Don't think to tell *me* about my rights, woman,' she snarled. 'I know exactly what they are and I've come here to remind *you*, since you appear to have forgotten.'

Anneys had risen, and now Rhoese saw how lovely her figure was in the simple rose-coloured linen chemise, how curvaceous and alluring, how the heavily lidded eyes slanted slightly upwards at the corners beneath plucked eyebrows. The hairline had been plucked too, and her ears hung with cascades of gold droplets, and any man, Rhoese thought, would have to be made of stone not to desire her.

'What *are* you talking about?' said Anneys, angrily.

'I'll tell you,' said Rhoese, 'so as to leave you in

no doubt. I'm talking about *my husband*, Judhael de Brionne, the man you once knew, the man you think you can take from me because *your* lofty protector is in trouble, the man you think will never be missed if he slips into *your* bed instead of mine. Remember who I'm talking about now, do you?'

'You're wrong. We haven't...I haven't...'

'No...oh, no! I'm never wrong where my property's concerned,' Rhoese snapped like a shower of falling icicles, 'and I have no charity for women like you. I've met your kind before. I heard, you see.' She pointed to the window. 'Out there yesterday in the garden. Every word. Yes, you may well look like that, woman. Now tell me, if you dare, that I'm wrong and I'll damn you for a liar and scratch your eyes out at the same time.' Slowly advancing with each threat, she came within reach and saw Anneys stagger backwards in alarm, almost sitting down again as the bed pressed against her knees.

For Rhoese, this was a new role, entirely unrehearsed. But her jealousy was like a furnace that burned a painful path through her body, very close to fear in its guise, and twisting through her guts in fiendish savagery. The very idea of Jude lying entwined with this seductive creature brought a spasm of incandescent fury surging into her limbs, shooting out a hail of words in stinging shots that made the woman wince.

Anneys made an attempt to defend herself. 'No, I think I ought to explain that—' she began, clutching at her chemise as it slipped again.

'No!' Rhoese barked. 'I want no explanations. I

know what I heard, and I'm telling you once and for all that if you so much as look at my husband again I'll lay a curse on you that will turn you into a crick-backed old hag with neither teeth nor hair, and pebbles for eyes. You've heard of my powers, I see,' she added, heartened by the woman's expression of sheer terror. 'Good. So be warned.' She wagged a finger. 'Jude is *mine*. He was always mine, and I shall not be giving him up. Do you understand me?'

'Yes…yes, I heard you, but—'

'Do you *understand*?'

'Yes.'

'*So…leave…him…alone.*' The words had a force all their own, emerging from deep down in her throat, snarled like a wild animal.

'Yes.'

With the slam of the heavy door hurting her ears, Rhoese marched back along the passageway and out into the brightening day, her feet moving without any steering device to tell them where to go. Beneath the light wool kirtle and the mulberry linen chemise, her heart hammered like a blacksmith's forge, heavy and clamorous, a beat she could feel in her throat and as far down as her knees. Often she had scolded the servants and torn strips off the reeve once or twice, but never had she threatened a woman of her own rank, and never had she been fired by the searing emotion she had felt up there, fighting to keep Jude. Is that what real love did? Was it the effects of the potion, and had she made it double-strength by mistake? Master Flambard had been right again; a talking-to was more immediate than a purge, though to the donor as well as the recipient it was almost as exhausting.

She found herself in the garden in the company of blackbirds and a darting wren. Echoing through the cloister, the cathedral bell summoned a file of monks towards the Chapter House and their daily meeting. Unseen by Rhoese, the last black-robed figure hung back then slipped away, made as if to approach her, hesitated, then went quickly through the archway to the stables in the courtyard, where he was sure to find the man he wanted.

'What is it, Brother?' said Jude. He was surprised to see Rhoese's chaplain in the stables. 'If it's about the book, it can—'

'No sir. It's not. Will you come…please?' He hovered by the half-door, waiting to show Jude out.

Puzzled, Jude gave a brief instruction to the groom and followed Brother Alaric as far as the arch in the wall, where they stopped. 'Tell me,' said Jude.

'Sir,' said the chaplain, 'there's something you need to hear. If you will trust me?'

The expression of deep sincerity on Brother Alaric's face could not be ignored. Jude did trust him, and respect him too. If he said there was something he ought to hear, then it must be important. 'Of course. What is it you have to say?'

'Not I, sir. The Lady Rhoese. Will you follow me? You must remain out of sight. And silent.'

Still not understanding, Jude was led along the grassy path to the place where he and Anneys d'Abbeville had thought they were private. And there, through sign language, he was instructed to wait in silence and to leave the rest to Brother Alaric. It was only then Jude realised that, for the first time, he and the chaplain had been conversing in English instead of French.

'My lady?' the gentle voice said, approaching from one side.

Rhoese sighed, fighting the urge to send the intruder away. But if she must suffer someone's presence, it might as well be her chaplain. Even so, a greeting of any kind was beyond her.

As usual, he spoke to her in English. 'Something has happened?' he said. 'Would it help to talk about it?'

Rhoese shook her head, still too overwrought to trust her feelings to words, even in her mother tongue.

The chaplain was not discouraged. With unusual familiarity, he touched her elbow and invited her to walk with him up the path to the bench backed by the spreading pear tree where, through its loaded arms, she had heard Jude's conversation yesterday. There they sat together, the troubled lady and a man of God who was all set to break the rule of confidentiality in the name of true love. The stalemate, he believed, would never be resolved otherwise, and a little rule-bending was better than a broken marriage.

He had seen the signs before, more than once, the sparkling aggrieved eyes, the flushed cheeks, the clenched fists and ramrod straight back. Even the long plait might have been carved from a single plank. He took the plunge. She would be sure to contradict him. 'You've had a fight,' he said. 'Was it with Jude?'

'Tch!' she said, looking away. 'It's that damn woman. That's who I've had a fight with, not Jude.'

'And presumably you won?'

'Of course I won,' she growled, her voice scalding with contempt. 'She didn't have a leg to stand on. She'd have taken him *off* me,' she squeaked, still outraged. 'I *heard* them. Here, in this very same spot.' She jabbed a finger in the direction of her feet.

'What? Heard what, my lady?'

'Yesterday.' It didn't take long for her to relate the story, but even the telling did not reduce by one iota the offence she had felt then. And the hurt.

'That's serious,' said Brother Alaric when she had finished. 'I can see why you're so upset but, from what you say, it sounds as if the lady was far more eager to renew the friendship than your husband. And what makes you think it's going to develop? Is it because of the journey ahead and the days spent travelling together? She may not be coming with us, you know.'

'She obviously expects to, to stay close to him. And things *have* developed.'

'Are you sure?'

'Yes, I have it on good authority. No, not her. She denied it, naturally. But I'll *not* have that low-bred Norman harpy trespassing on my marriage.' Her voice shook with passion. 'He's mine. I know he'll break my heart one day. But not yet…not yet.'

Brother Alaric had had his suspicions from the start

but now he was sure. 'So the purge was intended for her? To keep her here in Durham?'

'Yes, it was. But I wouldn't have tricked her into drinking it, Brother, after what you said, even though I could cheerfully have killed her just now. Is *all* killing unlawful?'

The chaplain reserved his smile. 'I can't think of any exceptions at this moment,' he said, gravely. 'But you've never felt like this before, have you? Not even when…' Artlessly, he paused to give her time.

'I know what you were going to say, Brother, but you need not hold back for my sake. My nerves are already tight-strung, and that's all in the past. No, then I thought I knew what love was, but now I know it was only the idea of being loved and wanted by a man. What I felt for Warin was never remotely like this, but recently I've thought how strange fate is and how, if I'd married him, I'd not have seen Jude and known the pain and heartache of loving him. It seems that, whatever I do, I'm destined to suffer loss in all its forms. My father, my lover, my property and now my husband. What else is there to lose when even my heart refuses to obey me? Can you wonder that I'm putting up a fight to delay the inevitable?' The words shook precariously.

'It's *not* inevitable,' Brother Alaric said, 'and it's good that you're taking control, even when it appears that others are controlling you. The problems arise because these events have no notion of timing, Rhoese. They don't spread themselves out in manageable portions to give us time to get used to them.

They come in packages, sometimes, just when we're at our most vulnerable.

'First your father was lost, then Warin, then all the distress of Ketti and your shattered dreams. But now you have happiness within your grasp, my lady, and you'll stand no chance with Jude until you've told him how you feel about him.'

'Some time. Perhaps,' she whispered. 'No good telling him now when I've just had a go at the woman he's starting an affair with. He'll not be so pleased with me about that. If only he—' here her voice broke, and the last words were gasped against the constriction in her throat '—could love *me* as much…as much as I…love him.' And because she didn't want Brother Alaric to see the full extent of her distress, she picked up her skirts and ran.

She ran through the stone corridors of the bishop's palace and out the other side, through the woodland that sloped away from the castle, down and down to an embankment by the river. Stumbling over her skirts and scattering squirrels, sheep and goats, and stirring sleeping owls from their roosts, she ran until she was out of breath, then walked, then ran on again.

Jude's immediate response was to dart after her, but Brother Alaric dissuaded him. 'Give her a few moments, sir. That's my advice. She'll have gone to her room.'

Jude's eyes reflected every nuance of the scene he had just witnessed of which the most pitiful was the not knowing. 'Why?' he said, standing with hands on hips. 'Why didn't she tell me? She's got it wrong.

There was never anything between me and the d'Abbeville woman.'

'That's not the impression she received, sir. You'll have some explaining to do, and a great deal of trust to build up. I thought you should know how she feels about you.'

'Yes, you're right. I had to know.' Jude shook his head. 'I must go and find her. But how did you know I speak your language?' he said, half-turning.

'From the very start, sir. In the compound at York, you said something to the reeve at the gate as you left, and he answered you. He told me. I knew that you understood all we said.'

'Huh! So the Lady Rhoese doesn't know?'

'No, sir.' There were other things neither of them knew. 'About the book, sir. We've discovered—'

Jude was already moving off. 'Oh, damn the book, man. Do what you like with it,' he said impatiently. 'It's to go down to Barking,' he called, 'without fail. Just fix it, will you?'

'You mean we can…?'

There was something in Brother Alaric's half-finished question that made Jude stop and retrace his steps as if knowing that he must say more. He stood like a young lad being asked for an explanation of his conduct, not knowing quite where to begin. 'Look,' he said, apologetically, 'I think it's better if I don't know.'

'Sir?'

Jude studied the chaplain's bewildered face. 'There's something about the book. I know that much. There'd not be all this concern for it otherwise, and

Rhoese is convinced it will be taken from her after all she and her father did to get it back and keep it from Archbishop Thomas into the bargain. So don't tell me about it, eh? She is the temporary owner, not me, and what *she* wants for the book must be done, whatever it is. I don't want recriminations about unfulfilled promises hanging over my head. We have enough to sort out between us without all that.' He had begun to move away in the direction that Rhoese had taken, the last words thrown over his shoulder as he strode through the arch out of sight.

Having quickly established that she was not in her room, nor indeed in any other room, Jude followed his instinct. Nevertheless, it was a good half-hour before he knew himself to be on the right trail after making a circuit of the long promontory forged by the loop in the river. He came at last to a small clearing ringed by trees on the southern side where the sun had begun to dapple the deep piles of leaves underfoot. Here they were dry and crisp, and to reach the lone figure in silence would be impossible.

Standing motionless by the fast-flowing river with her deep red kirtle and hair blending easily into the landscape, Rhoese waited for her breath to settle into its usual rhythm. Mocking her thoughts was the picture of rippling black tresses and one bare enticing shoulder and, almost without realising it, she had unbound her plait and shaken it free to fall where it would. She had won that bout, but unless she could win Jude too, and keep him, the victory would be short-lived. Now, she would have to decide how to continue, whether to pretend to know nothing of his last night's activities or whether to confront him too. The idea was not appealing, for his loving last night had apparently not been diminished by his previous engagement with that woman. Had it been as good for her? she wondered.

Sadly, she looked round for a boulder to sit on, and it was then that she saw him, leaning against a tree with his arms folded, quietly watching her. Ideally, she would have liked her indecision to resolve itself in that moment, but it didn't. Instead, the possibility overshadowing all others was that he had heard of her threats to Anneys d'Abbeville and had come to demand an explanation. And although she was prepared to explain things now and then to her chaplain, her experience of Jude could not guarantee so easy a ride.

Like a startled doe, she made a dash for freedom, heading along the river bank into the denser woodland rather than uphill, the way she had come. But she stood no chance against his agility, his speed and long arms, and in only a few frantic leaf-swirling yards he caught her round the waist like a wrestler and threw her down into the carpet of leaves, spilling them over her as they rolled.

In desperation she beat at his shoulders, angered by everything that had brought her to this, angered by her own helplessness when she had only just learned how not to be, and by the agonies of love that she had vowed never to know. 'No…no!' she panted. 'I'm not going to explain *anything*! Go away! Think what you like. I don't care…let me *go*!'

Her struggles made no difference; her wrists were

caught and he was over her, holding her with his hard-muscled body against which she could make no impression. She could see by his face that he was taking this seriously, and probably angrily, too. Deep brown eyes beating into hers, dark-lashed, bold and unwavering as they had been at their first meeting, firm mouth and perfect teeth. And he was whispering something. In English.

Incredulous, she watched and listened to his perfect pronunciation of the difficult sounds, to his fluency and word power, never dreaming that she might hear from him words that she herself had used, and more. Words of love and longing, of uncertainty, hope and loyalty too, rarely heard except in the context of arms and the king.

'I'm dreaming,' she whispered. 'Am I dreaming, Jude?'

'No,' he said, gravely. 'No, beloved. You're not. We know so little about each other. We have to put that right. We cannot go on like this, can we?'

Still, she could scarcely believe it. 'But...but you must have heard...things...that you were not sup-posed to hear. You *knew*. All this time you kept it from me. Why?'

'Several reasons, my beauty. You've kept even more important things from me, haven't you? And now it's time to get a few things straight. First, you can rid yourself of the notion that there's something going on between me and Anneys d'Abbeville. There isn't.'

She squirmed at that, already at the limit of her

trust. 'There *was*,' she said. 'In the past. You know there was.'

'In the past, woman, if you'll allow me a word in edgeways, she was my father's concubine, not my mistress. Yes, all those years ago before Gerard and I left Normandy. She's much older than you think. See?'

The relief must have shown in her wide eyes, for she had no words to express how the picture had suddenly changed, posing no threat. She watched his mouth come closer, then felt the sensual warmth covering her thoughts as a soft blanket hides winter's frosts, comforting her, playing upon hers as he knew so well how to do, submerging her in the sweet overtures of excitement.

'Jude,' she said, when he slowed. 'Did you know that I love you? Did you?'

'I had no idea,' he said, hoping she would forgive the lie. 'Tell me more, woman. Tell me what I've been waiting all this long time to hear. I want your love, Rhoese of York. I need it. Tell me of it.'

It was not nearly as difficult as she had anticipated. 'I love you, Judhael de Brionne. I don't know why, or how, or exactly when it started, but I think it must have been there from the beginning when you strode into my yard. And now I find that my heart has turned disobedient, against all my commands. I want you, Jude. I was close to killing that woman for you. I cannot lose you now. I beg you not to—'

'Shh, lass,' he crooned. 'Hush. There's no need to beg me. There's nothing to fear.' He released her wrists to stroke her hair back from her face, lifting a leaf out of it. 'I've loved you from that very first sighting, my beauty, when you stood there defying me with your amazing eyes and lashing me with your tongue. Even then, I'd decided to have you whether you liked the idea or not. No, not your property, lass. I have more of that than you can imagine, both here and in Normandy. It was ever you that I wanted, even when you fought me and tried everything you could to make me pay for it. Don't you know it only made me love you more?'

'Love me, Jude? Are you quite sure? You've had experiences like this before, I know.'

'No, I haven't,' he said, laughing. He rolled off her and pulled her into his arms, holding her between his great long legs so that she couldn't move away. 'No, I haven't. Not love. There's a difference, sweetheart. But I know nothing of what happened between you and Warin. Will you tell me the whole story now?'

'No, Jude. I can't. Not the whole story.'

'Yes, you can. No more secrets.'

'It hurts.'

He studied her in silence for a moment, then placed his hand gently over her womb so that she felt its warmth. 'There?' he said. 'Is that where it hurts? And here, too?' The hand moved to caress her breasts. 'Is this where a small head might have lain? Here, upon your lap?'

A shuddering sob turned her head into his shoulder, nodding in response to each perceptive enquiry. 'He never knew,' she said. 'I didn't see any point in telling him.'

'I see. Then you were expecting his child? And lost it?'

'Yes. It was the shock of my father, I expect. I vowed to revenge myself for the pain. It was almost too much to bear on my own, Jude. It took hold of my life.'

He swayed her gently in his arms, kissing her hair. 'And that's what you were doing on our last night in York? Saying farewell?'

'Yes. It was my heart's desire. But I never wanted Warin to suffer the way he is doing, Jude. That's something I never intended. And I can't undo that damage now. I'd not have wanted to take my revenge so savagely.'

Jude's thoughts on the matter were less compassionate. 'And you kept all this to yourself,' he said. 'My poor sweet lass.'

'It was not a good experience. Only a few know of it. You won't love me any less for it, will you Jude?'

'*Chérie,*' he said, pulling her closer to him, 'if I could love you more, then I do for your courage. But you can let it all go now, my love. Put the whole thing behind you. No more yearning. I shall give you all the infants you can manage, and I shall never leave you alone.'

'How did you know?'

A deep bass note sounded within his chest and his voice held a smile. 'I'm learning about you,' he whispered. 'I think I have a fair idea now of what pains you most, what makes you most fierce, *chérie*. Eh?'

Chérie. 'That's what you called her, Jude. I heard it.'

He seemed not to be surprised at that revelation, and he did not question how she had heard. 'Sarcasm, beloved. For her, sarcasm, that's all. She's wanted me since she lived under our roof. Yes, she wanted Gerard too, but not after he was injured. Concubines were not unusual then, and my mother had little choice in the matter, God rest her soul. The more Anneys tried, the less I was interested. I've never taken her to bed, Rhoese. Not even halfway.'

'And last night?'

'I spent last night with you. Have you forgotten so soon?'

'No, but Master Flambard told me—'

'What, that I took—?'

'Well, no, not exactly. It doesn't matter. I got hold of the wrong end of the stick, that's all.' *Clever, manipulative Master Flambard.*

'As you have done from the beginning, my lady.'

'And no wonder. You said I'd never reach your heart. Brute.'

There was no sign of contrition on his face. 'My heart was already lost by then, but I could see no use in telling you that, when you were set on holding yours so fast. You don't win a fight by telling your opponent what your plan is. And I was determined you'd find no softness in me that you could turn to your advantage. I know how to play a waiting game, woman.'

'That was unfair, Jude,' she whispered, 'when I had

no advantages at all after that embarrassing charade at York. How could you be so unkind?'

His arms tightened about her again, pulling her hard into him until her head was wedged into the crook of his elbow. 'Was it kindness you needed from me, woman? Eh? I think not,' he growled. 'No, kindness would have been useless when you'd set your heart on ice. Brute strength is what's needed when that happens, and I chipped away at it, didn't I? Undermined it and melted it. And now I have you, all of you, and I love your fierceness and independence, and I want such a woman for the mother of my bairns and the keeper of my heart. A woman who cares enough to fight bulls for me. A woman like you, my beauty.'

'You scared me, Jude. You crept into my dreams, and I adore you.'

'Forgive me. It was the only way to win you without taking forever. Will you have me, all over again, harshness and all?'

'A thousand, thousand times yes, beloved.'

He swung her down again into the bed of crisp leaves, already burning with desire and now unfettered by the weight of misunderstandings that had slowed them to a point where neither of them would admit anything to the other.

His kisses set her on fire, just as his bold words and his admission of love had done, raging through her with a joy that made her gasp as he pulled her kirtle down to bare one shoulder and breast. 'Superb creature,' he said, cupping the fullness in one large hand. 'My magnificent woman. I cannot get enough

of you, Rhoese. Be warned.' It had been his intention
to tease her a little, to make her wait and plead with
him to take her. But the first greedy touch of his
mouth upon her breast acted like a trigger for them
both and, in a torment of recklessness, they came together as powerful magnets do in a coupling of fierce
turbulence, shaking them with its intensity.

Resting his weight on his hands, he rocked her
body with powerful thrusts and then, at her cry into
the brightly dappled canopy above, sped to the conclusion with dizzying prowess, joining her in a groan
of pure ecstasy that set the waiting woodland to silence. Then it was over, with gasps of laughter and
the kind of deep overwhelming peace that neither of
them had achieved before with so many doubts to
plague them.

At last, she turned her head to him. 'Jude,' she said,
'there's something else you should know.'

His hand slid gently over her thigh beneath the soft
woollen fabric. 'Yes, sweetheart,' he said. 'I heard
about that. I expect it's the first fight she's had on her
hands for quite some time.'

'You know about that, too? How?'

'Oh, word soon gets around in a place like this.'

'It was very one-sided. I expected some opposition.'

'Whatever caused it, my love, I am honoured to
have you on my side. If she has any sense at all, she'll
stay clear of us both.'

'You fought for me, Jude, on several occasions.
I've not forgotten that. Will she be coming with us?'
There was an anxiety in her voice that would not

remain hidden, despite the attempt at lightness in her tone.

He sat up and leaned over her, watching her lovely eyes change from autumn brown to deep midwinter. 'So that's what was bothering you, eh? Her being with us? Well, don't. Just trust me.'

'I do, Jude. Only…'

'What is it, lass? Tell me.'

'What when I'm breeding? Will you want others then, instead of me?'

His fingers were tender on her forehead, lifting stray locks of hair and placing them carefully aside. 'Nay,' he said, softly. 'I'd have to be extremely crass to take another woman while my own was giving me a family, and I'm not as heartless as that, my love. Truly I'm not. I said provocative things to you that I'd never have said if I'd known the truth of it. You've had bad experiences, I know, but you're mine now, and you'll never find me wanting in that department. I've never had to fight so hard for a woman, Rhoese of York, nor have I ever had a woman fight so hard for my sake. I'm so proud of you. You're worth fighting for.'

She did not tell him of the potion, for she was not proud of the more desperate measures she'd employed, nor of the reputation that seemed daily to extend in repertoire without much help from her. 'Shall we ever make love in a rose-petalled bed with scented sheets and blossom to garland our nights?' she sighed wistfully, closing her eyes to hide the mischief there.

'Mm…m, no. Probably not for a while, my love.

Not until you start being an obedient and submissive wife to me. Is that something I might expect?'

'Mm…m, no, Jude. Probably not for a while,' she whispered. Through her closed lids, she could feel the warmth of him as he bent to her lips again. 'But I have nothing against you trying to persuade me, now that my heart is yours.'

Epilogue

⁓⁓⁓⁓⁓⁓

They had been away from York for two weeks, all told, in which time there was no reason for Rhoese to think that anything much would have changed at Toft Green in their absence. The greatest change of all, she knew, was to her and Jude, whose release from the strain of pretence had caused a collective sigh of relief to pass over their closest servants and friends, including both chaplains, neither of whom dared to tell Rhoese of the wager they had won from those who had doubted the outcome. Which went some way to explain their determination, by fair means and foul, to make the course of true love run a little faster, if not necessarily smoother.

True to form, Ranulf Flambard got most out of it on a material level by accepting Anneys d'Abbeville's offer of company each night and then telling her with all the regret he could muster that she would not be going with them down to York and beyond. It was Jude's decision, he told her, as if he had only just heard of it.

When she confronted Jude, in a state of near panic,

he assured her it was Flambard's decision, taken days ago. She was far from pleased, even when Jude told her that, if she waited at Durham long enough, Flambard would almost certainly turn up as bishop, one day. His light-hearted prediction was correct, but neither of them were to know that at the time.

Jude's cousin, Brother Gerard, restored the gospel-book to its former glory under the eagle eyes of Prior Turgot and Brother Alaric, who had quickly given the go-ahead for the English message to Abbess Christina of Romsey to be removed and replaced with the correct translation of the last pages of text. And so well did Gerard conceal the offending words that neither Jude, nor Flambard, nor Rhoese knew that anything had been changed except that it was seen by Rhoese as yet another manifestation of Jude's love when he kept his promise that it should be returned to Barking Abbey.

The change that no one had quite expected, except perhaps Hilda, was to Els, who proved to be with child, after all. It took quite some time for the empty-headed young maid to reveal that the father was Warin, of all people, and that they had been meeting in secret during the summer months whenever she could slip away. So one of the first things Rhoese attended to when they reached York was to take Els to see him and make him aware of the problem. He really could not, she said firmly, escape his responsibilities just because he could not see them.

But an even greater change had taken place at Toft Green, after all, for Ketti had met with an accident on York's busy thoroughfares. She had been run down by an ox-cart, never an easy vehicle to stop quickly at the best of times, and they had buried her only one week ago. Warin was already sitting outside in the October sunshine, being taught how to weave baskets by the local blind basket-maker. It had seemed appropriate then to leave him and Els together to discuss their future, and, as Els preferred to stay in York, the matter was soon settled.

In spite of his losses, it seemed that Warin would be a father after all, and now there was nothing to be gained by telling him about Rhoese's miscarriage last winter, after what had happened. During their absence, Eric had introduced Neal to several local beauties who had lost no time in veering his thoughts away from the fickle Els to other more interesting matters. Not surprisingly, it was Eric who permanently gave himself into the loving care of a capable and lovely young woman, the daughter of a London merchant, who showed none of Rhoese's former traits regarding men. He was delighted and relieved to find his sister and Jude so well suited, even if they did still spar with each other quite noisily. He was sure Jude had the upper hand, however.

Jude did, in fact, have the upper hand, for to do otherwise in such a relationship would have been disastrous for both of them. With limited success, Rhoese pretended to be piqued by his commanding manner, though she knew she was not the only one to receive the sharper end of his tongue when Master Flambard ventured to ask him how he knew that Anneys d'Abbeville had spend the last few nights with him. Jude's answer was less than subtle. 'Well, you may be the king's chaplain, man, but I'm his captain, and he doesn't employ *me* to sit around on my arse with my eyes shut, I can tell you.' And with that explanation, Flambard had to be content.

At night, of course, and in private, Jude employed quite a different manner that made Rhoese accept that the king, in spite of being obnoxious in most things, had been right in his choice of captains. And one year later, at their grand stone-built house on the outskirts of London, Rhoese gave birth to the first of their three sons, and no mention of a litter was ever made again.

*   *   *   *   *

MILLS & BOON®

has teamed up with

OLD ENGLISH INNS
a more enchanting choice

to offer you a fantastic 2 for 1 break

Escape to the beautiful countryside with super savings! Each and every inn has their own special charm and delightful surroundings – historic buildings, cosy bedrooms, oak beamed bars and restaurants, freshly cooked food, fine wines and real cask ales – perfect for quick get away!

With the emphasis on relaxation, the traditional inns and hotels offer a warm and friendly welcome and above all, excellent value for money! Perfect for walking, cycling, sightseeing, visiting historic houses and gardens and golf breaks.

To take advantage of this fantastic offer and for a list of participating hotels, Call FREE

0800 917 3085

quoting "Mills & Boon"

Terms & Conditions

1. The offer entitles two people sharing a standard twin or double room to 2 nights' accommodation for the price of one including breakfast. 2. Offer subject to availability. 3. Single supplements may apply. 4. All rates are based on current rack rates and could be subject to change during the promotion. 5. Must be booked through central reservations on 0800-9173085, not with hotel direct. 6. Excludes Bank Holidays 7. Offer valid until 30th September 2005 8. OEI reserve the right to remove/change the hotels during the promotion. 9. Cannot be used in conjunction with any other offer. 10. Applies to new bookings only. 11. Calls will be recorded for training purposes.

www.millsandboon.co.uk

0505/024/MB126

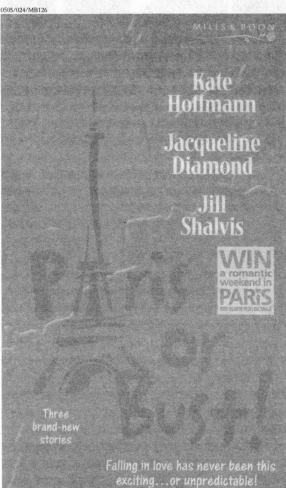

FREE

2 BOOKS AND A SURPRISE GIFT!

We would like to take this opportunity to thank you for reading this Mills & Boon® book by offering you the chance to take TWO more specially selected titles from the Historical Romance™ series absolutely FREE! We're also making this offer to introduce you to the benefits of the Reader Service™—

    ★ **FREE home delivery**
    ★ **FREE gifts and competitions**
    ★ **FREE monthly Newsletter**
    ★ **Books available before they're in the shops**
    ★ **Exclusive Reader Service offers**

Accepting these FREE books and gift places you under no obligation to buy; you may cancel at any time, even after receiving your free shipment. Simply complete your details below and return the entire page to the address below. You don't even need a stamp!

YES! Please send me 2 free Historical Romance books and a surprise gift. I understand that unless you hear from me, I will receive 4 superb new titles every month for just £3.65 each, postage and packing free. I am under no obligation to purchase any books and may cancel my subscription at any time. The free books and gift will be mine to keep in any case.

H5ZEE

Ms/Mrs/Miss/Mr...................................Initials ....
                                                            BLOCK CAPITALS PLEASE
Surname ....
Address ....
....
....Postcode ....

Send this whole page to:
The Reader Service, FREEPOST CN81, Croydon, CR9 3WZ